MW01134226

FORGET
ME

Kristen Middleton

Kristen Middleton

NY Times and USA Today Bestselling Author

Fantasy, Horror, and Romance.

Books By Kristen Middleton

Searching for Faith
Looking For Lainey
Forget Me Not

Blur
Shiver
Vengeance
Illusions

Venom
Slade
Toxic
Claimed by the Lycan

Jezebel
Deviant

Enchanted Secrets
Enchanted Objects
Enchanted Spells

Origins
Running Wild
Dead Endz
Road Kill
End Zone

Paxton VS The Undead

Planet Z
Blood of Brekkon

Romance under pen name K.L. Middleton

Recommended For ages 18 and older due to sexual situations and language.

Tangled Beauty
Tangled Mess
Tangled Fury

Sharp Edges

Billionaire at Sea
Billionaire at Sea Book 2

Gritty biker romance under pen name Cassie Alexandra

For ages 18 and older. Vulgar language and sexual content.

Resisting the Biker
Surviving the Biker
Fearing the Biker
Breaking the Biker
Taming the Biker
Loving the Biker
Luring the Biker
Christmas With The Biker
Destroying the Biker

Prologue

HIM

May 20th, 11:14 p.m.
Summit Lake, Minnesota
Fairfield Rest-Stop

I WAITED IN the shadows, my heartbeat in sync with a lone cricket chirping nearby. The night was cool, but I found myself sticky with sweat for what was about to unfold. After weeks of planning, revenge would soon be mine; I'd waited so long for it. Too long.

Headlights approached in the distance and a rush of excitement roared through me.

He's here.

I backed further into the darkness, knowing the fool would soon be getting out of his car. I imagined what was going through his head, which made it so much easier. He believed he was meeting up with an

6

eighteen-year-old high school football player. A confused young man exploring his sexuality, without his peers finding out and casting judgment.

I watched, my heart pounding as he parked his sedan in the vacant lot. He turned off the engine and climbed out. From the distance, I could see he'd gotten flabby and it pleased me considering how vain the prick used to be.

You're So Vain…

The lyrics from the song echoed in my head and I began to whistle the tune softly as he turned toward me. His eyes scanned the empty rest-stop until locating my gray mountain bike, which I'd left in clear view, by the picnic tables.

"Come on," I murmured under my breath, my stomach swirling with excitement.

He remained frozen for several seconds—more than likely wondering if it was a trap. But, as I anticipated, his deplorable appetite overrode caution, and soon he was moving toward the pavilion.

And me.

"Hello?" he whispered loudly, stopping at the entrance.

I could see his silhouette almost perfectly under the light of the moon; he had not aged well. His face was pasty white, there were jowls running along his jawline, and he had puffy circles under his eyes. It was pleasing to see that his bad habits had caught up with him. If he only knew how much.

7

"Terence?" he called out, his voice echoing in the pavilion.

"I'm here," I replied.

Relaxing, he smiled. "Why are you hiding? Why don't you come on out?"

"I'm nervous. I've never done this before," I replied. For this to work successfully, I needed to lure him closer.

"It's okay," he said in a soothing voice. "Neither have I. This is all new for me, too."

Liar.

I knew very well that he'd met up with others. I'd followed him to another rendezvous, just a couple of weeks earlier. He'd met someone behind a bookstore. It had been another young man, definitely in his teens. They'd gone to a motel, where it hadn't taken long to do their business. Ten minutes to be exact. I'd clocked it.

He looked over his shoulder, toward his vehicle. "Let's go to my car. We should get out of here before someone approaches."

"I thought that maybe we could just stay here? I skateboard in this area all the time. Nobody ever comes out this way," I replied.

He turned my way again, not looking too convinced.

I decided to try a different approach. One that he wouldn't be able to resist. "I have something for you.

Something you're going to love," I said with a smile in my voice. I'd sent him nude photos of a stranger just the night before. A randy young man I'd found posing on the Internet. Someone he now believed to be me. I'd labeled the email, "Something You're Going To Love."

He grinned and stepped toward me. "Oh, Terence. I have something for you, too," he replied, moving his hand toward his fly.

Repulsed, I ran my finger over the blade of my knife. Any hesitation I may have had vanished completely. He deserved what was coming to him. "I can't tell you how long I've waited for this moment."

"I've been anticipating it, too. It's all I could think about today. Come out, Terence."

Ironically, I was now aroused by the thoughts running through my head. All of them dark, but not sexual.

"Very well." I stepped out of the shadows.

His eyes widened in confusion as he stared at my face. He looked down at the knife and my gloves. "What the hell is going on?"

"Don't you recognize me?"

He squinted. "No. You don't look like the guy in the photo. Are you even Terence?"

I felt like he'd punched me in the stomach. How could he not remember me? "Yes and no."

He looked down at the knife. "What is this about?"

"Look at my face. How can you not recognize it?" I asked sharply.

"Look, man, I didn't sign up for this," he said angrily. "Obviously, there's been some misunderstanding. I'll just be on my way."

"On the contrary. There's no misunderstanding. You came here to meet with me and here we are. Now, look at my face," I ordered again, the vein in my temple throbbing. "You should know exactly who I am."

"I've never seen you before in my life." He began backing away.

Maybe he did remember me and was now panicking? No, that's not it. I smiled coldly. "You're lying."

He raised his hands in the air. "I swear to God, we've never met. You're confusing me with someone else. Take it easy with that knife now, man."

Maybe he had forgotten?

The thought sent me into a rage.

Growling, I lurched forward with the knife and slashed it across his Adam's apple.

Shocked, he let out a strangled cry and his hands flew to his neck. Blood gushed from between his pudgy, bloated fingers as he stared at me in horror and disbelief.

"No. This isn't right," I said, biting my lower lip as he staggered backward.

He was dying, but I wanted much more. The bastard needed to suffer. He needed to pay for what he'd taken from me.

Thankful I'd chosen, thick wool gloves, I reached down, grabbed his flaccid penis, and yanked it upward. Staring into his eyes, I told him my name and then buried my knife deep into his sack.

His eyes widened in recognition and horror. He let out one final gargled scream and then collapsed down onto the concrete.

I leaned down, cleaned the knife off on his jacket, and grabbed his car keys. I had much to do and felt only slightly appeased. He wasn't the only one on my list. There was another… and she would pay, too.

Chapter 1

Amanda

Summit Lake, Minnesota
Wednesday, June 29th, 11:05 p.m.

"HEY. WE'RE HERE," I said, reaching back into the SUV and shaking my eight-year-old son awake.

Kevin opened his brown eyes and stared at me in confusion. He was a deep sleeper and it usually took him a while to fully wake up.

I turned off the engine. "We made it Grandma and Grandpa's. Let's go."

"Oh. Okay." He yawned and rubbed his eyes.

"Lacey, I bet you're ready to get out, aren't you?" I called out.

Our Golden Retriever, who was kenneled in the back of the Tahoe, barked.

Smiling, I got out of the SUV and looked up at the aging Victorian house where I'd spent the first eighteen years of my life. My eyes traveled upstairs to my old bedroom window, where I used to sneak out in the middle of the night as a teenager. I'd make my way over to the old apple tree, climb down, and run off with one of my friends—usually Tara Flyhill. I also remembered the struggle of trying to get back up the tree, which had been no laughing matter. One fall and I would have easily broken my neck. Still, the threat of death hadn't been enough to stop me from going out to a keg party or even just… escaping for a while. Unfortunately, the tree was no longer there. Apparently, it had been struck by lightning a few years back.

As fond as those memories were, my childhood had been less than desirable. Both of my parents had been alcoholics, fighting constantly and blaming each other for their misery and regrets. Now my dad was gone, having died of a stroke, only months after I left the nest. Mom was still alive, however. And thriving.

She actually came to life after he passed away. Not only did she join AA and quit drinking, but she went back to college, earned a teaching degree, and started to really live. As ashamed of her as I'd been growing up, I was now proud of how she'd turned her life around. Our relationship was stronger than ever, which I felt made up for the earlier years.

As I was letting Lacey out of the kennel, the front porch light turned on and the door opened. Rocky, my stepfather, walked outside first, followed by my mother.

"You're here! Thank goodness," Mom called out, rushing down the steps and toward us. She approached Kevin first and pulled him into her arms. "We were getting so worried about you."

"Sorry. My phone died along the way and we stopped off for food. Of course, I couldn't find my car charger, either. I didn't mean to worry you. *Lacey*, down!" I scolded, as she jumped up on Rocky.

"She's fine." Laughing, Rocky began petting her. "Such a good dog," he said in a higher pitched voice. "Who's a good dog? Yes, I know, you are. Good girl."

I chuckled.

"Kevin, you've grown a whole foot, haven't you?" Rocky said, standing back up. "Come over here and give me a hug."

He smiled and rushed into Rocky's arms. Although they didn't get to see each other much, they were every bit "grandpa and grandson." Kevin adored Rocky as much as he did my mother.

"You should have had your phone plugged into your charger from the very beginning. What if you had problems with your truck and the battery had died?" Mom said, not letting it go.

We lived almost eight hours away and the trip here had only added an extra forty minutes, tops. She'd always been a worry-wart and a bit of a hypochondriac, however. Even worse, she'd learned how to surf the Internet for answers on ailments. That's how she'd met Rocky, who was now retired. He'd been a paramedic and they'd met when she'd called for an ambulance one day, convinced she was having a heart attack. Fortunately, it had been nothing more than severe heartburn.

"We were fine," I said. "Right, Kev?"

"Yep," he said.

"Maybe, but you just always have to be prepared," she said. "I'd hate for you to be stranded in the middle of nowhere. Relying on some stranger passing by to give you and Kevin a lift. These days, women and children are getting kidnapped left and right. You can't even go to the grocery store without the risk of disappearing."

"Really?" Kevin said, his eyes wide.

"She's exaggerating," I said to him, but glaring at my mom with irritation.

"No, I most certainly am not," Mom replied with a disapproving look. "Kevin needs to know these things, too. It's safer that way for him, too."

I sighed. I didn't want Kevin boarding the "paranoia train", the one my mother frequented. He was already somewhat of a worrier himself.

Rocky sighed. "I knew you were fine. But, you know your mother and her overactive imagination. She was convinced that you two were in mortal danger."

I raised my eyebrow. "Mortal danger, huh?"

She shrugged.

"Mom. Where do you get these ideas from?" I asked, smiling.

"Ideas? They're facts. You just have to watch the news to see. You know, there are a lot of crazies out there. I'm just thankful that you've decided to move back here from Chicago," she replied, pushing a strand of hair behind her ear.

I hadn't made that a final decision yet. My first-husband had recently died in a tragic car accident and had, apparently, left me everything. Talk about a shocker. We hadn't spoken in fifteen years and to learn that he'd named me *sole* beneficiary—for his entire estate—had been totally unexpected.

"Are we moving here for good?" Kevin asked with a frown. "You told me that we were just staying here for the summer."

"I'm not sure yet," I replied.

"But, I don't want to move away from my friends," he whined.

"Kevin, you'd make so many wonderful friends out here," Mom said, wrapping her arms around him again. She smiled warmly. "And you'd get to see me and Papa Rocky that much more. Wouldn't it be wonderful?"

"Yes, but…" his lip quivered. "I'd miss Aaron and Tyler and my other friends at school."

"Hey," I said, stepping closer to Kevin. I leaned down and stared into his eyes. "I haven't decided anything yet, okay?"

He nodded.

Kevin's best friends, Aaron and Tyler, lived on the same street as us. We'd been renting a house in the neighborhood for the past four years, and the three had become best friends. I knew that moving would be hard on Kevin, which was why I wasn't totally sold on returning permanently to Summit Lake. As for myself, I could move anywhere. I was a writer, so it didn't matter where I planted my laptop.

"Let's get into the house," Rocky said, frowning and swatting at mosquitos. "I'm sure you're both tired and could use a good night's sleep."

"Yes, let's go." Mom looked up at the sky. "The weather report said we should be getting a storm here soon."

As if on cue, we all noticed a distant bolt of lightning, followed by the rumble of thunder. Lacey, who'd been exploring the yard, froze and then came running back to us. Like most dogs, she hated storms and couldn't be outside when they erupted.

"It's okay, girl," Kevin said, scratching behind her ears. "We're going inside."

I pulled out two of the four suitcases from the back of the SUV.

"Let me help you with that," Rocky said, taking them.

"Thanks." I grabbed the other two and closed the trunk.

"Other than your phone dying, how *was* the drive up here?" Rocky asked as we all headed toward the porch.

"Fine," I replied. "Same as usual."

The traveling was something I'd always enjoyed. Not only was it nice to get away from Chicago, but it gave Kevin and I a chance to really talk. When he wasn't at school, he usually hung out with his friends, played baseball, or watched television. As for me, when I wasn't feeding him, or chauffeuring Kevin around, you'd find me in my office, working on a new book. I often felt guilty for the amount of time I spent there, but it was hard being a single parent with what seemed like endless bills. As much as I felt horrible about my ex's tragic accident, I was grateful for what it might mean for us—less financial worries.

"Good. Well, we've missed you. I'm glad you're back," he said.

I smiled. "Me, too."

We walked into the house and I was greeted with all of the old smells I'd grown up with—Pine Sol and remnants of whatever had been in the oven earlier. It was comforting.

"Come on, Kevin," my mother said, moving toward the dark-cherry wood staircase. "Let's get you upstairs so you can put your jammies on and get some sleep."

He yawned and then asked for something to drink first.

"Sure," she replied, taking his hand. "How about some lemonade?"

"Yes, please," he answered.

"I'll bring Kevin's suitcases upstairs," Rocky said. "And then I'd like some of that lemonade, too, if I may?"

"Of course. What about you, dear? Would you like anything?" she asked, looking at me.

I told her I was fine.

"Lacey," I said, noticing she was sniffing around my mother's knitting basket. "No."

"I picked up some chew-toys for her at the pet store last week," Mom said. "I bet she's hungry and thirsty." Her voice raised an octave. "Do you want something to eat, Lacey?"

At the mention of food, the dog's ears perked up and she barked.

Mom smiled in amusement. "I thought so." She looked at me. "Did you bring a bag of food for her?"

"Of course," I replied. "It's still in the SUV, though."

"Don't worry. I'll grab it after we get everything upstairs, Amanda," Rocky said, heading up the staircase. "That way you can focus on unpacking."

"Thank you," I replied.

Mom led Kevin into the kitchen, with Lacey following quickly behind. Meanwhile, Rocky and I went upstairs with the luggage.

"Do you want Kevin with you or in the guestroom?" he asked, setting his two suitcases down on the carpeting next to my old bed.

"He can stay with me."

I'd purchased a twin-sized air-mattress so we could share the same room. Kevin had a tendency to get spooked at night, especially when sleeping at someone else's place. Grandma and Grandpa's was no exception.

"I heard you had to pick him up from a sleepover a few weeks back," he said in a low voice. "You mother mentioned he had some kind of a panic attack?"

My thoughts returned to that night. He'd been at a friend's birthday party and the boy's mother had called me in the middle of the night. "Yeah. He has this wild imagination and it seems to be just be getting worse."

He gave me a concerned look. "What do you mean?"

"The night I had to pick him up, Kevin was worried sick that something was going to happen to me," I explained and sighed. "It's been like this ever since a friend of his, Tyler, told him that he'd seen some man sneaking around our yard late one evening. Since then, he's been paranoid."

Rocky looked shocked. "You had a *Peeping Tom*?"

"Honestly, I don't know if that's even true or not. The night Tyler said he saw someone, Lacey didn't bark, and she would have if someone had really been prowling around on our property. Anyway, Tyler has a history of telling tales and I'm sure it was just another doozy he'd concocted."

Tyler lived directly next door to us and his bedroom was on the top floor. Apparently, he'd seen a shadow creeping around our backyard, on a Friday night. At first, I'd been quite disturbed by the idea. After not finding any evidence, like footprints in the dirt, I eventually brushed it off. Kevin still believed him, however.

"Well, you never know. Don't discount it too easily. Your mother is right about one thing—there *are* a lot of nutcases out there. Especially in the big cities."

I let out a weary sigh. "Yeah, I know. At least it's not something I have to worry about right now. If there is a Peeping Tom, hopefully he'll forget about me."

"Let's hope there isn't." He scratched his chin. "So, who's watching your place while you're here?"

"Tyler's parents are going to keep an eye on it for us," I replied. "I gave them a key. They promised to water my plants and bring the mail in."

"That's nice of them."

"Very. They're a nice couple. Oh, here." I reached into my pocket and gave him my key fob so he could get Lacey's food.

"I suppose we'd better not keep her waiting any longer. I'll meet you downstairs," Rocky said, leaving the bedroom.

"Okay."

I smiled in amusement as I looked around my old bedroom. Nothing had changed since high school. My rock posters still hung on the walls. My favorite satin purple comforter was on the bed. Then there was my collection of Beanie Babies, which still lined the shelves above my bed, the ones my father had built all those years ago. I'd spent a lot of time in my bedroom, especially when I hadn't been off gallivanting with Tara. It had been my refuge, and thankfully, my parents hadn't bothered me too much. They'd been too busy arguing and drinking. Thank goodness those days were over. I missed my father, but not the man he'd become after his second beer.

Yawning, I began unpacking Kevin's pajamas and realized I still needed to grab the air-mattress from the SUV.

I left the room and headed back downstairs, passing Rocky as he brought in the large bag of dogfood.

"Where you going?" he asked, setting it down in the foyer.

"I left the air-mattress in the car."

"Hell, I can get that for you. Let me haul this into the kitchen first," he said, nodding toward the six-pound bag of dogfood.

My mother had no idea how good she had it. It seemed like Rocky was always offering to do the grunt work and was a true gentleman. He was also no spring chicken, and after sitting for so many hours behind the wheel, I didn't mind a little exercise.

I waved my hand. "Don't be silly. I can grab it. Just worry about Lacey's food and I'll take care of this. I need to stretch my legs anyway after driving so long."

"Okay." He handed me the key fob.

I thanked him and then walked outside to our SUV. I opened up the back and pulled out the box containing the air-mattress. I glanced up toward the sky and was relieved to see that the storm clouds had passed already.

The rain must have missed us.

Enjoying the soft breeze, I began humming softly and headed back toward the house. The crickets were chirping and I could hear an owl hooting somewhere in the distance. I'd almost forgotten how peaceful Summit Lake could be, especially in the summer. It was a far cry from where we lived in Chicago. Our neighborhood wasn't the worst, but there were some rough areas just north of us. It was getting to the point that I was afraid to let Kevin ride his bike by himself, even on our block.

I should have moved back to Summit Lake long ago.

The only reason I'd originally left Minnesota was to put distance between myself and Brad after our gut-wrenching divorce. He'd actually been the one who'd filed and it had cut me deeply. Yes, we'd fought quite a bit, but it had been mainly about him wanting children and me needing to wait. I'd been twenty-two at that time and hadn't wanted to jump into late-night feedings, changing diapers, and chasing after children. Especially after running a daycare for the first three years of our marriage.

My mind went back to that time. I'd started running the daycare in our home at nineteen, right after Brad and I'd married. The money had been decent, but I'd been young and it had turned out to be a pretty stressful job. Eventually, I gave it up and enrolled at the community college, while doing some administrative work at a real estate company. It was during that time when Brad started nagging me about wanting kids. He hadn't understood why'd I'd wanted to wait, although I'd tried many times to reason with him. But, the man had been so stubborn, even refusing to go to counseling with me.

"The only way I'm going is if you give me what I've always wanted—a child," he'd told me. "We talked about this when we became engaged."

"I know, Brad. I just didn't realize you expected them right away," I'd fired back. *"Give me some time."*

Not having the patience to wait, he shocked me by filing for divorce. Ironically, it had been Brad acting like a child that had torn us apart. In the end, I moved to Chicago, to stay with a friend from college, and we never spoke again.

As for Brad, he never remarried, or had children of his own. When he was still alive, Mom would sometimes mention seeing him around town with different women on his arm, but apparently, nothing ever progressed and he remained single until he died in the car wreck.

Thankfully, I moved on and eventually met Kevin's father, Jason. He'd been fifteen years older than me and a high school science teacher. We met one summer, at a barbecue, and hit it off right away. Handsome and funny, he quickly swept me off my feet and soon we moved in together. Then came marriage and, of course, Kevin. Unfortunately, just when I thought our lives were perfect, Jason had a horrible stroke and died before our son was old enough to remember much about his father. It had been a devastating time in my life, even worse than the ordeal with Brad. I'd loved Jason with all of my heart and losing such a wonderful man put me into a depression that lasted for several months. Thank goodness for Tara, who drove out to stay with Kevin and me during that dark period.

A sudden whistling noise interrupted my thoughts as I headed up the steps to the porch. Alarmed, I quickly turned around and listened.

Silence.

Squinting in the darkness, I scanned the line of trees that surrounding both sides of the house and wondered if I'd imagined the noise or if it had merely been the wind. After not hearing anything further, I decided that I was just tired and needed to go inside. I took another step and then heard it again. This time, I knew it wasn't my imagination, because someone started whistling the tune *Pop Goes The Weasel*.

"Who's out there?" I called out.

They ignored me and continued whistling the nursery rhyme.

Was it Tara?

Was she trying to creep me out?

Admittedly, she had a dark sense of humor. But, I was pretty sure Tara had never learned to whistle.

The noise continued and I clenched my jaw. It was obvious that whoever was doing this wanted to scare me.

Asshole.

The front door opened abruptly, startling me.

Rocky stepped outside. "Need some help with that box, young lady?"

"Someone's out there," I murmured, noticing the whistling had stopped again, leaving just the sound of the leaves rustling in the wind.

Rocky's smile fell. "What?" He stepped out onto the porch. "Where?"

"I don't know, exactly," I replied as I searched for movement around the trees. "I just heard someone whistling. I called out to them and they ignored me."

He looked angry. "Whistling?" He turned and opened the screen door. "Come on. Let's go back inside."

I quickly scurried into the house.

Rocky took a shotgun out of the entryway closet, along with a box of bullets. He began loading the gun while I stared at him in bewilderment.

"Don't you think this is a little extreme?" I asked, feeling anxious now.

He grunted. "I hope not. We had some issues here a couple of weeks ago, though. Probably teenagers messing around, but you never know. They freaked your mother out, as you can imagine."

Knowing her, she would have been utterly terrified. "What did they do?" I asked, surprised she hadn't mentioned it.

"Not much. Just the damn whistling and an occasional glimpse of someone wearing a dark hoodie." He walked outside with the gun and stood on the porch. "Listen up! Whoever you are, get the hell off of this property or I'll call the sheriff and have you arrested!" he hollered.

Silence.

Rocky waited another minute. When there was still no response from the trespasser, he walked back into the house and locked the door.

"Do you think we *should* call the sheriff?" I asked as he stepped over to the window and peeked through the curtains.

"Nah. Like I said, this happened a couple of other times. It's probably just kids messing around. Trying to freak people out for kicks." He looked at me over his shoulder and smiled wryly. "I'm sure I scared them off with my gun."

Having seen enough horror movies in my time, I was starting to get the heebie-jeebies. Admittedly, knowing he had a gun was somewhat of a relief, though. In case it wasn't just "bored" teenagers messing around and some guy carrying a chainsaw.

28

"What's going on?" Kevin asked, walking out of the kitchen with Mom and Lacey following closely behind.

"Nothing," I lied and forced a smile to my face. "You ready for bed?"

Ignoring me, Kevin froze when he saw the hunting rifle and his eyes went wide. "Whoa, is that a real gun, Grandpa?"

Rocky smiled. "Yeah. I was just about to ask your mother if she'd like to go target shooting tomorrow."

Relieved that he didn't mention the whistler, I walked over to Kevin and put my hands on his shoulders. "Speaking of *tomorrow*, it's almost here. Let's get you to bed, kiddo."

"If you go shooting with Grandpa, I want to come and watch," Kevin replied, excited.

"I'm going to be very busy, so I don't think it's going to happen. Anyway, a shooting range isn't a place for an eight-year-old," I replied before walking over and picking up the air-mattress box. "Now, let's march upstairs. It's late and I think we could all use some rest."

"What about Lacey? Where is she going to sleep?" Kevin asked.

"Wherever she wants," Rocky said. "Does she need to go outside and do her business?"

The last thing I wanted was my dog outside with the whistling asshole. "She'll be fine. She just went before we brought her into the house."

He looked relieved. "Sounds good. Night, Kevin."

"Night, Grandpa," he replied and looked at my mother. "Goodnight, Grandma."

"Goodnight," she replied, looking distracted.

"Is there something wrong?" Kevin asked, noticing her troubled expression.

"Wrong? No. Nothing is wrong, dear." She smiled wanly. "I'm just tired. Now, get some sleep. I'll make you pancakes in the morning. Just like we talked about."

He started up the stairs. "Okay."

"I'll be back down in a bit," I said to them as I followed Kevin.

"Nonsense, Amanda. Get some sleep," Rocky said. "You're meeting with the lawyer tomorrow. You'll be too exhausted to think straight. If something comes up, and we need you, you'll know."

"Okay. Goodnight," I replied.

"Goodnight," they said in unison.

Chapter 2

Amanda

AFTER BLOWING UP the air-bed, which was admittedly more comfortable than my old mattress, and putting Kevin to sleep, I snuck another glance outside, but didn't see anyone lurking around on the property. Deciding that Rocky must have scared off whomever it was, I took a quick shower and then went to bed myself. Sleep didn't come for me right away, however. My mind raced with thoughts of the asshole whistler, my upcoming meeting with the lawyer, and then I thought about Brad. I still couldn't get over that he'd left me everything. Of course, the last I knew, he'd disowned his parents and brothers, Ben and Barry, for some unknown reason. Brad and Barry had actually been twins, while Ben had been the

youngest. All I knew was that the family had some
kind of a falling out and that he'd moved to
Minnesota when he was nineteen. Before moving to
Summit Lake, I knew he'd attended college at the U.
of M. As far as what happened between Brad and his
family—he refused to talk about it and they weren't
invited to our wedding.

Yawning, I rolled over and tried picturing Brad as
a man in his forties. It had been so long since I'd seen
him, although I could still remember our first
encounter. He'd just purchased, and restored, the
town's only video arcade. It had been during the
grand-reopening that I'd first laid eyes on him. He'd
been twenty-three, tall, with wavy blond hair, muscles,
and a smile that made all the girls swoon, especially
me. Back then, he'd reminded me of a surfer,
especially with his tousled, sun-bleached hair. Of
course, I'd only been eighteen at the time and he'd
barely noticed me, not with all the other girls flirting
like crazy with the handsome newcomer. For me it
had been love-at-first-sight and I'd been determined
to get him to notice me. So, I spent every free
moment at the arcade, trying to win his attention,
usually to no avail. It wasn't until he put a *Now Hiring*
sign in the window that things changed. I applied and
ended up getting the job. I immediately started
working for him, and we soon became much more
than boss and employee. He told me later that he'd

known all along I'd had a crush on him, even before hiring me, and was glad that I'd applied for the job. Apparently, the attraction had been mutual, although he'd thought I'd been older and had been a little disappointed to learn my true age.

Sighing, I turned back over and stared down at Kevin, sleeping peacefully. I wondered what would have happened if I'd have given Brad the child he'd wanted. Of course, I wouldn't have my son and he meant more to me than anything in the world. I also wouldn't have met Kevin's father, and I'd loved the man with all of my heart.

It was strange, and sad, that both guys were now gone and at such a young age. As angry as I'd been at Brad for breaking my heart, I would have never wished an early death upon him. Especially one so tragic.

It had been reported that his car had gone over a cliff, up near the North Shore somewhere. Shuddering, I imagined how terrifying those last few seconds must have been for him. As far as why it had happened, some thought he might have killed himself. The Brad I'd known used talk down about suicide, however, so I believed that his death had been an accident. Of course, it was always possible that his views had changed. He never remarried or had the children he'd wanted, and that might have taken its toll. Regardless, my heart felt heavy for the man I once loved and I hoped that wherever he was, he'd found some kind of peace.

Chapter 3

Amanda

"WHY ARE YOU putting on makeup?" asked Kevin, watching me from the doorway.

Staring into the bathroom mirror, I leaned forward and added some mascara to my lashes, which complemented the eyeshadow and eyeliner I'd also applied. I normally wore just a little pressed powder on my face and the mascara, so he wasn't used to everything else. Of course, I also didn't go out much. I'd devoted most of my time to him and working to pay the bills.

"I have a meeting today. Remember?" I replied, screwing the mascara cap back on.

"Oh, yeah. How long will you be gone?"

"Hopefully just a couple of hours."

"Okay."

Bored of watching me, Kevin left and went downstairs.

I pulled my blonde hair into a chignon, added some bobby-pins, and took one final look at my reflection. I had to admit, I didn't look half-bad for a woman approaching forty. Most people told me that I looked much younger, which I'd always chalked up to them just being friendly. Today, however, I almost believed them.

After I finished getting ready to meet with Brad's lawyer, I found Rocky on the porch, drinking his morning coffee and reading the paper. Lying by his feet was Lacey chewing on a raw-hide bone. I could tell right away, by the bags under his eyes, that he hadn't gotten much sleep.

I asked him if there'd been any more trouble from the whistling asshole.

"No. Like I said before, it's probably just kids," he said, looking up at me. "They might have been scared off by the gun. I didn't bring it out the time before. Now they know I mean business."

"Let's hope that's the case. Hey, girl," I said, bending down to pet Lacey. "I was wondering where you'd taken off to."

"She followed Kevin out here, and then stayed after he went back in for your mother's famous pancakes. Did you eat?"

I nodded.

"Good." He patted his stomach and smirked. "She put me on a diet so I can't have anything but oatmeal in the morning. It's only the third day and I'm about ready to sneak off into town and have some pancakes at Auntie K's Diner. You need a ride to your meeting?"

I smiled. "No. Why are you on a diet?" He didn't look overweight, although he did have a small pot belly.

He sighed in exasperation. "Let's see, my blood pressure is high. My cholesterol is high. My sugar levels are high. I'm so high… I reckon I should be seeing pink elephants and unicorns by now."

I laughed.

He glanced down at my blue short-sleeved sheath dress and then looked back up at my face and smiled. "Look at you all dollied up. You look very pretty."

I smiled. "Thank you."

"Do you have any idea what Brad left you?"

"No, I don't have a clue. Like I said before, we hadn't talked in ages. I was stunned when his lawyer called me. I thought Brad hated me, to be honest."

"Apparently, he didn't. In fact, he used to ask about you," Rocky said.

My eyes widened. "Really?"

He nodded. "Yep. Not that we talked much, but he would ask how you're doing upon passing each other in town."

I sighed. "Yeah, well, I'm *still* surprised that there wasn't anyone close to him when he died. Closer than me, at least."

"Your mom mentioned he was stubborn, and sometimes bossy. These days, if you want a woman in your life, you can't be either of those things. You choose your battles, too, which is why I'm on this damn diet. Your mother put her foot down and now I can't even open the refrigerator without her busting my chops."

I chuckled.

"Anyway, back to Brad. All I know is that he sold that video arcade of his awhile back, and apparently traveled a lot. That's what I heard, at least."

"He loved that place. Hopefully, he didn't lose money on it. You don't see many arcades around anymore."

"Nope, you don't."

"It's kind of sad. Anyway," I said, pulling my phone out of my purse to check the time. "I should get going. My meeting is in twenty minutes."

He glanced up at the sky. "Drive safely. I heard we're getting another storm soon. This one might not pass us by like the last one"

"Good to know. See you soon. Take care of Kevin for me."

"Your mother will smother him with over-protection and too many pancakes. Believe me, he's in good hands."

I laughed.

THE LAWYER'S OFFICE was in the center of town. I arrived a couple of minutes early and waited in the lobby with mixed emotions. Part of me was deeply saddened by my reason for being there. The other side was intrigued about the inheritance. Money had been tight for as long as I could remember, which was why'd we'd continued to rent the house in Chicago. We hadn't been able to save for a decent down payment on a home of our own. It was too bad that our situation might change for the better because of someone's death. I couldn't help but feel a little guilty about it.

"Mrs. Schultz?"

I looked up from the magazine I'd been rifling through at the older man standing in front of me. He had white hair, a moustache, and a tuft of fuzz under his mouth, reminding me a little of Colonel Sanders. All that was missing was the white suit and dark string bow tie.

"That's me." I put the magazine down and stood up.

"Mathew Bower," he said, holding out his hand and smiling warmly. "Nice to meet you."

"You as well." I shook his hand and then he invited me into his office.

"I'm sorry we're meeting on such grim circumstances," he said, after inviting me to sit down. "I'm very sorry for your loss."

"Thank you," I replied, not mentioning that our relationship had been estranged. I was uncomfortable enough as it was, being Brad's lone beneficiary.

He sat down across from me and pulled out a file. For the next hour, we went over Brad's will and discussed the assets he'd left behind. Apparently, there'd been a life insurance policy of fifty-thousand dollars, along with fifteen-thousand left still sitting in his savings account.

"He also owned some stock," Mr. Bower said. "I have his portfolio right here. As of this morning, the value of his investments appear to be just over two-hundred-and-sixty grand."

My jaw dropped. Had I heard him correctly? "You're kidding?"

"No. He sold the arcade a few years back and invested the money. You are the sole beneficiary to all of his stock holdings as well."

My head felt like it was swimming. "This is crazy. There wasn't anyone else he named in his will? Just me?"

"Just you." He smiled sadly. "I know you two divorced many years ago. I think he regretted his mistakes and probably still had feelings for you."

So, Brad had talked to him about our marriage?

I leaned back in the chair, still trying to take it all in. It felt so surreal. "As much as I'm grateful for him leaving all of this to me, I wish there'd been someone closer to him," I replied softly.

"I know he dated, but obviously, you'd left the biggest impression in his life."

I smiled sadly. "It's funny because he never tried getting in touch with me."

"You remarried, right? I'm sure he didn't want intrude on that."

"My husband died a few years ago. It was… unexpected."

Mr. Bower's eyes softened. "I'm sorry. You have my condolences."

"Thank you."

"So sad to hear that both men died so young. I imagine he wasn't an old goat like me?"

I couldn't help but smile. "No. I mean, you're not a goat. Or an old one."

He chuckled. "Tell my wife that."

I laughed.

"Anyway," he said, getting serious again. "Brad wasn't wise in regards to feelings of the heart, but he did make some sound investment choices."

"Apparently." I thought about Brad's funeral, which I'd missed. It had been during the last week of school and there'd been so much going on. Unfortunately, we hadn't been able to get away. Mom and Rocky had gone, however, as did most people in Summit Lake. It didn't matter that Brad had almost always kept to himself. People in town always paid their last respects to their neighbors, no matter how close they were. Of course, there'd been a big write-up about his death in the paper, so I imagined many also showed up out of curiosity.

"He pre-paid for the funeral a couple of years ago," Mr. Bower replied.

I frowned. "Really? He was only in his forties. That's quite young to be thinking about death, isn't it?"

He shrugged. "Brad wanted to be prepared, in case something happened. It might seem a little odd, but a lot of people are making arrangements earlier and earlier these days." He leaned back in his chair. "And funerals are damn expensive. He didn't want anyone to be burdened with having to pay for his."

"That was very thoughtful of him," I replied, my eyes getting misty remembering some of the tender, romantic moments we'd had together before our marriage had started to disintegrate. As frustrating as he could be, I would never regret the times we'd shared together.

"Yes," agreed Mr. Bower. His brown eyes began to sparkle. "Of course, I might have planted a seed or two about the importance of estate planning."

"Nothing wrong with that."

"Well, it certainly paid off this time. Sadly." He started paging through the paperwork again. "Now, as far as his liabilities go…"

Fortunately, Brad had little to none, I learned. His mortgage had been paid off long ago and the only vehicle he'd owned had been the one in the crash. That loan had also been paid off.

"It looks like you have a lot of thinking and planning to do," Mr. Bower said, after I signed all of the legal paperwork and was given the keys to Brad's home.

"Indeed. Thank you so much for everything," I replied, my head still spinning from everything that was happening.

He held out his hand. "If you have any questions or ever need legal advice, give me a call."

"I actually do have a question," I said, shaking his hand. "Do you have the address for Brad's place?"

He chuckled. "I suppose that would help. He's right on the lake. The address is in the file. I'd show you the cabin myself, but I have another appointment coming up in twenty minutes."

"It's no problem at all," I answered, intrigued. During our marriage, we'd lived in a small home, close to town. We'd sold it after our divorce, splitting the meager proceeds.

"It's a nice place. I think you'll like it."

"You've been there?" I asked as he walked me to the door.

"Not when he owned it. I was friends with the previous owner, though. We used to go fishing together."

"Did Brad have a boat?" I asked, not recalling one being on the list of assets.

"No. There's a dock, though. You should get one. You certainly have the money for it," he replied, smiling.

"*If* I decide to move into the cabin."

"When you see the house, I have a feeling you will have a hard time parting with it," he replied with a wink.

Now, I really was intrigued.

Chapter 4

Amanda

I WALKED OUT of the building and headed to my SUV, which was parked across the street. After getting in, I called my mother and told her the news.

She gasped. "You're kidding? All of that's *yours?*"

"Apparently," I replied, wishing I didn't feel so giddy, but unable to help myself. This would be life-changing for me and Kevin.

"When do you get the money?"

"I have to contact the life insurance company and put in a claim for the fifty-thousand. As far as the investment money goes, I need to talk to a financial advisor and decide what I should do with it. Maybe invest it myself?"

"Good idea. And the house?"

"I'm going to look at it right now."

"Can we meet you there?" she asked excitedly. "I've always wanted to see the inside of that place."

"Is it really *that* nice?" I asked.

"Wait until you see it," she replied with a grin in her voice. "You're going to want to move in."

"Funny, the lawyer basically said the same thing to me."

"You'll see why. I'll grab Rocky and Kevin and we'll meet you out there. Unless… you want to be alone for a while? I know you didn't live together at that place, but I'm sure this must all be pretty overwhelming. Not to mention that I know how much you once loved him."

"Actually, why don't you give me an hour and then meet me there?" I replied, realizing that I did need a little time to myself. Having talked with the lawyer had brought back some old feelings. I wasn't sure how I would handle stepping into Brad's cabin and thought it might be better to do it alone.

"I understand," she said softly.

We talked for a few more minutes and then hung up. As I was about to start the engine, I noticed a white envelope on my dashboard. Frowning, I opened it up to find a flowery greeting card that read "Welcome Back" on the front. I looked inside and found a handwritten note.

Roses are fickle

Violets are sweet
I'm glad you returned
You're in for a treat…

There was nothing else with the card and nobody had signed it.

I raised my eyes and looked around as people walked by, most of them with their heads bent to stare down at their phones. I wondered who'd left the odd note. Even more-so, I wondered how the sender had gotten into my vehicle, which I know had been locked. One learned to do that, living in Chicago.

As I was staring out my passenger window, I heard a loud knock on the driver's side, startling the hell out of me. I gasped and then smiled when I saw who it was.

Tara Flyhill.

I rolled down my window. "Tara! Hi. How are you?" I asked, noting that she actually looked very well. She was tall and still very slim, with long, dark hair and light-blue eyes. The previous summer, she'd appeared so gaunt and tired. We'd gotten together for dinner and that's when Tara had confided in me that she'd caught her husband cheating. Although they'd started counseling soon afterward, she'd been having a tough time trying to forgive him. Things must have gotten better, however, because today her face was glowing and she looked more attractive than ever.

"I'm doing well," she said, leaning down. "And you?"

"Great."

"Good. I heard you were stopping back into town." She gave me a pouty look. "Why didn't you call me?"

"We just got in last night. I was going to call you later this evening."

"Eh, I figured you would when you got the chance. Someone has to give you a hard time. It may as well be me." She smiled, and tucked a strand of hair behind her ear. "Girl you are a sight for sore eyes. I can't tell you how good it is to see you. How is Kevin?"

"He's doing very well."

She smiled and clucked her tongue. "That kid. He's adorable. I'm sure he's shot up a few inches since the last time I saw him, right?"

"A little." Kevin was short for his age, although his father had been relatively tall. I was only five-two, however, and knew that Kevin's final height was going to be a toss-up. I only hoped he'd take after his father. He already looked so much like him—a handsome boy with wavy brown hair and puppy-dog eyes that had me wrapped around his finger. I knew I was biased, but he *was* damn cute.

48

"I loved his Halloween costume last year. The one you sent me a photo of. What was that? A swashbuckler?"

I laughed. "He was a vampire pirate."

She chuckled. "Oh, of course. What was I thinking?"

"I know. He's very creative. When he couldn't decide over being a pirate or a vampire, he combined the two."

"Makes total sense. The kid is as smart as a whip."

I agreed.

"You know, I was thinking that we should get together and have a couple of drinks. Catch up on things?"

"Of course. How about tomorrow?"

She nodded. "Yeah. That'll work. You want to meet at Shoop's?"

Shoop's was the newest nightclub in Summit Lake. I'd never been there, but it sounded like fun. "Sure. What about Josh? Is he going to be okay with it?"

She grunted. "He has no say. Josh and I have been separated now for six months."

My eyes widened. "What? I had no idea. I'm sorry to hear that." Even more so, I was sorry we'd lost touch.

"Don't be. I'm just sorry that I wasted time going to counseling with him. Do you know that the bastard cheated on me *again* after I caught him the first time?"

I scowled. "Wow. What a jerk. I always thought you were too good for him."

Josh and Tara had met when they were in the eleventh grade. It had been the familiar story of prom-queen and star-quarterback falling madly in love and marrying right out of high school after expecting the unexpected—twins. Of course, Josh had always been a heavy flirt, so the fact that he'd cheated on her, again, hadn't totally surprised me.

"I wish you would have expressed those thoughts a little more loudly," she said with a smirk.

"Hey, I tried telling you back when I saw him hitting on Emma Murphy at that one party, remember?" I replied, thinking back. Josh had been wasted and I'd seen him grabbing Emma's butt when Tara hadn't been looking. Unfortunately, he'd given some excuse about being drunk and of course, she'd forgiven him.

Tara let out a ragged sigh. "I know. I know. I was so naïve back then. Anyway, forget about him. How is your mother doing? I've seen her in town, but we haven't had a chance to catch up."

"Doing very well. Rocky is taking great care of her."

"Those two love-birds," she mused. "He's adorable. I always thought he looked a little like Harrison Ford."

I nodded in agreement.

"And your mom, she always reminded me of Meg Ryan. What a handsome couple they are. And why in the hell haven't *you* aged?" she joked. "Are you still single? Is that why?"

"I'm not with anyone. Of course, I don't get out much," I admitted.

Her eyes sparkled with amusement. "Keep it that way. I swear, look at what my boys and husband have done to me. I look like hell."

"You look great, especially now that you've kicked Josh to the curb," I replied. "Not all guys are like him, you know. Untrustworthy."

"I know," she said, her smile fading. "I probably always knew the kind of man he was, I just didn't want to admit it to myself."

I could tell the subject was bringing her down, so I changed it. She was past all of that, anyway. "Speaking of your boys, how are they?"

Her "boys" were now grown and in college. Both handsome young men with promising futures. Tara herself worked for some strategic marketing firm that was based out of New York. Fortunately, she was also able to work from home, but was always flying around the country for meetings.

"They're doing well. Pissed off at their father for being a cheating jerk."

"You raised them right, then."

She grinned proudly. "Yeah, well… someone had to. Josh was always at 'the office'—the lying asshole.

Anyway," she looked at her watch, "I've got to get my ass home. I have a group chat about some potential new accounts that I can't miss. So, what do you say? Eight o'clock at Shoop's tomorrow?"

I nodded. "Yep. See you then."

"Great. Don't forget."

"I won't."

"You'd better believe you won't. I still have your number and I'm not afraid to use it."

I laughed.

She leaned in and gave me a hug. "I've missed you."

"I've missed you, too, Tara."

Chapter 5

Amanda

BRAD'S HOME WAS an expansive, one-level log cabin. It was located at the end of a long gravel road and on the northern side of Summit Lake. From what I could tell, a newly constructed deck wrapped around the front of the place and there was a large storage shed just beyond the house.

Impressed, I got out of my SUV and headed to the front door, excited to see the interior of the house.

I was not disappointed. I gasped in pleasure as I opened the front door.

Walking inside, I immediately found myself in a large, open space where the kitchen, dining room, and living room were all connected. Long, wooden beams stretched across the tall ceiling, making the home even more rustic-looking. As I stepped closer to the kitchen, I noticed the wood was painted white, making it not only bright, but very charming. There was also a huge butcher-block island, which separated the gourmet kitchen from the dining area, and imagined myself making Kevin's meals while he played with his baseball cards or worked on his homework.

After inspecting the cupboards and the large pantry, I walked over to the fireplace, which was definitely one of the main focal points in the house. Running my hand over the mantel and stonework, I could see myself curled up on a sofa and reading in front of a warm fire. Or coming up with my own book ideas.

Inspiration, I thought. *This place might be exactly what I need get me over my writer's block.*

Smiling to myself, I headed around the corner to the hallway, and found three bedrooms. The first one was the master. I walked through the double-doors and found myself staring at a large king-sized bed with a dark mahogany head- and foot-board. There was also a tall dresser, two nightstands, and an armoire that matched the bedstead. It was masculine, bold, and beautiful. Exactly what I would have pictured in Brad's bedroom.

I walked over to the closet and opened it. Of course, his clothing still hung from hangers and his shoes lined the bottom. Stacked above were old car magazines, some sweaters, and several shoeboxes. Knowing I'd have to go through everything later, I started closing the closet when I caught the scent of Brad's cologne, which obviously hadn't changed over the years. The smell brought back more memories, making my heart heavy again and caused tears to prick my eyes.

I quickly closed the closet and checked out the other bedrooms. One had a full-sized bed and the other had been used as an office.

My new office?

I continued walking around, falling more in love with the cabin with each passing second. It wasn't until I stepped out onto the ground-level deck, however, that I really appreciated the place.

"Wow," I murmured, leaning my hands against the wood railing as I stared at the lake.

The view was breathtaking.

Knowing I could look out every day to such natural beauty, without having to even go on vacation, made me want the place even more.

How could anyone say no to this?

I certainly didn't want to. Hopefully, Kevin would fall in love with it, too.

My phone suddenly began to buzz and I received a text from my mother that they were on their way.

MOM, KEVIN, AND Rocky showed up fifteen minutes later.

"Well… what do you think?" Mom asked, after getting out of their pickup truck.

I grinned. "You were right. It's very nice. Brad definitely had wonderful taste."

"Of course he did," Rocky said, twirling his key chain around his finger. "He chose you once, too. He just didn't have very good common sense. Which… apparently worked out for you in the long run." He put his arm around Kevin. "Right, kiddo?"

"Huh?" he replied, looking confused.

"It means that Brad had a good woman and let her go. That worked out better because then she met your father and you were born," Mom answered for Rocky.

"Oh," he replied and smiled.

"And I wouldn't have changed that for the world," I added, ruffling Kevin's hair. "So, are you ready to see the place?"

"Yes!" Kevin hollered, now looking excited himself. "I've never been to a cabin before."

"And what a cabin it is," I replied with a wink. "I think you're going to love it."

We walked into the house and Kevin sucked in a breath. "Wow, does that fireplace really work?"

"It should," I replied.

"I'm sure it does. We'll help you get it going." Her eyes danced as she looked around. "Wow, this has a nice open floorplan, too. Don't you think, Rocky?"

"Yes. I like how you can watch television and still be in the kitchen," he replied.

"Of course that's what you love about it," she said, rolling her eyes and smiling. "The woodwork is simply gorgeous. And look at those beams above."

Rocky looked up. "Yeah, great craftsmanship." He walked over to the built-in media center and ran his hand along the top. "This is made from black walnut. Wow, I'm impressed."

Mom turned around and looked at me. "You know, if you don't want it, maybe Rocky and I will take it off of your hands."

"I'm game for that," he said, smiling. "Ours is too big for just the two of us now anyway."

She walked over and put her arms around his waist. "And I don't know about you, but my knees aren't getting any younger and that staircase of ours isn't helping."

"I hear you," he said, hugging her. "No matter what Amanda decides, we should really think about downsizing anyway."

Mom nodded. "I agree."

"Is this house really yours, Mom?" Kevin asked me, staring at everything with wide eyes.

I smiled. "It's *ours*, Kev. To do whatever we want with it."

"Can we keep it?" he asked.

I stared at him in surprise. "You want to *move* here?"

He frowned. "No. But, I would like to stay here sometimes, though."

I chuckled. He was too young to understand. Oh, to be so young and unaware of mortgages, taxes, and utility bills. "Sorry, kiddo, but we can't afford to have both places."

Kevin sighed.

"Let's look at the rest of the place. Come on, Buckaroo," Mom said, grabbing Kevin's hand.

The three of them toured the house while I put my sunglasses on and went back outside. I headed down to the lake, where there was a floating dock. I walked down to the end of it and sat down on the bench, sighing happily.

The water was alive with boaters and a couple of jet-skiers, enjoying the eighty-degree weather. Sitting there in the sun, and staring at such a lovely view of the lake, I imagined Kevin and me living there permanently and how nice it could be.

"He'll adjust," Rocky said, startling me.

I gasped and laughed. "I didn't hear you," I said, looking up at him as he walked around and sat down next to me on the bench.

"Sorry. This place is something else, isn't it?" he said, looking out toward the lake.

I nodded. "Yeah. It's amazing. Everything about it."

He sighed. "You'd be silly if you let it go. Even to us. This could be a nice home for you and Kevin."

"I know. I was thinking the same thing. He'd be so angry with me if I decided to stay, though."

Rocky shrugged. "Not for long. He just needs to make some friends in town and he'll be fine. You know, life is always changing and it's good for kids to learn how to adapt at an early age. It will make him a better adult."

For someone who'd never had children of his own, he had a very good point. I also knew I usually gave in too easily to Kevin. It would definitely be a good learning experience if we kept the cabin.

Rocky smiled. "Besides, your mother would be ecstatic if you moved back, too."

She'd been begging me to for so long. "I know."

Suddenly, we could hear someone running on the dock. We both turned to find Kevin heading toward us, my mother behind him.

"This is cool! Can I go swimming?" Kevin asked excitedly as he looked around the lake.

"Not right now. We didn't bring along your swimsuit," I replied.

"I can wear my shorts," he said.

I looked down at the water. "I don't even know how deep it is here."

"I'm thinking it's pretty shallow," Mom said as she reached us. "But, he should wear a life-jacket, just in case. There could be some drop-offs. At least until we know for sure."

"Can we go back home and get my suit and a life-jacket?" Kevin begged.

I was tired and was about to tell him we'd have to wait until tomorrow, but then changed my mind. The more time we spent at the cabin, the more likely Kevin would fall in love with the place. The easier it would be to convince him to want to stay.

"I think that's a great idea," I said and looked at Rocky. "Do you have a life-jacket that will fit him?"

"Of course. We still have the one from last year when we went fishing. There could also be some in that shed back there," he said, motioning toward the shore.

I looked back at the shed. We hadn't yet explored it, but I imagined that it was where Brad had kept his gardening supplies and lawn mower.

"I don't know. He didn't have a boat, or kids, so chances are there wouldn't be a life-jacket that could fit Kev," I replied.

"No worries. Like I said, we've got one for him," Rocky replied.

I smiled. "Okay. I'd like to go back home and change out of this dress. We can grab some boxes from town on the way back here, too." I wanted to start packing Brad's things so we could donate them to a local shelter.

"Boxes? For what?" Kevin asked.

I explained.

"So, you're just going to give away everything?" Mom asked, looking surprised.

"That's what I was thinking. It's certainly the easiest way to clear this place out. If you see something you want, take it," I replied. "Anything."

"Why don't you have a garage sale?" Rocky said. "People in this town love those things. I bet you'll make some good money, too."

"That's a great idea," my mother said, her eyes lighting up. "We can help you with it."

To me, it sounded like a lot of work. But then again, so did packing and making several trips to the shelter. A little extra cash wouldn't hurt, either.

"Okay. Good idea. Let's do it," I replied, standing up.

"I bet we can get everything ready by this weekend," Mom said, the wheels in her head already spinning. "In fact, I'll go into town tomorrow morning and buy some pricing stickers and signs."

"I'll give you money for that," I said.

"Whatever," she said. "You know, I have a feeling that Brad has some expensive items hidden away.

Whatever you make, you can use for Kevin's college fund."

"I will, but… I'm splitting whatever we make with you guys," I replied.

Mom waved her hand. "You don't have to do that."

"Nonsense. It's either that or you're not helping," I said firmly.

"You'd better listen to her," Rocky said, chuckling. "We both know she's as stubborn as you are, Jan."

"Don't I know it," Mom replied with a small grin.

"Can I help with the garage sale?" Kevin asked, biting the side of his fingernail.

"You sure can," my mother said, putting her hand on his shoulder and squeezing it. "Getting it ready will probably be a lot of work. We're going to need all the help we can get."

"Okay. But I can still go swimming today, right?" he asked, looking at me.

I glanced down at my watch. "Of course. Let's get going now, so we have enough time for all of this."

"Hurray!" Kevin hollered before running back down the dock toward shore.

"Something tells me that he's going to be begging you to move here before the end of the week," Rocky said with a smirk.

"Let's hope so," I replied.

"So, you're thinking about keeping it?" Mom asked.

"Unless you really want it," I answered.

"I'd rather have you in it," she said with a loving smile. "Here, back in Summit Lake."

"Then help me convince Kevin to want to stay," I replied.

"Leave it to me and Rocky," Mom said as the three of us headed back toward shore. "We'll change his mind."

"Good luck," I replied, knowing how stubborn Kevin could be.

"By the way, have you had a chance to look through the shed yet?" she asked as we passed it on the way back to the cabin.

"Nope," I replied.

"I'm sure it's the usual—lawnmower, grass seed, spiders, mice, maybe a snake or two," Rocky said.

I shuddered, thinking back to when I was a teenager and had stumbled upon a snake one summer. It had been eating something small and furry and had freaked the hell out of me.

"Stop that. You know how much she hates snakes," Mom scolded.

"Yeah. Just for that, *you're* looking inside," I told him. "With my luck, there really *is* something living in there."

"Don't worry. I'll inspect it tomorrow," he promised.

"Thank you," I replied.

"This is going to be fun," Mom said. "I haven't held a garage sale in ages."

"Good Lord," Rocky said. "If that's really your idea of *fun*, I'm a shitty husband who needs to take his wife out more."

She laughed. "Oh, Rock, you're wonderful. I just love a good sale and catching up with old friends. When folks around here find out we're holding one, they'll be throwing money at us. Especially when they find out we're selling Brad's things."

"Why is that so special?" I asked.

"Because of how he died. People around here are friendly, but they're also nosier than hell," Rocky said. "They're going to flock here when they find out."

"You got that right," Mom said dryly.

One reason why I'd left Summit Lake in the first place—gossipy neighbors. Still, things seemed to be falling into place. First the inheritance money and now a beautiful cabin on the lake. I just needed Kevin to come onboard and things would be perfect.

Chapter 6

Amanda

AS PLANNED, KEVIN and I changed at Mom and Rocky's, and then made our way back to the cabin. Along the way, I stopped at a local supermarket and scored some empty boxes for packing. As we were leaving the store, a man called out my name. I turned around and saw a face I hadn't seen in many years.

Parker Daniels.

We'd dated briefly in high school, but stopped after he went off to college. Parker had been a grade higher and we only went on a handful of dates, but I'd really liked the guy. Seeing him again brought back some good memories.

"Hey!" I said, smiling as he approached.

"Look at you. You haven't changed a bit," he said, his blue eyes twinkling. "Is this your son?"

"Yes," I replied. "This is Kevin."

"Hi, Kevin. I'm Parker. Nice to meet you," he said.

"You, too," Kevin replied shyly.

I noticed that Parker had changed, but only in a good way. The skinny, lanky boy had filled out into a broad-shouldered, athletic man who filled out a tank top better than most. Not to mention, he was still very handsome, with his light-brown hair and icy blue eyes. Just seeing him again gave me butterflies.

"How's Jan?" Parker asked me.

"She's doing great. She remarried a few years ago."

He nodded. "Yeah, I know. I've met Rocky a few times. He's a good guy."

"Yeah. So, how long have you been back in town?" I asked.

"A couple of years. I moved back to Summit Lake after my divorce," he replied.

From his expression, he seemed like he wasn't bitter about it, but in a good place. Of course, one never knew. "Divorce? I'm sorry to hear things didn't work out between you and your wife."

He smiled and shrugged. "It is what it is, and... we're still friends. For the most part. Anyway, what's with the boxes?"

Before I could answer, Kevin chimed in. "We're going to have a garage sale!"

Parker stared at him in amusement. "Really?"

"We're helping to clear out Brad Shaw's old stuff," I explained, not wanting to get into it too much.

"I saw in the paper that he'd died recently. You're selling his things?" he asked.

I nodded. "We, um, we were married once. A long time ago."

"I thought I heard something about that. You know, his cabin is not too far from my place. It looks like a nice place. Are you thinking about buying it?"

"Honestly, I don't know. Maybe. We're pretty comfortable in Chicago, though. It's hard to say," I replied cryptically.

"I imagine it's hard to just drop everything and move back here. Especially, if you and your husband are settled into your jobs," he replied.

"Actually, it's just me and Kevin now," I said. "I'm a writer, so I can work from home. He has friends in Chicago and isn't thrilled about leaving them," I explained.

"Yeah, that can be difficult. Well, if you need help with anything, like I said... I'm close."

"Thank you."

He looked at Kevin again. "By the way, my son Austin is joining me tomorrow. He just turned twelve. Maybe we could get the boys together to go fishing sometime soon? I have a pontoon, so there'd be plenty of room. I'd love it if you could join us."

"That would be nice," I replied, thinking it sounded like fun. "Thank you."

He grinned. "Great. I'll have to get in touch with you," he said as his cell phone began to ring.

"Sounds good," I replied.

Parker's face fell as he stared at his phone.

"Is everything okay?" I asked.

He let out a weary sigh. "My mother is in a nursing home. She has dementia and they've been having issues with her. I'm actually nervous about calling them back," he said with a grimace. "She's been getting a little violent lately."

I was about to ask about his father when I remembered Mom telling me that he'd been killed in some kind of boating accident, a few years back.

"That's too bad. I'm sorry about your mother," I replied.

"Thanks." He stared off into the distance. "I feel so guilty sometimes. Leaving her there. I even tried looking out for her when I first moved back to Summit Lake, but she needs round-the-clock care now. It just became too much."

"I can only imagine," I replied, not knowing what else to say. He certainly didn't have to explain anything to me. "You're doing the best you can. You have to know that."

He sighed. "I keep telling myself that. It doesn't make me feel any better, though."

"You always were tough on yourself," I replied, remembering how serious he could be at times. "I guess some things never change."

He chuckled. "No. I guess they don't."

Our eyes met and the butterflies started up again.

"Well, it's been good seeing you. I missed that smile of yours."

I blushed. "I missed yours, too."

He gave me a lopsided grin. "Don't be a stranger."

"Um, you neither," I replied.

"Nice meeting you, Kevin," Parker said, holding out his hand.

Kevin shook it and let go. "You, too, sir."

"Wow, the kid not only has great manners, but a Kung-Fu grip. Those are some deadly weapons," Parker joked, shaking out his hand like it hurt.

Kevin smiled.

"You keep your mama safe, now, you hear?" Parker said.

He nodded.

"He always does. My little bodyguard," I said, putting my hand over my son's shoulder.

Kevin blushed.

"You're obviously in good hands. Both of you. See you, later," Parker said, winking at me.

I smiled. "Goodbye."

"I CAN'T WAIT to go fishing on his pontoon!" Kevin said when Parker was out of earshot. "What is it, anyway?"

I smiled. "A pontoon?"

Kevin nodded and I explained.

"Cool!"

"We'd better get a family fishing license," I said as we headed back to my car.

"You're going, too?"

"I hope so. I like to fish, too, you know."

Sort of.

I liked watching the bobber go under and reeling in my catch. But, that was about it.

He gave me a confused look. "But, you never go with me and Rocky."

As much as I loved Rocky, he wasn't Parker Daniels, and somehow I knew he would make fishing much more enjoyable.

WHEN WE FINALLY made it back to the cabin, it was three o'clock. I took Kevin back out to the dock with his life-jacket on, and we both slowly got into the lake. The water was cool and felt wonderful in the eighty-eight-degree heat. It was definitely deeper than we'd anticipated, over Kevin's head, so I was relieved to have the life-jacket Rocky had provided.

"Mom, watch this!" Kevin cried before doing a cannonball off the dock for the fourth time.

Laughing, I wiped the water away from my face and watched as he dog-paddled his way back to the dock.

Kevin climbed back up and was about to do it again, when he stared past me and waved. I turned to see a stranger waving back at him in a slow-moving black Monterey boat. He was shirtless, wore a *Twins* baseball cap and sunglasses, but other than that, I couldn't make out the guy's features. Thinking it might be Parker, I raised my hand and also waved, but the stranger ignored me. I watched as he gunned the boat and took off.

I looked up at Kevin just as he jumped back into the water, splashing me in the face again and loving every minute of it.

"You turkey," I cried, splashing him back playfully while both of us laughed. We stayed out in the lake for almost two hours and then dried off in the sun.

"Can I go back into the water?" he asked when I finally stood up and grabbed my towel.

"No. It's time to go inside. I want to go through a few of Brad's things before we head back to Grandma and Grandpa's."

He began to pout.

"Grab your life-jacket," I said, ignoring his pout.

Reluctantly, he did what I asked and then ran up toward the shore with his towel wrapped around his shoulders. I followed him, but as I reached the deck, I realized I'd left my cell phone on the bench.

"Kevin, change your clothes. You can have a snack before I order the pizza we talked about. I'm going back to the dock to grab my phone."

"Okay."

I walked back to the bench where I'd left it and was about to head the opposite direction, when I heard the sound of an approaching jet skier. I turned and noticed a man hauling ass in my direction, wearing what looked to be a skull-mask bandana. Just before reaching the dock, he turned sharply and deliberately splashed me. I gasped, shocked and annoyed that my phone was now wet. Instead of apologizing, he raced away and disappeared on the other side of the lake.

"Asshole!" I screamed inspecting my phone.

Fortunately, it wasn't completely drenched and seemed to be working fine. Grumbling to myself, I headed back up to the house, thinking about the boater and the jet skier.

Was it the same guy?

They both had similar athletic builds, although the boater had been too far away to get a good look at. Not to mention, the jet skier had been wearing the freaky skull mask. I wasn't sure what their problems were, but I decided not to let it ruin my day. Especially after it had started out so well.

AFTER CHANGING OUT of our swimsuits, I ordered a pepperoni and mushroom pizza, Kevin's favorite. I then handed him one of the apples my mother had packed in a small cooler, while we waited.

"Can I watch TV?" he asked, polishing the apple on his T-shirt before taking a bite.

"The electricity is off," I replied, grateful Brad's lawyer had hired someone to empty the perishables from the refrigerator and freezer before the power company had turned everything off.

He sighed. "I'm bored."

I arched my eyebrow. "Really? I can find you something to do."

"Like what?"

"For starters, you can help me go through some of Brad's things."

He groaned. "Can I play on your phone instead?"

I nodded toward his apple. "No. You'll get it sticky."

"After I'm done eating?"

"My phone is almost dead. Wait until we get back to Grandma's and Grandpa's."

"Fine," he huffed.

I grabbed a couple of boxes and headed toward Brad's bedroom. "You want something to do… without doing *anything*? Listen for the doorbell."

"That doesn't make any sense."

I bit back a smile. "It will when you have your own kids someday."

He didn't reply.

I walked into the main bedroom and set the empty boxes down. Opening up the closet, I looked around and decided I'd start with the shoeboxes on top and work my way down.

I reached up, grabbed the first box, and set it down on the bed. When I removed the cover, I saw that it was filled with credit card statements and other financial receipts. Not wanting to be nosy, I shoved the paperwork back into the box and decided that in the morning, I'd contact the lawyer and ask him what to do with all of Brad's bills and legal paperwork.

"Mom," Kevin said, walking in the room as I searched quickly through the other shoeboxes. "Can I go outside?"

"The pizza will be here soon," I said, not really wanting him outside or near the lake without me. Especially after the rude jet skier. He'd really rubbed me the wrong way.

"I can watch for him. I'm bored in here," he said.

"You can go outside, but… stay on the deck."

He groaned. "Why?"

"Just do what I ask, Kevin. Please."

Sighing, he mumbled something under his breath and then walked out of the room.

"Don't leave the deck!" I called out.

"I won't," he grumbled.

Wondering if maybe I was being a smother-mother, I began going through Brad's clothing and sorting them in piles on the bed. As I examined everything, I noticed he'd gone up quite a few sizes since we'd been together. Unfortunately, there weren't any photos around, at least none that'd I'd found yet, so I had no idea what he'd looked like before his death. It was kind of odd, considering he used to love being in front of a camera.

The doorbell rang and I raced out of the bedroom to answer it, wondering why Kevin hadn't warned me. Oddly enough, when I opened up the door, nobody was there.

I stepped outside and looked around.

"Kevin?" I hollered, thinking he might be so bored that he had resorted to playing ding-dong-ditch on his own mother.

"Yeah?" he replied loudly, peeking his head around the house from the back of the deck.

Surprised, I asked if he'd seen anyone around.

"No, why?"

"I could have sworn I heard someone ring the doorbell. It wasn't you, was it?"

He shook his head. "No. I've been right here."

I knew I hadn't imagined it.

Was he still trying to mess with me?

I calculated the time it would have taken Kevin to ring the bell and then race back behind the house. It was definitely feasible, but, he didn't look out of breath and had appeared surprised when I'd asked him about it.

"I must be hearing things," I replied, frowning.

"Is the pizza here yet?" he called out.

"You're the one who's supposed to be watching for the delivery person," I said.

Kevin looked past me and his eyes lit up. "It's here!"

I turned around and saw a white pickup approach with a pizza sign on top. As I was about to head back inside to get my purse, I noticed a small, brown box sitting between two, large empty planters. Tied around it was a sparkly red bow. Curious, I walked over, picked it up, and then went inside to get some cash.

"What's that?" Kevin asked, walking into the kitchen, from the deck.

"I don't know. Looks like some sort of gift, doesn't it?" I said, setting the box onto the kitchen table and then reaching for my purse.

"Can I open it?"

Suddenly feeling apprehensive about the box, I told him that I would have to do it.

"Why?" he whined as the doorbell rang.

"Because we don't know who it's from."

"Maybe it's from that guy. Parker?"

"Maybe."

I headed to the front door and let the deliveryman in. After paying for the pizza and a two-liter bottle of orange soda, we brought everything into the kitchen. I then began searching the cupboards and found clean plates and glasses.

"Can we go home after this?" Kevin asked as I opened the pizza box. The smell of tomato sauce and freshly baked dough filled the air, making my stomach growl.

I snuck a piece of pepperoni and popped it into my mouth. "We'll see. I'd like to go through more of Brad's things."

"But you said we had to leave before it got dark."

I pulled out a piece of pizza and put it onto a plate. "It's early still," I said, sliding it over to him.

"I'm tired," he pouted. "I want to go back to Grandma's and see Lacey."

I sighed. Clearly, if we stayed, I wouldn't get much done because he would continue to whine until I relented.

I sat down across from Kevin and picked up my piece of pizza. "Fine. We'll go back. We both need showers anyway."

Plus, I hadn't gotten a lot of sleep the night before.

"Good," he said, looking relieved.

When we were finished eating, we packed up the leftovers and grabbed our damp swimsuits.

"Don't forget about the gift!" Kevin said as we headed to the door.

"That's right."

I picked up the box, feeling another wave of apprehension as I examined it.

"Open it," prodded Kevin, his eyes glittering with excitement.

Using my key, I cut through the packing tape and opened up the box. Inside, was a cell phone.

"What in the world?" I pulled it out of the box and began examining it.

"Whose is that?" Kevin asked, scratching his head.

"I have no idea."

It definitely wasn't new, either. In fact, there was a small crack on the screen and it looked pretty beat-up. I turned the phone over and found four numbers typed onto a small piece of paper taped to the back of the phone. I punched them into the keyboard on the screen and it unlocked the phone.

"Is it a phone for me? Maybe someone got me a phone?" Kevin said with a hopeful look.

"No, Kev. This is not for you."

I checked the *contact list* and began doing a search. Not seeing anyone's name I recognized, I went to the photos to see if I could figure out who owned it.

Strangely, most of the pictures were of children and the majority seemed unaware that someone had snapped a photo of them.

"What are you looking at?" Kevin asked as I thumbed through more images.

"Nothing," I said, a little weirded out by the number of photos taken of kids. They were all done at public places and the subjects were anywhere from toddlers to children not much older than Kevin.

He sighed. "I want to go home."

"Okay." I put the phone back into the box, still bewildered as to why someone had left it for us. Even weirder is that I knew it had to be the person who'd rung the doorbell and disappeared.

Parker?

No. It didn't make sense. Why would he send me a used cell phone?

"Let's go," I said to Kevin.

We walked out of the house and headed to the car. As I started the engine, I heard a buzzing noise and realized it was coming from the strange phone. Surprised, I took it out and saw that someone had sent a text message with the words "Looking Good." It was followed by a photo. I enlarged the picture, not sure what I was seeing at first. When I realized what it was, I gasped in horror and dropped the phone.

"What's wrong?" Kevin asked.

My heart raced as I looked around the property, wondering what in the hell was going on.

"Mom?"

"It's nothing," I lied, trembling.

Unfortunately, it was something. Something that scared the hell out of me.

Chapter 7

Amanda

MY HEAD WAS spinning as we drove back to my mother's. As terrified as I was, I'd decided to wait and talk to them before going to the police. Not only did I not want to freak Kevin out, but I thought they might be able to make sense as to what was happening.

"Mommy, are you okay?" Kevin squeaked from the backseat.

Mommy?

He never called me that anymore.

Realizing that my silence was scaring Kevin, I looked at him in the rearview mirror and forced a smile to my face. "I'm fine, sweetie."

"Okay," he said, still looking unsure.

I turned the radio on, grateful that one of his favorite songs was playing. We turned the music up and he began singing with Bruno Mars.

When we finally made it to Mom and Rocky's, I was a nervous wreck.

"Come on, Kev. I'll race you inside," I said, both anxious and apprehensive. For all I knew, the person who'd left the phone, and sent the message, could be close by. I wondered if it could have even been the whistling asshole.

Fortunately, Kevin thought it was all still just a game and he bolted up to the house. When we stepped inside, my mother and Rocky were in the living room watching television, and our dog was barking with excitement.

"Lacey!" hollered Kevin, laughing as she jumped up and began licking his face. "Sorry, girl. Next time we'll bring you."

After what had just happened, I knew I wouldn't be leaving her behind anytime soon.

"She kept watching for you out the window," Mom said, smiling up at us from the sofa. "Anyway, did you have fun swimming?"

"Yes," Kevin said excitedly. "You should have seen me doing cannonballs. I made these huge waves, didn't I, Mom?"

"You sure did. Which reminds me, you need a shower to wash off all that yucky lake water. We both do." I looked at my mom. "I hate to ask, but could you bring him upstairs and get him started?"

"Of course," she said, getting up from the sofa. "Let's go, buckaroo."

"Do I have to go to bed afterward?" he asked.

"No. You can probably stay up for another hour or so. It depends on how well you clean behind those grubby ears, though," Mom joked as they headed up the staircase with Lacey following.

"Whatcha got there?" Rocky asked, smiling at the pizza box.

"Don't you worry about what she has," my mother said loudly, as she reached the top of the stairs. "It's pure sodium and cholesterol. It's bad for your heart."

He let out a weary sigh. "What fun is having a healthy heart when it's depressed all the time?"

"Fine. One piece," Mom replied, looking down at him. "And that's it."

He blew her a kiss. "And that's why you own my heart. You know how to make it smile again."

She grunted.

"Come on," I said, heading toward the kitchen with the pizza and my beach bag, which held the cell phone. "We need to talk."

"Uh, oh. Sounds serious." Rocky got up from his chair and followed me inside. "So, what's wrong?"

I turned around and took a deep breath. "When we were at the cabin, someone rang the doorbell and disappeared. They also left me a little present. A cell phone."

"A cell phone, you say?" He scratched his whiskers. "That's rather odd. And it was addressed to *you*?"

"Not exactly, but it was meant for me." I pulled the box out of my beach bag and took the phone out. "Someone sent me a message and a photo."

His forehead wrinkled. "Really? That sounds creepy."

Nodding, I pulled up the message and handed him the phone. "Check it out."

Rocky stared at it in confusion. "I don't get it. It's a picture of someone bending over. Definitely female," he said, with a funny look on his face.

"Yeah. It's me in that photo."

There was no doubt, either. I'd been wearing my favorite yoga pants and one of the tank tops I typically used for exercising. I was in the downward-dog position in what appeared to be my living room.

"It was taken when we were back in Chicago. I think Kevin's friend Tyler was right," I mumbled.

"Wait a second, are you saying the person who took this photo of you is your *Peeping Tom*? And now he's sending you messages?"

I nodded. "It appears that way. It looks like he's followed us here," I said, walking toward the kitchen window. I looked outside, wondering if my stalker was lurking in the woods nearby. Watching us.

"We need to call the sheriff," Rocky said angrily. "Do you know whose phone this is?"

"I have no idea," I replied.

The mysterious phone buzzed again, startling Rocky, who let out a curse and almost dropped it.

"Another message?" I asked, my stomach knotting up as I moved over by him.

He nodded. "Looks that way."

"Let me see it first," I said, holding out my hand. "Who knows what other pictures this guy might have of me?"

Rocky handed me the phone.

I looked at the screen. This time, there wasn't a photo, but a message.

Him: *Are we having fun yet?*

I growled in the back of my throat and began to type.

Me: *Who is this?*

Him: *I am HIM.*

Me: *HIM who???*

Him: *Take a guess.*

Me: *I have no idea. This isn't funny.*

Him: *It's not meant to be.*

"What are you doing?" Rocky asked me.

I looked up from the phone. "I'm trying to find out who this bastard is," I muttered.

Me: *What do you want from me?*

It took the person several seconds to respond.

Him: *Retribution.*

"What in the hell is *that* supposed to mean?" I said, about to type back.

"Stop. Quit messaging him," Rocky said angrily. "You're giving this wacko what he wants. Attention."

Trembling with rage, I erased my message and stared at the phone, waiting for another one from him. None came.

"Can I see that?" Rocky asked.

Sighing, I handed the phone to him.

"You don't recognize the number this person messaged you from?"

86

"Nope. It's a Minnesota area code, though," I replied.

He nodded. "If this guy knows what he's doing, he's either spoofing someone else's phone number, or using a disposable phone. One that we won't be able to track."

"*If* he knows what he's doing. He might just be a nut-job without a lot of common sense." My gut told me I was wrong, however, and that this guy knew exactly what he was doing.

"Hopefully."

"Maybe it's not even a guy," I said, staring off into space.

"You have any female enemies?"

"No." I looked at him. "Not that I'm aware of, at least."

"Women can be catty and you're a good-looking woman. Could someone be jealous of you?"

I snorted. "I highly doubt it."

"You recall attracting unwanted attention from any of the married men in your neighborhood? You just never know. Some jealous wife could have gotten the wrong idea and is after you now."

I closed my eyes briefly and rubbed my temples. "No."

Rocky began searching through the cell phone and after a few seconds, he gasped. "I'll be damned…"

"What is it?" I asked, alarmed.

His eyes locked with mine. "I hate to say this, but I think this might actually be Brad's phone."

I stared at him in shock. "What? You're kidding?"

"I looked through the *contact list* and recognized some of the names in there. I know he used to hang out with some of the guys listed."

This was growing more disturbing by the moment. "How could this wacko get ahold of Brad's phone?"

"I don't know. Maybe he lost it before his accident?"

"But... wouldn't the service have run out?" I replied.

"Maybe someone else is still paying the bill."

"Wait a second," I said, my mind spinning. "Do we know for sure that Brad is even dead?"

Rocky's eyes widened.

"I know it sounds crazy, but are they certain it was really *him* at the bottom of that cliff?" I asked.

"Look, I think we're way off course here. Obviously, the medical examiners knew what they were doing. Anyway, if Brad was alive, do you really think he'd play games like this? Not to mention, leave you everything? That doesn't sound logical at all."

He was right. Brad had been a fairly serious guy and not someone this devious. The only games he'd enjoyed were the ones in his arcade.

"None of this makes sense," I mumbled, leaning against the counter. I closed my eyes and rubbed my temples again.

"You okay?"

I nodded. "Just a slight headache."

He smirked. "Your mom has an entire pharmacy upstairs. She'll find you something."

"I bet," I replied.

"Let's just get the phone to the police and see what they have to say. Hopefully, they'll track the number that's been texting you and we'll figure things out." He held the phone up. "I have a feeling this is Brad's, though."

"Hmm… Did you see the photos of all the kids?" I asked.

He nodded. "Yeah, it was a little weird, I have to admit. Taking random pictures like that. Did Brad get into photography, I wonder?"

"No clue." I wondered if it had anything to do with him not ever having children of his own.

Maybe he'd become obsessed?

The photos had seemed innocent enough, although as a parent, I definitely wouldn't want some stranger taking ones of Kevin. It definitely seemed very odd and out of character from the Brad I'd known.

"Maybe it's not even Brad's phone. The stalker could be trying to confuse us."

"I guess we'll know soon enough."

"Stalker, what stalker?" my mother asked, walking into the kitchen.

Chapter 8

Amanda

MY MOTHER WAS horrified when she heard the news.

"You need to go to the police," she said angrily, staring down at the picture of me in the yoga pants. "This person sounds like a complete nutcase."

"Oh, damn right we are," Rocky said as he reached for the keys to his truck. "We'll get to the bottom of this."

She held the phone up and pointed at the photo. "How long ago was this picture of you taken?"

"I can't be for certain, but I imagine it was a couple of months ago. When Tyler claimed he'd seen someone snooping around the yard," I replied.

Her face turned pale. "So, the Peeping Tom, the one that Kevin's friend mentioned, is the same guy stalking you *here*?"

"It looks that way," I replied with a grim smile. "Is Kevin done with his shower?"

"Almost." She handed me back the phone.

I sighed. "Do me a favor, don't tell him what's going on. It'll frighten him."

She nodded. "Don't worry. I won't say a word."

I put the phone back into the box and shoved it into my beach bag. "I'm going to talk with Kevin and then we can get going."

"Okay. I'll meet you outside," Rocky replied and then began mumbling about nutcases and perverts.

I left the kitchen and headed upstairs, running into Kevin, who'd just walked out of the bathroom in his Transformers pajamas. He smelled like fresh apples and I wanted nothing more than to cuddle with him, like I used to when he was younger. Unfortunately, he was becoming less and less of a momma's boy and I dreaded the teenage years.

"Hey, Kev. I'm leaving with Rocky for a little while."

"Where are you going?" he asked.

"Just into town to run a few errands."

His forehead scrunched up. "I thought we did that earlier?"

My son was too smart for his own good. I hated lying to Kevin, but I didn't want to put him into a panic. "I have more errands, ones involving the cabin and the garage sale we're going to have. You stay here and take care of Grandma, okay?"

He yawned and nodded.

I gave him a hug and a kiss and then we walked downstairs together.

"Kevin knows we're going into town for errands," I emphasized to my mother.

She nodded. "Okay."

"Can I watch TV?" Kevin asked.

"Yes. Just until nine and then it's time for bed," I replied, sliding my feet into my flip-flops.

"But, it's the summer," he whined.

"I don't care. We're going back to the cabin again in the morning," I said, ruffling his damp curls. "You need a good night's sleep."

Huffing, he sat down on the sofa and picked up the remote control.

"Bye, Mom," I said, giving her a quick hug.

"Call me if you find out anything useful," she whispered near my ear.

"I will."

WHEN ROCKY AND I arrived at the police station, we ran into Sheriff Dan Baldwin, who greeted us warmly. He appeared to be somewhere in his fifties, with friendly green eyes that crinkled around the edges, short, white hair, and a stocky physique.

"Rocky, you old dog, it's good to see you," the sheriff said, holding out his hand. "It's been awhile since we've run into each other."

My stepfather shook his hand and chuckled. "Considering you're always working, that's probably a good thing."

"With your lead foot, I imagine you're right," he said with a wink and a smile. "You still own that GTO?"

"No. I sold it long ago. You remember that, huh?"

"I remember racing you with my Mustang." The sheriff looked at me. "Before I was in law enforcement, of course. We graduated high school together and hung around the same circles."

"Ah," I said.

Rocky introduced me and then began to explain why we were here.

"Come on back to my office," the sheriff replied, his expression now serious. "You have the phone with you?"

I opened up the beach bag and handed him the small, brown box. We then followed him into his office and sat down at his desk.

Sheriff Baldwin put on a pair of spectacles and plastic gloves. He then took out the cell phone as we continued to fill him in on the details.

"Rocky seems to think that the phone was Brad's," I said. "But, I'm not so sure."

"Brad Shaw was your ex-husband, correct?" he asked, looking up from the phone.

I nodded.

"Tragic, how he died. I met him a few times, back when he owned the arcade. He seemed like a nice enough guy." The sheriff began examining the messages and then wrote down the texter's number. "So, the picture this person sent was of you, back in Chicago?"

"Yes." I told him about the Peeping Tom.

"You ever report it to the authorities?" the sheriff asked.

I shook my head. "I just thought it was my son's friend, trying to scare him. Also, our dog never barked that night either, so I just brushed it off."

"Retribution, huh?" the sheriff said, reading the text. "Obviously, this jackass—pardon my language—is trying to scare you. The idea that he followed you here is disturbing, though. Have you noticed anyone trailing you lately?"

"No, but I haven't really paid attention, I guess," I replied, folding my arms under my chest. The idea that I may have been followed for a while gave me the chills.

"Has there been anything else that's happened out of the ordinary?" he asked, peering at me over his spectacles.

I suddenly remembered the card I'd found in my SUV earlier.

"I can't believe I forgot about this, but earlier today, someone left a card in my vehicle," I said.

"A card?" repeated Rocky, frowning. "What kind?"

"A greeting card. Like the kind you'd buy in store. Inside they wrote a personal message," I replied, feeling like a knucklehead for forgetting about it.

"What did it say?" asked Sheriff Baldwin.

I thought back. "*Roses are fickle. Violets are sweet. I'm glad you returned. You're in for a treat.*"

The sheriff looked at Rocky. "Interesting. It definitely sounds like her stalker might be from this area and knew her before she moved to Chicago."

"It sure does," he replied, tapping his fingers on his the desk

"You bring the card with?" the sheriff asked me. "Maybe we can track it to one of the stores around here."

I sighed. "Sorry. It's still in my vehicle and Rocky drove here tonight. I can drop it off tomorrow."

"No problem. Was it handwritten, typed, or did this person paste words together?" he replied.

"It was handwritten," I said.

"Either this guy is arrogant or a simpleton," the sheriff replied with a grim smile. "Hopefully, it's the latter and we'll be able to get to the bottom of this fairly quickly."

I nodded. "That would be nice."

"Is there anything else you can think of that might help?" Sheriff Baldwin asked.

"Nothing that comes to mind," I replied.

Rocky cleared his throat. "Actually, we did have someone on the property last night… whistling."

The sheriff frowned. "Come again?"

Rocky told him about the annoying trespasser. "That wasn't the first time it's happened, though. So, I don't think it has anything to do with Amanda's stalker. Hell, I think it's just some teenagers doing it for kicks."

"It could be, but we can't look past it. Did you ever get a good luck at the whistler?" he asked him.

"Not really. The one time we saw him, he was wearing a hoodie and it was dark. Tell you one thing—that asshole can whistle louder than anyone I've ever met. He always whistles the same nursery rhyme, too. Creepy as hell, I tell you."

"Which one is that?" Sheriff Baldwin asked.

"*Pop Goes The Weasel*," said Rocky.

The Sheriff gave a derisive snort. "Now I'm *sure* it's the same guy messing with Amanda. He's definitely playing games."

"Well, I've had enough of it," I mumbled. "I hope you can help us, Sheriff. I'm not just worried about me, I'm frightened for my son."

"I understand. We'll do what we can to find this joker and at the very least, get a restraining order," he replied.

My jaw dropped. "A restraining order? That's it?"

"Do you have actual proof that he was on your property?" he replied.

"Yes. The photo," I said, waving toward the phone.

"This clown could say he used a high-powered lens and wasn't actually in your yard," he replied.

"But… Tyler *saw* him on my property," I answered, frustrated.

"Would he be able to identify the perp and testify in court without any doubt?" Sheriff Baldwin asked.

I sighed. "I don't know."

"I'm sorry. I know it's frustrating and I'll do what I can to help, but at this moment, even if we catch him, there's only so much we can do," he said.

"If I get my hands on him, *I'll* get him to stop for good," Rocky said angrily.

"Yeah, by calling *us*. Remember, if you catch him on your property, then we can get him for trespassing," Sheriff Baldwin reminded him.

Rocky muttered something under his breath.

He frowned. "Don't take this into your own hands. You'll be the one ending up in jail, old friend."

"I hear you," he grumbled, looking away.

The sheriff began searching through the phone again. "What's up with the kid photos?"

"I know. It's definitely weird," Rocky said.

"Why do you think this is Brad Shaw's phone?" he asked.

"I don't know. The *contact list* has some of Brad's friends' numbers," Rocky replied.

"I have an idea." The sheriff went into the *recent call* list and dialed one of the local numbers. "I know this guy. Andy Newman."

The sheriff put the phone on speaker and someone picked up from the other end.

"Is this Andy?" Sheriff Bradshaw asked.

"Yep," the caller replied, sounding stunned. "Who in the hell is this?"

"Sheriff Dan Baldwin."

Andy laughed. "Oh, hey, Sheriff. What's going on?"

"Do you recognize the number I'm calling from?"

"Yeah. It's Brad Shaw's."

"You were right," I whispered to Rocky, stunned by the revelation.

He nodded.

"I have to say, seeing this number pop up on my phone shocked the living hell out of me," Andy said, still sounding amused. "I thought I was getting a long-distance call from the Great Beyond there for a second."

The sheriff chuckled. "Sorry about that. We located Brad's cell and I just wanted to make sure it was his and knew this would be the quickest way. Thanks for your help."

"Anytime," he replied. "Have a good night."

"You, too, Andy. Take care."

"I guess we have our answer," Sheriff Baldwin said, after ending the call. "Not one I was expecting."

"Me either," I said breathlessly.

He sat back in his chair and folded his hands across his stomach. "Now the next question is—how did your stalker get Brad's phone?"

Chapter 9

Amanda

AFTER MULLING OVER the situation for a few more minutes, the sheriff rubbed his eyes. "Listen, why don't you two go home and relax. I'll do some checking on the texter's phone number and get back to you."

Rocky stood up. "We appreciate it."

"Thanks, Sheriff," I added, also standing up.

"Just, remember—if this idiot shows up, don't get trigger-happy. Got it?" Sheriff Baldwin warned.

"What if he starts shootin' first?" Rocky asked.

"Duck," he replied with a smirk.

Rocky snorted.

"Look, if your life is in danger, you do what you gotta do. But don't go shootin' at anyone just because they're on your property and you're pissed off. It won't end well for anyone," The sheriff said wearily.

"I hear you," Rocky said.

He grabbed a business card and handed it to me. "Amanda, call me if you think of anything else and don't forget to bring in that greeting card. If he purchased it here in town, hopefully we'll find record of it and nail this jerk."

I nodded. "I won't forget. Thank you."

"You're welcome. Another thing—I wouldn't go to Brad's cabin again by yourself," he said. "We don't know what kind of a freak we're dealing with."

"Don't worry. She won't be there alone," Rocky said firmly. "Not on my watch. Nobody messes with my family."

I smiled and slipped my arm through his, happy that my mother had ended up with such an amazing guy. "Thanks, *Dad*," I said softly.

He gave me a gentle smile and looked back at the sheriff. "Talk to you soon, Dan."

"Yep. You take care," he replied. "And stay safe. Both of you."

Chapter 10

Amanda

BY THE TIME we returned home, Kevin was in bed sleeping.

"How did it go?" Mom asked anxiously as I calmed Lacey down in the foyer.

We filled her in on the details.

"So, the phone was actually Brad's?" she said with a shocked look on her face. "What was this creep doing with his phone?"

"Hopefully, we'll find out when the police catch this idiot," Rocky said, locking the door.

Mom sighed. "Maybe he broke into the cabin and stole it?"

"That's what I'm thinking," I replied. "I imagine it might have happened before Brad died, though. I doubt he'd have gone on a trip to the North Shore without it."

"Who knows, maybe Brad had two phones and didn't realize he was missing one?" Rocky said.

I hadn't thought of that. "That might be."

"It's probably the case," Mom said. "Are you planning on going to the cabin tomorrow, Amanda?"

I nodded.

"We're going with her. We were planning on helping with the garage sale, anyway," Rocky said.

"For sure. What about Kevin?" Mom asked, biting her lower lip. "Should we say anything?"

"I don't want to frighten him but… if we don't say anything, it leaves him vulnerable." I sighed. "I'm going to tell him that someone is playing practical jokes that aren't funny and to keep a lookout for strangers."

"That's a good idea," Rocky said, nodding in approval. "I agree, too. He shouldn't be kept completely in the dark."

"He's a smart kid, too. He's going to figure out something is going on if we keep talking around him like this," Mom added.

"Hopefully, they'll catch the guy before he has to figure anything out," I replied.

WE TALKED A little more and then I went upstairs to take a shower. Afterward, I headed back down and noticed Mom had also gone to bed, but Rocky was sitting in the living room, alone in the dark. He'd left the curtain open and was staring outside from his favorite chair.

"See anything?" I whispered.

"Nope," he said, looking exhausted.

"You know, if someone shows up, Lacey will probably start barking," I said, scratching behind the dog's ears. "You don't have to stay up."

"Maybe she will, but I might not hear it. I'm a pretty sound sleeper," he said, picking up the can of diet soda next to him and taking a swig.

"We could take turns?" I suggested, sitting down across from him on the rocking chair.

"No. You go to bed. I couldn't sleep if I wanted to," he said. "Besides, if Kevin wakes up and finds you gone, he'll get worried."

Rocky was right.

"Okay. Goodnight," I said, before giving him a peck on the cheek. "Thanks again, by the way."

"No need. We're family and we take care of each other," he said, smiling up at me warmly.

I agreed.

BEFORE CRAWLING INTO bed, I plugged my cell phone into the charger and noticed I'd received a voicemail from Tara.

"Hey, Amanda. It's me, Tara. I'm so sorry to have to do this, but tomorrow night isn't going to work. My boss just called and asked me to fly to Dallas to meet with a potential client. They're looking for a new marketing firm and we really need their account. Anyway, how about next week? I'll call you soon so we can discuss another night to get together. Sorry, again. Love, ya."

After the craziness of the day, I'd forgotten about meeting her at Shoop's. I sent her a quick text telling her that next week was fine and that I'd talk to her soon.

"Mom," Kevin murmured, half-asleep.

"Yes, buddy. I'm here," I replied softly, moving over to him.

"Where's Lacey?"

"Downstairs with Rocky."

"Okay. Can we go swimming again tomorrow?"

"Sure. Unless it rains."

He smiled and closed his eyes.

My heart swelled as I stared down at my innocent little boy. I'd walk through fire to keep him safe and prayed that whoever was stalking me would get caught and quickly.

I leaned down and kissed his temple. "I love you, Kev."

"I love you, too," he whispered back.

I slid under the sheets and tried falling asleep. Once again, it didn't come easily. All I kept thinking about was the stalker and who in the hell this person might be. It was frightening to think that this person, *HIM*, had been spying on me in Chicago and now he was back in Summit Lake. I had no enemies, at least none that I'd been aware of.

Brad?

Could he be alive?

It was too hard to believe that he'd fake his own death—and what would be the point? The only one who'd gained anything by it had been me.

I wasn't sure what was happening, but something told me that this wasn't over. If this guy was willing to travel, to frighten me, he was on one serious mission. I just didn't understand why I was his target and what kind of retribution he was looking for.

Chapter 11

Amanda

THE FOLLOWING DAY was hectic. After breakfast, the four of us made plans to return to the cabin and worked on getting Brad's things ready for the garage sale. Before we left, I sat Kevin down and told him about the "practical joker", leaving out the part about the photo.

"I don't think this person means any harm. He just has a weird sense of humor," I explained.

"Like playing ding-dong-ditch?" he asked.

I nodded. "Yes. And sending me the cell phone. So, if you see anyone trying to play tricks or doing anything odd, I want you to let me know right away. Okay?"

"Okay," he said, chewing on his lower lip as he stared ahead, obviously now deep in thought.

I ran my fingers through his hair, trying to distract him from worrying too hard. "You've got quite a garden growing up here. I think it's time to get a trim."

His jaw dropped. "But, Tyler's hair is longer. I want to grow mine out, too."

I had to admit, he looked adorable with the curls framing his face. "I suppose we could leave it this way for the summer. When school starts, we'll talk about it again. Okay?"

He nodded. "We're not going to move here, are we?"

"Honestly, I don't know. It's a big decision so it's going to take some time to think about it."

Kevin looked like he was about to cry.

"Listen," I said, staring into his big brown eyes. "Let's not think about moving. Instead, let's enjoy our summer vacation. Okay?"

"Okay," he replied, still looking at me warily.

The truth was, as much as I wanted to stay, I really didn't know what our future held in Summit Lake. Especially under the new circumstances.

"DO YOU HAVE a key for the shed?" Rocky asked, an hour later, when we were back at the cabin.

"I think it could be in that drawer," I said, pointing toward the other end of the counter. "I noticed a large assortment of keys inside."

He walked over and began rummaging through the drawer. He pulled one out and examined it closely. "I think I found it. This looks like the brand."

"Good," I replied.

He shut the drawer and smiled wickedly. "So… do you want to come out and check out the shed? See if anything is living in it?"

"About as much as you'd like to help me buy feminine napkins," I replied, reaching for the stack of brown and burgundy dinner plates from the cupboard.

He grimaced. "You didn't have to go there, did you?"

I laughed. "Men are so squeamish about that stuff."

"You mean like you are with snakes and spiders?"

"Point taken," I said.

"I'll be back and let you know what I find," he said, opening up the patio door. "Unless I don't make it out of there alive. Did you know that a python could swallow an alligator whole?"

"Stop," I said.

He winked at me. "Sorry. I couldn't resist. There shouldn't be any pythons in these parts. Unless someone had one for a pet and it got out."

"I'm not listening to you," I said. "Ever again."

He laughed and went back outside.

I glanced through the window, toward the lake, where Mom was watching Kevin swim. We'd promised him an hour in the water and then he was to help us clean the garage. Thankfully, Brad had been a very organized guy, which was something I'd forgotten about. Almost too organized at times. I recalled one time when he'd gotten all bent out of shape because I'd cleaned the bathroom and had moved his toiletries to different spots.

"Next time, let me do it," he'd complained. "You don't know where my things go and it's going to make me late for work if I have to hunt them down."

I thought he'd been joking, but had found out later he'd been dead serious. It was his way or no way.

"I like order," he'd said.

"You like YOUR order."

"Obviously, my way makes the most sense. Don't worry, you'll catch on one of these days."

His little digs had been constant and irritating, but I'd put up with them because I'd been young and in love.

I opened up the cupboard where he'd kept the glasses and remembered another time when I'd been cleaning and had done a little rearranging. Of course, that hadn't gone over well, either.

"The glasses should always be to the right of the sink. That makes it easier and more efficient if you're thirsty,"

"Yeah, but wouldn't it also make sense to put glasses next to the refrigerator then? In case you'd want a glass of something cold? Or get some ice for the water?"

He'd brushed away the answer, mumbling something about common sense and not fixing what wasn't broken.

Thinking back, it was a wonder he'd allowed me to run a daycare for three years, which had been pretty chaotic at times. Fortunately, we'd sectioned off the basement of our old house, and it had made things easier. He'd complain once in a while about chalk on the driveway, toys in the yard, and late parent pickups. For the most part, however, he'd been pretty patient and reasonable about things.

The doorbell rang, startling me. I left the kitchen and went to answer it, hoping it wasn't another unexpected surprise from the stalker. When I opened the door and saw who it was, I smiled in relief.

"Parker. Hi," I said, noticing he wasn't alone. A lanky boy stood next to him, with the same features—obviously his son.

He grinned. "Hi. Sorry to bother you. We were riding our bikes and thought we'd swing by and say hello. This is Austin, by the way."

"You're not bothering me at all." I looked at Parker's son and smiled again. "Hi, Austin. I'm Amanda."

"Hi," he said, looking slightly uncomfortable.

"I was telling Austin that you also had a son and that maybe they could hang out this summer once in a while?" Parker said.

Although there was a four-year age difference, I knew Kevin would be thrilled to have someone to swim or go fishing with, other than an adult.

"I'm sure Kevin would love that. He's out by the dock right now, swimming. I'll take you down and introduce you," I said, stepping outside.

"Sounds good. So," said Parker, looking around the property. "What do you think of the place?"

"I love it. The cabin is great, but the lake view… it's gorgeous," I replied.

He smiled. "Yeah, I agree. Have you decided on whether you're going to buy it?"

Not wanting to get into things with him yet, especially with Austin standing there, I decided not to tell him that Brad had actually left it to me. That was a conversation for another day. "I'm not sure what I'm going to do yet."

"Well, like you said, it's a big decision," he said.

As we walked around the house to the back, I remembered the jet skier and asked if he'd noticed any craziness on the lake.

"What do you mean?" he asked.

I told him about the rude guy, with the skull-mask, who'd splashed me.

Parker looked shocked. "Really? What a jerk. He didn't apologize?"

"No," I replied. I was going to say that it had been on purpose when the words got stuck on my tongue.

Was the jet-skier my stalker?

And then there'd been the unfriendly boater as well.

"What is it?" Parker asked, looking concerned.

"Nothing," I said, not wanting to involve him.

"You sure? You look like you just saw a ghost," he replied.

"I'm fine," I said, forcing a smile to my face. "Really." I changed the subject. "By the way, how is your mom?"

"As well as could be," he replied. "She had another episode. Attacked an old man at the nursing home."

"Oh, my goodness. I'm so sorry," I replied.

He smiled grimly. "He's not exactly a saint. Kind of a crabby old man. Still, he didn't deserve to be hit."

"What happens now?" I asked.

He shrugged. "They're just going to keep a closer eye on her."

"That's good," I said.

Parker nodded.

Rocky, walked out of the shed with a shovel, hoe, and rake.

114

"Parker, nice to see you," he said, setting the gardening tools down onto the grass. "This must be your boy."

"Yep. This is Austin," Parker replied. He put his hand on Austin's back. "Say, hi, son."

"Hi," Austin said shyly.

Just then, Lacey, who'd been down by the lake with Kevin and Mom, came barreling up to us, barking happily.

"Down, Lacey," I said sternly as she tried jumping on Parker and Austin with her wet paws. "I'm so sorry."

"It's okay," Parker said, scratching between her ears and smiling. "I'm used to it."

"This is your dog? Cool," Austin asked. He kneeled down next to Lacey and began petting her.

Rocky wiped the sweat from his brow with his work glove. "I'm surprised she didn't hear you earlier. You know, I'm almost wondering if she's having hearing problems. Maybe we should have you check her out, Parker."

"Yeah, I can examine her ears and do a BAER test if needed. Is she a really sound sleeper?" he asked me.

"Actually, she has been lately. Are you a vet?" I asked, surprised and a little embarrassed that I didn't know. Of course, we'd barely talked the day before.

Smiling, he nodded.

Memories of old conversations rushed back to me. His father had been a surgeon and had wanted Parker to follow in his footsteps. But, Parker wanted to take a different route and had talked about becoming a veterinarian. Not *so* different, but something his dad hadn't exactly been pleased about.

"That's right," I said. "You used to tell me that you wanted to one day open up your own veterinarian practice here in Summit Lake. I can't believe I'd forgotten."

"Eh, don't worry about it," he said, now trying to look into Lacey's ears, who wasn't having any part of it. "Why don't you bring her by on Monday and we'll see what's going on? I'm working over at Summit Lake Pet Center now. You know where that is?"

I pictured the building, which was just north of downtown. "Yeah. Definitely."

"I took over the practice when I moved here, so in a sense, I accomplished what I'd set out to do," he said.

"Congratulations. You should be proud of yourself," I replied.

"Thank you," he replied.

"What time should I bring her by?" I asked.

"We open at eight on Monday. Call me in the morning and I'll fit you in somewhere. If she does have some sort of a hearing problem, it might not be anything major. See how she's twitching her ears in

116

response to sounds?" he said when we heard Kevin laughing loudly by the lake. "That's a good sign."

"Oh. Okay," I replied, watching Lacey's ears move. "Good."

"How old is she?" Rocky asked.

"Around four," I replied. "We adopted her from an animal rescue shelter. I don't know her exact birthday, but they figured it was in June sometime."

Parker nodded. "She looks pretty healthy."

"Do you have any animals?" Rocky asked Austin.

"No. My mom is allergic to dogs and cats," he replied with a frown.

"That's too bad. What about you, Parker? You have pets?" Rocky asked.

"I have a cat," he said.

My eyes widened in surprise. "I was expecting you to list off at least a half dozen animals, considering your profession."

He grinned. "I'd love to have more, but the truth is, I spend more time at the clinic than I do at home."

"Understandable," I replied.

"I'm trying to talk him into getting a puppy," Austin said, looking up at his father. "My birthday is coming up in a couple of weeks. Hint. Hint."

Parker sighed. "We talked about this before. You know you couldn't bring it back home with you."

"You could keep it for me," he replied. "Please, Dad? I've always wanted a dog."

"We'll talk about it later," Parker said firmly. "Now's not the time."

Austin sighed.

"In the meantime, you can play with Lacey all you want," I said.

"There you go," Parker said.

Austin looked frustrated, but didn't say anything else. As a pet owner, I knew it wasn't the same and almost felt bad for him.

"Let's go down to the lake," I said. "Come on, Lacey."

Lacey barked and then Parker, Austin, and I walked down to the dock, where Kevin was just getting out of the water. I quickly made the introductions and both boys stared at each other awkwardly.

"How's the water?" Parker asked Kevin after my mom walked back to shore.

"It's great," he replied and then looked at me. "Can I go back out again later?"

"Probably. I'd like you to help us clean the garage and set things up for the sale first, though," I replied.

"Okay," he mumbled.

"Would you like some help?" Parker asked.

"No. Thank you, though. It's kind of you to offer," I replied.

"If you change your mind, let me know." Parker looked at Kevin. "Have you fished in the lake yet?"

"Not this year," he replied.

"Austin and I are going Sunday morning," Parker said and looked at me. "We'd love it if you could join us."

"I really wish I could, but… I'll be busy organizing the garage sale," I replied. "Otherwise," I smiled. "I'd love to."

"That's right," he replied. "You mentioned that."

"Kevin can go with you, though." I glanced at my son, who looked excited.

"Great," Parker replied. "What do you say, Kevin? Would you like to join us?"

"Yes!" he answered. "I don't have a fishing pole, though."

"That's fine. We have plenty of poles for you to use," Parker said.

"Okay," he replied, looking relieved.

"Sorry. Kevin's only fished a couple of times, so we don't have any gear," I explained. "We usually use Rocky's."

"Hey, no problem. You know, there is a summer fishing camp for kids. The owners of Gibbons' Dockside Boathouse and Pub run it. It's a husband and wife team. They teach them the basics and bring them out on the lake Tuesday and Thursday mornings, around nine. I'm signing Austin up. He went last year and had a lot of fun."

"Really? That sounds like an interesting idea," I replied and looked at Kevin. "What do you think? You want to join a fishing camp?"

"Would I have to stay overnight?" he asked.

"No. It's a day camp. You're home before three. I can even give Kevin a ride," Parker offered, looking at me again.

"Can I, Mom?" Kevin asked, excited now.

I nodded and smiled. "I think it's a great idea," I replied. "Where do we sign up?"

Chapter 12

Amanda

AFTER CHATTING FOR a few more minutes, Parker and I exchanged phone numbers and then they left on their bikes. A few minutes after that, Rocky took Kevin to McDonald's.

"So, what's going on with you and Parker?" my mother asked as she swept the floor of the garage.

"Nothing. We're just friends," I replied.

She was quiet for a while and then said, "He's a good-looking man. And a veterinarian, too."

"Yeah," I said, biting back a smile. "I heard."

"I remember when you two went out. You were such a cute couple."

"Mom, stop that."

She looked at me and her eyes widened innocently. "What? I'm not doing anything."

"You and I both know exactly what you're doing," I said with a smirk. "You don't have to sell him to me. I already know that he's a great catch, but I'm not looking for a man right now."

"One never usually is when the right one comes knocking at the door."

I knew she was probably right, but I really wasn't looking to start anything with anyone. Especially since I didn't know what the future held. I reiterated that to her.

"Honestly, I don't know why you'd want to go back to Chicago. Summit Lake is so much safer. I mean, really… what exactly is holding you back there? You have the luxury of working anywhere you want."

"First of all, after the last couple of days, I don't think Summit Lake *is* safer, considering the person stalking me sounds like they're from here. Second of all, Kevin has roots there. I'd be pulling him away from his school. His friends. Everything."

"He's a kid. He'll adjust to change. It's good for him."

"I keep telling myself that, but it doesn't mean his heart won't be broken and I don't know if I want to go down that road when I have a choice not to."

"You're thinking too hard about it. Kids adapt very easily. Anyway, he just needs to meet new friends here. It will make it a lot easier. I think it's great that you're signing him up for the fishing camp he mentioned."

I nodded. Kevin had told her all about it before leaving with Rocky.

"As for the stalker, the police will hopefully catch him. Anyway, I don't care what you say—living in Chicago is still much more dangerous. At least you have family here and aren't alone. You and Kevin are much more vulnerable there."

I sighed. She was right. "I know. I know. Speaking of the stalker," I looked at the time. "I'm surprised we haven't heard back from Sheriff Baldwin. He was supposed to track the phone number that texted me."

"Call him," she replied.

"I think I will."

I went into the cabin and grabbed the sheriff's card. When I called him, he answered right away.

"Great timing. I was actually about to call you," he said.

"Really? What did you learn?"

"Unfortunately, not much. The perp used a disposable phone and probably a burner app, which reroutes calls through a different number. Anyway, Sorry, Amanda. We don't have anything useful for you at this point."

"What about the greeting card?" We'd dropped it off on our way to the cabin.

"I checked around and none of the shops carry that particular one. He must have picked it up out of town."

"Damn," I mumbled. "What do you suggest I do then?"

"Just keep a lookout for this dipshit and if you see anything unusual, report it."

I knew he was going to say that. "Okay."

"I wish I could have found out more information for you. Do you have any old boyfriends, or anyone you may have turned down for a date, that might be doing this?"

"No. Not at all."

"You mentioned that you write books. Has anyone sent you any threatening letters or emails? Maybe it's a disgruntled fan?"

"Nope."

"Anything odd happen to you on any social media sites?"

"No. Nothing strange at all."

"Did you get any more visits from that whistler, the one Rocky mentioned? Or any new presents on the doorstep?"

"Not that we know of," I thought, thinking back to when we arrived back at the house, after seeing the sheriff. It had been dark and quiet. I grunted. "He must have taken the rest of the evening off."

"Yeah." He let out a sigh. "I don't know what to tell you other than what I said before—be aware of your surroundings and call us if you see anything alarming."

"I will."

"Okay. I gotta high-tail it out of here. You have yourself a nice afternoon and tell Rocky and your mother I said hello."

"Will do."

After hanging up, I headed back into the garage and told Mom what the sheriff had said. Like me, she was frustrated, but knew there wasn't much more the police could do at this point.

"You should tell Parker what's going on. In case we need his help," she said. "I mean, he lives so close."

"I'm not pulling him into this," I replied.

"He should know if he's going to be taking Kevin fishing. You just never know."

She had a point.

I sighed. "I will. The next time I talk to him."

"In the meantime, Rocky and I aren't going to let you out of our sight."

Although the situation was a little unnerving, I didn't want to be babysat. I also knew that my mother wasn't exactly bodyguard material. Plus, I'd hope that in any situation, I'd do better than my petite, middle-aged mother who was usually afraid of her own shadow. Of course, being a mom myself, I understood where she was coming from. I'd stand up to a grizzly bear to protect Kevin. Hell, I'd stand up to one to protect her, too.

"And I'm not going to respond to any more unmarked packages or text messages. I'm handing everything over to the sheriff." Besides, I didn't have Brad's cell phone anymore. But, something told me that the stalker already had my number, and in more ways than one.

"Good idea. I do think that when you move into the cabin, however, you should consider getting a security system installed."

I smirked. "*When* I move in, huh?"

"Did I say 'when'? I meant 'if'," she replied with a smirk of her own.

"Right."

I could see by the sparkle in her eye that my mother wasn't going to give up. Considering our bitter past, back when she'd been with my father, I appreciated what she was trying to do. I always knew that she loved me, but as a teenager, there'd been a lot of resentment on my part. Most of my memories consisted of my parents drunk and arguing while I locked myself in my bedroom, angry and frustrated. I could remember many times wishing they'd either stop or get divorced, it had been so bad. The fights had always been about the same things, too—my father spending too much money on frivolous things and my mother not being supportive enough or respecting him. As much as my father's death had been heartbreaking, it had definitely given the both of us a second chance.

"What are you thinking about?" she asked, noticing I was staring at her. I could see by the look in her eyes that she still held some insecurities of her own.

"I was just thinking about how grateful I am to have such a supportive family, for as small as it is," I replied.

Mom smiled. "Small is right. That's why it's important to stick together, especially in times like this."

I nodded.

"By the way, are we selling everything of Brad's? Or are you keeping anything?"

"I'd like to get rid everything except for the riding lawn mower and gardening equipment. You know, in case I do decide to stay," I replied. "All I own is a push-mower and hose."

"Good thinking."

My phone began to ring. I looked at the caller ID and noticed it was Parker. Surprised that he was calling me so soon, I answered.

"Sorry to bother you. I just wanted to let you know that Austin and I biked over to Gibbons' Dockside and talked to Julie, one of the owners. She said the fishing camp only has a couple of spots left. So, you might want to act fast."

"Oh. Good to know. I'll stop by as soon as I can."

"You can always call, too."

"Okay. Thanks for letting me know, Parker. I think this will be good for Kevin."

"No problem. Would you like the phone number?"

"Yes. Please. Actually, could you text it to me? I don't have any paper available at the moment."

"Sure. By the way, I was thinking of barbecuing tomorrow night. If you and your family have nothing going on, we'd love to have you over."

I smiled. "I'll check with Mom and Rocky to see if they have plans. Kevin and I are definitely free, though."

"Great," he said, a smile in his voice. "Just let me know."

"I will. What time are you thinking?"

"Six?"

"Sounds good," I replied. "Thank you for everything."

"My pleasure."

After a few more words, we hung up.

"Who was that?" Mom asked.

I told her and mentioned the barbecue.

"Oh, how nice of him. I think we're free, but will check with Rocky."

"Okay. If not, I told him Kevin and I could still make it."

She winked. "Good for you. Nothing wrong with surrounding yourself with some handsome eye-candy while you're here."

I groaned. "Mom."

"Oh, you know very well that Parker has only gotten better with age. You two would make a darling couple."

I rolled my eyes.

She laughed.

My phone buzzed and I saw that it was Parker sending me the information about the fishing camp.

"Who's that?" Mom asked.

I explained.

"Kevin is going to have so much fun. You just wait—he's going to beg to move to Summit Lake after all of this."

"We'll see," I replied, not sure if that's what I wanted anymore myself.

Chapter 13

Amanda

AFTER CALLING GIBBONS' Dockside, and signing Kevin up for the camp, I went outside and noticed Rocky's truck pulling up, returning with our food. After cleaning off the picnic table on the deck, the four of us sat down to eat.

"By the way, Kevin, I signed you up for the fishing camp," I said, opening up my salad.

Excited, he started barraging me with questions.

"You start on Tuesday morning, but other than that, I don't know a whole lot," I said. "But, Austin will be with you. Remember, the boy who was here earlier?"

"Yes," he replied. "How old is he?"

"Twelve, I think," I said.

"He's a lot older than me," Kevin said, frowning.

"That's okay. He'd rather hang out with you than the old fogies," Mom said, handing Kevin some dipping sauce for his chicken nuggets.

Kevin's face brightened.

"Speaking of which, Parker invited all of us over to his cabin tomorrow evening for a barbecue," Mom said. "Doesn't that sound like fun?"

"Really? That's nice of him," Rocky said, removing the wrapper from his Big Mac.

"Rocky, what about your blood pressure?" Mom said, exasperated. "I thought we talked about this."

"I took my meds," he said. "Don't worry about me. I'll be good for the rest of the day."

Shaking her head, she looked at me. "It's funny how *his* diet is also giving me high blood pressure."

"That's your own fault. You worry too much," Rocky said, before taking a large bite of his burger.

"If you'd follow your diet, I wouldn't have to worry so much," she countered.

"I've been good," he replied between chews. "Hey, you should be happy I ordered the diet soda. I wanted a shake."

"He really did," Kevin said, raising his own to his lips.

"Why did you order *him* such a large shake?" Mom said to Rocky. "He won't be able to finish it."

Rocky winked at me. "I know."

"You're incorrigible," she huffed.

"What does that mean?" Kevin asked.

"It means she loves me," Rocky said. "And can't live without me."

"It doesn't sound like it means that," he replied.

"Smart kid," Mom replied, breaking into a smile.

"Mom, can I give Lacey some fries?" Kevin asked, as the dog watched him eat, her eyes pleading for food.

"Just a couple," I replied, standing up. "I should feed her. She probably worked up an appetite down by the lake."

"Okay." He pulled out a couple and threw them at Lacey. They landed on the grass and she gobbled them up.

"I'll be right back," I said. "Rocky, try to control yourself around my salad."

He laughed. "You can keep your rabbit food," he said before taking another bite of his burger.

Chuckling, I went into the house and poured some dog food into Lacey's bowl. As I was securing the bag, I heard a strange noise coming from the other room. Frowning, I brushed my hands off into the sink and went to investigate.

"Oh, my God," I gasped.

The front door stood wide open, and standing in the foyer, was a skunk. Noticing me, it turned and arched its back, raised its tail in the air, and began stomping its feet.

Worried it was going to spray, I turned and quickly ran into the kitchen and out the sliding glass door.

"Rocky," I said, my heart pounding. "There's a skunk in the house."

His eyes widened in alarm. "What?"

"A skunk. In the living room," I said.

"How in the world did it get inside?" Mom asked in a shrill voice.

"The front door was wide open. It must have snuck in," I replied, as Rocky walked over to the sliding glass door and peered inside.

"You don't want to leave doors open around here," Mom said, frowning. "There was a bear spotted just a few weeks ago. Only ten miles north of here. God forbid if one of those were to get inside…"

I stood next to Rocky and put my face to the glass. "I didn't leave it open. Someone else must have. Do you see it?"

"No. Did it spray?" he asked.

"I don't know. I hope not," I murmured.

"Lacey. Get back here!" Kevin hollered.

I whipped around and noticed her scampering around to the front of the house. Realizing she might be after the skunk herself, I raced after her.

"Lacey!" I called, angry and frustrated. "No! Lacey, come here!"

Ignoring me, the dog ran into the house.

Groaning, I was about to follow her when Rocky shouted at me not to.

"Then what are we supposed to do?" I asked.

"I've dealt with these things before. Let me go in and get her," he grumbled. Before he could get inside of the house, however, the dog ran out the door, passing us. I looked inside again to see the skunk scampering away and out the front door.

Rocky groaned. "Too late," he said covering his nose.

The next several minutes were a fiasco, but we eventually got the skunk out of the cabin. Unfortunately, not only did Lacey get sprayed, but the cabin itself now smelled horrible.

"Better call Parker back and see what he recommends for cleaning Lacey up," Mom said. "Meanwhile, keep the door open so we can air-out the cabin. Good thing for wooden floors. If there would have been carpeting, we'd of had to probably rip it out and start over."

"I'm bringing Lacey down to the lake for now," Rocky said. He patted his leg and began walking toward the water. "Come on, girl."

Lacey, who'd been whining, took off after him.

"She smells so gross," Kevin said with a grimace.

"This is why you have to make sure you don't leave the door open," I said, pulling my phone out. "Like Grandma said, there are too many wild animals out here. Not to mention snakes and… other critters."

"But, I didn't leave it open," he protested.

"Someone did." I sighed. "Maybe the latch on the door needs to be checked."

Or maybe the stalker had done it…

I shoved the thought out of my head. How would he be able to corral the thing all the way into the cabin without getting sprayed himself?

Maybe he was good with animals?

Parker was, but I refused to believe that he had anything to do with it.

Wondering if I was going insane, I called him and explained what had happened.

He groaned. "Oh, that sucks. Do you have hydrogen peroxide and baking soda?"

"I think so," I said, trying to recall what I'd seen in the cupboards and pantry.

"Good. You'll need some dish soap, too," he said and then explained exactly what I needed to do.

"Okay. Thank you."

"Do you have any dog shampoo?"

"Not here," I said with a sigh.

"I'll bring some over. I happen to have a jug here at the cabin. Start washing Lacey with the baking soda and peroxide mixture. Try not to get any in her eyes. I'll be over in a couple of minutes."

I sighed in relief. "Thanks, Parker."

"No problem. I need to do something to make sure you're smiling again."

I grinned. "This will definitely help."

"Good."

AN HOUR LATER, Lacey was drying off in the sun and we'd cleaned up the mess in the cabin with bleach and baking soda. Fortunately, the skunk hadn't gotten anything on the furniture, just the floor and part of the wall.

"Thank you so much for coming to our rescue," I said to Parker, as he was preparing to get into his Jeep.

"You're welcome. What a nightmare, huh?" he said with a grim smile.

"No kidding."

"How did the skunk get in?"

"Someone left the front door open," I explained. "Probably Kevin, although he claims it wasn't him."

"It happens. You lucked out. It could have been a lot worse."

"I know. That's what I keep telling myself."

He looked over toward the cabin. "I almost forgot—are Rocky and Jan joining us tomorrow?"

"I think so," I replied. "Can we bring over anything?"

"Nope. Just yourselves."

"You sure? My mother is going to insist on bringing something. She's very stubborn and usually doesn't take 'no' for an answer."

"Okay. Well, she's welcome to bring a dessert. How about that?"

I smiled. "I'll let her know."

He looked at his watch. "Speaking of food, I should go. Austin is home by himself and probably quite hangry by now."

"I'm sure he has quite the appetite now that he's almost a teen."

Parker smiled at me. "You'd better believe it. The kid eats more than I do."

I chuckled.

He started the engine. "Thanks again."

"Like I said before, anything to see that smile of yours," he replied with a wink.

I almost wanted to give him more than a smile at that moment.

Chapter 14

Amanda

FORTUNATELY, THE REST of the evening was uneventful. After cleaning and locking up the cabin, the four of us headed back to Mom and Rocky's place for a late dinner.

"I hope everyone likes chili-dogs and mac-n-cheese," she said as we walked into the house around eight. "Because that's what I'm making."

The three of us agreed that it sounded great.

"Kevin, why don't you go and take a quick shower before dinner?" I said.

He groaned.

"You've still got lake water and grime on you," I reminded him. "Come on. It won't take long."

Pouting, he stomped upstairs, grumbling under his breath.

"If all I had to worry about was taking a shower and cleaning behind my ears," Rocky said, sitting down in his recliner. "I'd be one happy camper."

I grunted. "No kidding. It's like pulling teeth, trying to get him showered and cleaned up."

"Most kids are like that," Mom said. "You were the same way, in fact."

My eyes widened. "I don't remember that."

"Oh, yeah. It wasn't until you were around ten that I didn't have to nag you about it anymore. But, believe me, you gave me just as much trouble," she said.

I sat down on Mom's recliner and kicked the footrest out. "That must be the time in my life when I though us girls always smelled like sugar and spice," I said with a smirk.

"Emphasis on the 'spice'," she replied, laughing. "Anyway, once he discovers girls, he'll be showering three times a day. Wanting to smell good for them."

"Yeah, *that's* why he'll be taking so many of them," Rocky joked in a low voice.

"Shush. Don't talk about my baby like that," I said, closing my eyes. "He's not going to be interested in girls until he's twenty-one. Not if I can help it."

"Good luck with that," Rocky replied. "I think I started liking them when I was in kindergarten. I still remember Josie Hamilton. She had the prettiest blonde hair and green eyes."

"You can't even remember what you had for dinner the night before, but you remember Josie Hamilton's green eyes?" Mom asked dryly.

"There's no comparison between kale and your first love," he replied.

"So, you *do* remember that healthy–rich-in-antioxidants-salad I spent hours cutting up vegetables for," she teased.

"I've tried to forget all about that horrible meal. Believe me," he drawled.

She threw a throw-pillow at him.

I listened to their lighthearted banter, smiling to myself. Even as they went back and forth, the love between them was so obvious.

"Woman, didn't you mention something about chili-dogs and mac-n-cheese?" he asked. "I'm starving."

"You can have a wheat bun, but no mac-n-cheese," she replied, getting up from the sofa. "I'll make you another salad instead."

His face fell. "But—"

"No buts. You had your Big Mac, remember? You're lucky to be getting the chili-dog. By the way, have you taken your meds?" she replied.

"Yes," he muttered.

"Good." She disappeared into the kitchen.

"Now I know why you moved all the way to Chicago," he joked, closing his eyes. "Was she a drill sergeant back then, too?"

"It was different back then," I replied. "She wasn't so involved with my life. Not while I lived at home, at least."

He opened his eyes. "She told me. She regrets a lot of things," he said in low voice. "Almost all of them pertaining to your childhood and how she wasn't there for you."

"She said that?" I whispered. Mom and I had never really talked about it. It was a subject we'd both avoided.

Rocky nodded. "There's not one night that goes by that she doesn't pray for you and Kevin or ask to be forgiven for her drinking."

My eyes filled with tears. "I wish she'd talk to me about it. She'd know that I'd forgiven her long ago."

He sighed. "She's still ashamed and doesn't want to dredge it all up."

"I should talk to her," I said, staring ahead.

He nodded. "I think it would be a good idea. Maybe she'll be able to put the past behind her, once and for all."

Lacey began pacing back and forth and then went over to the door.

"I bet she needs to go potty," I said, getting up off the recliner. "Come on. Let's go."

The dog barked.

"I can bring her out," Rocky said, standing up. He looked exhausted.

"No, I got her."

His face darkened. "It might not be safe."

"I'm just going outside. Plus, Lacey will protect me."

He sighed.

"Do me a favor, just listen for Kevin, if you could?"

He glanced toward the staircase. "Will he need help with anything? Turning on the hot water or finding a towel?"

"No. He should be fine," I replied, opening the front door.

Lacey bolted outside and I followed after. She began sniffing around the yard, and after a couple of minutes, found a place to relieve herself. When she was finished, the dog started making her way back toward the house but then spotted a rabbit near the trees and froze.

Crap.

"Come on, Lacey!" I hollered, clapping my hands.

Ignoring me, she ran off into the woods, chasing the animal as I suspected she would.

Frustrated, I followed, calling her name. Although, I didn't think she'd catch the rabbit, I wasn't in the mood to bathe her again in case she somehow got lucky.

"Lacey, get back here!" I ordered, seeing her up ahead, still hunting. Considering that she wasn't even pausing for my commands, I wondered again if it was because of her ears.

I stepped further into the woods, passing by the remnants of what was left of the treehouse Tara and I had once tried to build. We'd gotten as far as a few floorboards before giving up. Later, as teens, Tara and I had snuck back a few times to smoke cigarettes she'd snuck from her parents, and drink the alcohol I'd stolen from mine.

As I thought back to those days, and some of the wild things we'd gotten away with, I heard the snapping of twigs behind me and quickly turned around. When I didn't see anything, I told myself it was probably a squirrel, or bird.

Not the whistling asshole.

Please, not the whistling asshole.

Spooked, my heart began to race.

"Lacey!" I called, unable to see her any longer. "Come on, girl! Get back here!"

I scanned the woods in front of me, which went on for miles.

Suddenly, I heard a yelp in the distance, now stopping my heart stopping all together.

"Lacey?!" I hollered.

She began to bark and yelp some more.

Frightened that she'd been attacked by another animal, I raced toward the sound, too worried about

143

my dog to consider my own safety. When I finally found Lacey, she was alone but her foot was caught in some kind of a metal trap. Trying to remain calm, I knelt down next to her and was going to try and get the contraption off her leg, when she tried biting me.

"Stop. I'm trying to help you," I said, my eyes tearing up as she growled at me.

I tried once more, but Lacey was confused and in pain, so she snapped at me again. Knowing I couldn't help her by myself, I stood up and pulled out my phone to call Rocky. That's when I heard someone begin to whistle the familiar nursery rhyme I'd grown to hate.

Chapter 15

Amanda

BEFORE I COULD turn around, a gloved hand clamped over my mouth and pulled me away from Lacey. Frightened and shocked, I tried getting away, but the person holding me had arms of steel.

"Amanda," a voice murmured into my ear as I thrashed and wriggled to break free. "This is such a pleasant surprise."

I screamed against his hand.

"You know… it would be so easy to kill you now. But I prefer to prolong the fun. We *are* having fun, aren't we?"

Kill me?

Terrified, I kicked and fought with everything I had.

"Stop struggling," he ordered, digging his fingers into my skin painfully. "Or, I'll kill you, your dog, and the rest of your family."

I froze.

He relaxed. "That's it. Poor Lacey's had a rough day, huh? First the skunk and now the trap? It's funny how dogs are so predictable."

Asshole. I should have known...

"The skunk from earlier was all me. And I assume you found my *Welcome Back* card. But the trap? That's on you. Dogs should really be leashed at all times."

Noticing that he'd loosened his grip as he bragged, I kicked him in the shin and bit his gloved hand with everything I had.

Gasping, he let go.

I lurched forward and then turned around to have a look at him, almost wishing I hadn't. He wore some kind of a camouflage suit made of loose strips of various material, resembling leaves and twigs. It covered him from head to foot, making him look utterly terrifying. On his face he wore some kid of black, nylon mask with a pair of sunglasses.

The man pulled out a long, narrow gun and aimed it at me.

"Please," I begged, raising my hands in the air. "Don't kill me. My son—"

"Son? You don't deserve a son," he growled in a raspy voice, taking a step closer.

My eyes filled with tears. "Why are you doing this?"

"Because, you need to pay for what you did." He stepped toward me and I backed away.

"Pay for what?" I asked. His words made no sense.

Ignoring me, he fired the gun.

I screamed as something hit me in the shoulder. Realizing it was a dart, I pulled it out just as another one hit me in the thigh. Distracted, I didn't notice him move next to me, until it was too late. He jabbed a syringe into my stomach and injected me with something.

"Oh, my God!" I screamed, pushing him away. I turned and began running, already feeling strange. I didn't make it far before the effects of whatever he'd injected in me made me pass out.

Chapter 16

Amanda

SOMEONE SHOOK MY arm. "Amanda. Wake up."

I moaned, wanting nothing more than to sleep.

"What's wrong with her?" Mom asked.

"I don't know," said Rocky. "Amanda, honey. Wake up."

I was about to protest when everything came back to me. Frightened, I forced my eyelids open and saw that it was dark and I was lying on the ground in the middle of the woods.

"Where is he?" I asked, feeling a wave of nausea wash through me as I sat up.

Rocky, who was kneeling next to me, asked, "Who?"

"HIM. The guy. He was wearing camouflage clothing. Like a hunter or a soldier," I said, getting up off the ground with Rocky's help. "Where's Lacey?"

"We don't know," he replied.

"What happened to you?" asked my mother, who was holding a flashlight. Her voice sounded like she was on the verge of hysteria.

I looked around the dark woods, but couldn't see anything. "The guy who's been stalking me showed up out of nowhere. He injected me with something. It must have knocked me out."

Mom gasped.

I headed back to where Lacey had been caught in the trap and they followed. She was gone, along with the trap. My stomach twisted in fear. "Lacey!" I screamed.

"I told you we needed to call the police, Rocky," Mom said angrily. "Amanda, we've got to get you to the hospital and make sure you're okay."

"I'm fine," I said, my head slowly clearing. I called out for Lacey again, but there was still no answer. I knew there wouldn't be and it gutted me. "He... he must have taken her."

"You think the stalker took Lacey?" Mom asked, shocked.

"Yeah. Or he may have just killed her," I replied, blinking back tears. "And..." I couldn't get the rest of the words out. I didn't want to think of my dog as being dead.

"I'm calling Sheriff Baldwin," Rocky said angrily, pulling out his phone.

Mom put her arm around me. "Let's get you back home."

"Lacey!" I called out, trembling.

WHEN WE MADE it back to the house, Mom told me Kevin was upstairs watching television in the bedroom and had no idea of what had happened.

"When we thought you were missing, we didn't want to worry him," Mom said. "We locked him inside."

"You shouldn't have left him alone," I cried, racing up the steps.

"Where have you been?" Kevin asked as I entered the room.

"Outside," I replied, relieved that he was okay. I sat down on the bed and put my arms around him.

"What's wrong?" he asked as I held him.

I didn't know what to tell him, but knew he was no dummy. Lacey was missing and there was no hiding it from him.

"We can't find Lacey," I mumbled.

He stiffened up. "What?" Kevin pulled away and looked up into my face. "What do you mean?"

"She wandered off into the woods."

He quickly got out of bed. "I'm going to find her," he said, sitting down on the carpeting to put his shoes on.

"We've already looked," I said.

Kevin looked up at me. "She'll come for me. I just have to call her."

Sighing, I closed my eyes. The last thing I wanted to do was tell him what had really happened. As I tried coming up with an explanation, Rocky knocked on the door and then peeked his head inside. "Sheriff is on his way."

"Okay," I replied. "I'll be downstairs in a second."

Nodding, he looked down at Kevin, who was tying his shoes. "You okay, kiddo?"

Kevin looked up at him. "Yeah. Why is the sheriff coming? Because Lacey is missing?"

Rocky looked at me.

"Yes. Kind of," I said. "He's going to try and help us locate her."

Kevin nodded. "Good. I just know we'll find her if the cops help us."

Rocky and I looked at each other, our grim expressions mirrored.

Kevin stood up and headed toward the doorway. "She probably just got lost or is digging a hole somewhere. Excuse me," he said, moving around Rocky.

"What are you going to tell him?" Rocky asked when Kevin was out of ear-shot.

I rubbed my forehead. "I have no idea."

"He needs to know that there's a dangerous man out there. This guy's next target could be Kevin."

He was right.

We walked downstairs, where my mother was arguing with Kevin, who wanted to go outside and search for his dog.

"Kevin. Enough. We're going to wait for the Sheriff," I said, putting my hand on his shoulder.

He let out an exasperated sigh. "But, she might come if she hears my voice."

"I don't think it's that easy. Come and sit down. We need to talk," I said, dreading the conversation.

Kevin followed me over to the sofa and we both sat down.

"There is something you need to know," I began.

My mother interrupted me. "Do you think this is a good idea?"

Rocky answered for me. "At this point, it's safer if he knows what's going on."

Kevin's face turned white. "What's going on? Is it Lacey?" Tears filled his eyes. "Is she… is she dead?"

I took his hand in mine. "We don't know where she is. But, I think that someone took her."

"*What?* Who?" he asked.

"There was a man in the woods. He," I paused, knowing that this was going to frighten Kevin, "he shot me with a couple of darts and then injected me with something. I fell asleep, and when I woke up, Lacey was gone."

"With a needle?" Kevin asked, looking stunned.

I nodded. "It's the same man I told you about. The one who is playing bad pranks on us."

He sucked in a breath. "Are you okay?"

I nodded. "Don't worry about me. I'm fine. He just knocked me out."

Kevin was silent for several seconds and then his face turned red. "Why did he take my dog?" he asked angrily.

"Because he's not right in the head," I replied. "Which is why you need to stay close to me, Grandpa, and Grandma."

"Exactly," Rocky added. "And don't worry, kiddo. I'm sure the police will catch this guy soon and everything will be fine."

"What about Lacey?" he asked.

"Hopefully, they'll find her, too," I said.

Kevin was silent for a few seconds. "Maybe she'll run away from him and come home?"

"Maybe she will," I said, pulling him into my arms. I didn't think there was any chance of that happening, because she was hurt. But that wasn't anything he needed to know. It would only make him more upset.

A loud knock on the door startled us.

Rocky got up and peeked outside.

"It's the sheriff and a couple of deputies," he said, looking relieved.

Chapter 17

Amanda

AFTER INTERVIEWING ME, we walked back to where I'd been accosted by the stalker. They searched the area, but unfortunately, didn't find any sign of Lacey.

"I know you said the perp tried hiding his voice, but is there anything else that seemed familiar about him?" Sheriff Baldwin asked, when it was just me, him, and Rocky.

"No. Nothing at all. He acted like he knew me, though. He kept making statements about me not deserving a son and that this was a game he was playing with me." I told him that the man had made threatening comments about not killing me *"yet."*

Sheriff Baldwin frowned.

"You know, I've been wondering—could this somehow be related to Brad?" Rocky suddenly asked.

"I can't imagine why," I replied. "Unless someone is upset that Brad left me everything."

"Now that's an interesting concept," Sheriff Baldwin said, perking up. "Did Brad have any family?"

"Yes. I don't know if his parents are still alive, but he had a twin brother, Barry, and a younger one named Ben. They were estranged the entire time we were together, though," I replied. "He never liked talking about his family."

"Hmm... Do you think you might be able to find some names or addresses for any of his family members?" the sheriff asked, writing things down.

"I can try searching the cabin," I replied. "There were quite a few boxes of bills and other paperwork. Maybe I can find something."

"Okay. Otherwise, I'm sure we can track them down, too," he said.

"Twin brother, huh?" Rocky said. "Twins are usually pretty close. It's too bad he never told you why they weren't on speaking terms."

"Barry could be the nutcase stalking you. Or even the younger brother," Sheriff Baldwin said. "Maybe Brad wanted nothing to do with them because he knew that he, or someone else in the family, wasn't right in the head."

"Honestly, I can't think of anyone else who'd be doing this, so I guess it's possible," I replied, shivering at the thought of one of Brad's brothers trying to kill me.

"How are you feeling?" Sheriff Baldwin asked.

I shrugged. "Tired. Whatever he injected me with seems to have worn off."

"You need to get down to the hospital and have them run some blood tests, pronto," the sheriff said. "We need to find out what it was."

"Will, do," I replied.

We talked for a few more minutes and then Sheriff Baldwin warned me again about going anywhere alone.

"Hopefully we'll find this jackass quickly, but he's obviously not done with you. In fact, it might be a good idea for you to stay somewhere else. Maybe a hotel room in town?" he said.

I shook my head. "No. I feel safe here. At my parents'. If he tracks me down again, and I'm alone in a hotel room, that could be much worse."

"We could have a deputy stay with you for a couple of nights," he suggested.

"And then what? Thanks, Sheriff, but I'd rather stay here with Rocky. He's my deputy," I replied.

Rocky smiled. "You're damn right." He looked at the sheriff. "I'll protect her. Just don't go putting me in jail if I have to use my gun to do it."

"Act wisely," the sheriff warned.

"I'll act accordingly," Rocky replied stubbornly.

"Please find this jerk," I said in a shaky voice. "And Lacey, too."

"We'll do our best," Sheriff Baldwin replied and scratched his chin. "Tell you the truth, I think we might be on to something with Brad's family. I'm going to start looking into that possible lead. I'll see if this Barry, or little brother Ben, have records and we'll try to find out where they might living."

"Thank you, Sheriff," I said, feeling hopeful.

Chapter 18

Amanda

ROCKY DROVE ME to the hospital, while the sheriff waited back home with Mom and Kevin. After I was examined by a woman named Dr. Fisher, a nurse drew my blood and then promised to get the results back within twenty-four hours.

When we arrived back at the house, Kevin was sound asleep, and Mom and Sheriff Baldwin were talking in the kitchen.

"That didn't take as long as I thought it would," my mother said, looking up at us in surprise.

"That's because I called ahead and told them they were coming," Sheriff Baldwin said, looking weary. "How did it go?"

"Fine. They'll contact us within the next day with the test results," I replied.

"Okay," he replied.

"Thank goodness he didn't kill you," Mom said, her eyes welling. She looked at the sheriff. "You *have* to catch this guy. And soon… before he does something even worse."

He nodded. "I know. I know. We'll do everything we can. I promise you. I want to catch this freak as much as you do."

Mom sighed and stared down at her coffee.

"I should get a gun," I said suddenly. It wasn't anything I'd ever considered, but my life had never been in danger before.

Everyone looked at me.

"You'd need to get a permit first," Sheriff Baldwin said.

"A gun? No," Mom said, staring up at me. "What if he gets it away from you?" She shook her head. "I don't like it. It's just asking for more trouble."

"He's already shot me with a dart gun and injected me with who knows what. He's a lot bigger than I am. I need to be able protect myself," I argued.

"Even if you get one, you'd need a Carry-And-Conceal permit if you're going to keep it close to you at all times. That means taking a class," Sheriff Baldwin said. "It's not something you can do by tomorrow."

I sighed.

"We'll talk about it later," Rocky said, looking at me.

I nodded.

"Well, I should get going," the sheriff said before drinking the rest of his coffee. "Let me know if you remember anything else about the perp."

"I will," I replied.

AFTER HE LEFT, I went upstairs and crawled into bed. Just like the last couple of nights, I couldn't sleep. I kept thinking about Lacey and the maniac in the woods. I was frightened, but also furious. If he really was one of Brad's brothers, or even another family member all together, I could definitely understand why he'd wanted to put distance between them.

I turned over in bed and stared toward the window, worried about Lacey. Something told me that if he had kept her alive, it was only because he was planning on using her for his sick game. The idea made me ill, but I refused to get pulled into his twisted fantasies any longer. If the man wasn't caught soon, I would take the money Brad left us, hire a real estate agent, and disappear. I didn't want to live in fear and something told me that the stalker was going to be stepping up his game. I refused to be around for that. I wasn't going to allow him to hurt my son.

THE NEXT MORNING, while Kevin and I were finishing up breakfast, he asked if he could go out into the woods and continue searching for Lacey.

"I don't think she's there," I told him. And the hell if I was going to let him wander around in the woods with a maniac on the loose. "But, hopefully we'll get her back soon."

His eyes filled with tears. "But, what if she is out there? Maybe she's hurt and scared?"

I wanted to punch the man in the face who was breaking my child's heart. "The police checked all around for her last night. She's gone."

"So, where is she?"

"I don't know, Kevin. I'm sorry. Hopefully we'll get her back soon, though," I said softly, touching his hand.

He brushed the tears from his face. "I miss her."

"I do, too." I put my arm around him and kissed the top of his head. "We just have to try and not lose hope."

He sighed and nodded.

I looked up at the clock. It was almost nine-thirty. "We need to get back to the cabin. I want to finish getting everything cleared out and into the garage." I also wanted to see if I could find anything on Brad's family. Letters, pictures, or anything else that might be packed away.

My mother walked into the kitchen with the mail. She looked like she hadn't gotten much sleep either.

"Where's Grandpa?" Kevin asked, standing up.

"Outside," she said, sorting through the envelopes in her hand. "On the porch."

"I'm going out there, too," he said.

"Put your dishes in the sink," I reminded him.

Kevin obeyed and then left the kitchen.

"How are you doing, Mom?" I asked, pushing my plate away.

She shrugged. "I'm fine. Still trying to wrap my head around everything that's been happening, though. What about you?" she asked, putting her hand on my shoulder.

"Managing. It's just so hard to believe that this is really happening. I keep thinking that I'm going to wake up and find it's all been nothing but one crazy, messed up dream."

"I feel the same way. Hopefully they catch this guy soon," she said in a low voice. "Rocky is about ready to take matters in his own hands and hunt this guy down. I don't want him getting hurt."

"Me neither," I replied. "Would you like any coffee?"

"No thank you. I've had enough already."

"Do you have plans this morning? I'd like to get back to the cabin and go through more of Brad's things," I said, standing up. I walked over to the coffee pot and poured myself another cup. "Maybe I'll get lucky and find something on his family."

"Do you really think it could be Brad's brother?"

"I don't know."

She sighed. "I wish Brad would have told you more about his family."

"I know. Me, too," I replied, thinking back at the times I'd tried questioning him about his childhood. He'd been so aloof about his past. "Speaking of the past…"

"Yes?" she asked, with a sudden guarded look on her face.

I wasn't exactly sure how to bring it up, so I just jumped into it.

"Growing up here, wasn't easy," I began.

Her face fell and she looked away. "I know it wasn't. I—"

I interrupted her softly. "Mom, let me finish. Please."

She nodded and our eyes met.

"I just want you to know that even though it wasn't easy, I knew that you did the best you could with what you were given."

"No, I didn't," she said, looking ashamed. "I was a bitter woman. A drunk. Not the mother I should have been."

Kristen Middleton

"I know it wasn't intentional, though. And, even though life here wasn't perfect, I always knew that you loved me."

Her eyes filled with tears. "You were all that really mattered to me. You kept me sane, even though it may have looked like I was anything but," she said with a grim smile.

"I always thought you were sane, just not happy."

"I wasn't. But, it had nothing to do with you."

"I know." I studied her face. "It was Dad who made you unhappy."

She nodded.

"Did you love him?"

She stared off into the distance. "I did, but…" her voice trailed off.

I waited for her to continue.

Mom's lip curled under. "He was always so super-critical of everything I did. My meals were never good enough. I didn't vacuum the right way. I folded the sheets wrong." She sighed. "I couldn't please the man if I tried. Do you ever remember me driving with him in the car?"

"No."

"Because he would nag the hell out of me. From the moment I'd start the engine, he'd act like I didn't know how to drive and always, *always* treat me like I was an idiot."

I did recall my father always bossing my mother around and being super anal about everything. He'd

165

even started on me, when I was a teenager. It was another reason I'd kept my distance.

"It not only wore me down, I began to resent being with him, especially when I saw how happy my friends were in their marriages."

"Is that why you drank so much?"

"Originally, I drank with your father, because he was nicer after he'd have a couple of beers. He'd relax and not complain that his remote control wasn't in the spot he'd left it or that dinner was running late. He was actually 'normal', I guess you could say."

She sighed and went on.

"I *kept* drinking, because I eventually realized that things were never going to get better between us. It made me depressed and I needed something to get by."

"Why didn't you divorce him if you were so unhappy?"

"Because, to answer your earlier question, I did love your father. As miserable as I was, I never stopped. It's why I kept drinking. To cope with his unending nit-picking."

I nodded.

"Anyway, enough about the past. We need to focus on right now and the creep who's after you."

"Yeah."

Mom reached over to my neck and straightened the amethyst pendant she'd given to me last

Christmas. "I've been meaning to ask—was there any other guy in your life, from around here?"

I shrugged. "No. I mean, other than Parker…"

Her eyes widened. "Wait, you don't think…?"

I snorted. "Heavens no. Whoever is doing this is obviously a psychopath. Parker is everything but. He's a nice, normal guy. Besides, when we did break up during high school, it was a mutual thing." Admittedly, I'd been a little saddened by it, but had understood why.

"I guess you're right. He seems too 'normal' and nice to be HIM," she said. "I can't imagine Parker doing anything so horrible. Maybe it really is Brad's twin? He's probably jealous that he left everything to you."

"Maybe. How would he know about it, though?"

"Could they have reconciled?"

That was always possible.

I took a drink of my coffee. "I don't know, Mom."

"I just hope they catch this person soon. I've never been so frightened in my life. I used to give Rocky a hard time about owning a gun, but now I have to admit, it's comforting."

I also remembered the times she'd given him grief about it, while on other visits. Now that all of our lives were threatened, I was pretty relieved myself.

"I'm going to ask him to show me how to use it," I said. "Just in case."

She sighed and nodded. "I guess it wouldn't be a bad idea."

Chapter 19

Amanda

A SHORT TIME later, Rocky and I went into a clearing, far away from the house, where he showed me how to load and use the shotgun. My aim wasn't the best, but something told me I wouldn't need to fire from a long distance anyway.

"We'll practice some more later," he said, picking up the empty soda cans that were still standing. Most hadn't moved, but I'd managed to knock a couple down. At close range, of course.

"Okay," I said.

"Meanwhile, don't go wandering off by yourself again," he said with serious look. "I know you weren't expecting what happened last night. But, until he's caught, we need to stick together and assume that he's not going to stop what he's doing.

I nodded.

WE ARRIVED BACK at Brad's cabin around eleven and went right to work, cleaning out drawers and closets, and hauling things into the garage. This time there was an urgency in what we were doing. Kevin was given some chores to do as well, although he wasn't terribly happy about it. Eventually, he begged to go swimming again, and Rocky took him down to the dock.

As Mom sorted through the linen closet, I searched through Brad's mail and other personal documents, trying to find information on his family. Unfortunately, there wasn't anything. Not even an old photo album, which was frustrating.

By the end of the afternoon, the garage was filled with most of Brad's belongings, except for the large furniture items.

"Things are looking good," Rocky said, as we began pricing items. "Now, let's just hope the sheriff comes through and finds Lacey."

"Yes," I replied, my heart wrenching as I thought about Lacey again. If only I'd gotten her microchipped, I imagined that we could have easily found her by now. "Let's hope he also finds out who took her."

His face darkened. "He'd better. Or I'm going to find him myself and kick the—"

"Rocky," Mom warned, nodding toward Kevin as he stepped into the garage.

He grumbled something under his breath.

"When is the garage sale going to be?" asked Kevin, sitting down on a metal folding chair.

Mom, who was pricing a pile of old books, answered. "It's starting tomorrow morning."

"I hope we get Lacey back before then," he mumbled, opening up a package of string cheese and pepperoni sticks.

I ruffled his hair. "I hope so, too."

"Speaking of which, I'm going to call the sheriff and see if he's learned anything new." Rocky pulled out his phone. As he made the call, my own phone began to ring. Noticing it was Parker, I groaned inwardly. He was more than likely calling about the barbecue, which I'd forgotten all about it.

"Who is it?" Mom asked.

"Parker. I'm sure it's about dinner. What should I tell him?" I replied, not really in the mood for socializing.

"That we'll be over," she said. "Besides, we should fill him in on what had happened. Maybe he can help somehow?"

"True," I replied.

Before I could dial Parker, I noticed he'd left a message. I listened to it and learned that he was actually canceling with us.

"I hate to do this," he said in the message, "but, I'm having problems with my grill. I'm not sure if we're going to be able to have dinner at my place tonight. If you're free tomorrow, I'll hopefully have things figured out by them."

I deleted the message and returned his call.

"The worst thing is, I already went shopping and purchased everything," he said to me. "I planned this remarkable meal and now it looks like it's going to be a no-go for tonight."

"Don't worry about it. I'm sure it will be just as wonderful tomorrow," I replied.

"What's going on?" Mom asked, listening in to our call.

I explained.

"There's no need to cancel. Tell him that we can have it here," she replied. "We'll just use Brad's grill. It's big enough to cook for an army."

Thinking it was a great idea, I told Parker.

"Are you sure?" he asked. "I feel like an idiot."

"Of course I'm sure, and don't feel bad about it. Things happen. Just bring everything over here. One thing you should know, though, is that we don't have any electricity."

"No problem. I'll bring over a large cooler and some ice. Is it a propane or charcoal grill?"

"Charcoal. We have some, too," I said, remembering the bag Rocky had found in the shed.

"Perfect."

We talked some more and then he promised to be over by five.

"I'm still in charge of the cooking, so that I can impress you with my exceptional culinary skills," he said with a smile in his voice.

I chuckled. "No problem. I'm looking forward to it."

"Okay... maybe, just *maybe* I'm overselling a little bit. Although I can grill one mean ribeye, the rest is compliments of Donatello's Deli, you know the one off of Main Street? I cannot take credit for the salad, baked beans, and cheesecake. Hope you like strawberry, by the way."

"Strawberry cheesecake? I love it. I'm a big fan of Donatello's, too," I replied. Everything was a little pricey, but the food was worth it. The deli offered everything from lasagna to potato salad. The place had been around forever, and most of the recipes had been handed down from Mama Donatello, who'd passed away many years ago. Her granddaughter, Maria, who I'd gone to school with, had taken over the business recently.

"Good. I even picked up a couple of rawhide bones for Lacey," he said. "By the way, have you noticed anything else with her hearing?"

My stomach dropped thinking about her.

"No," I said, turning to look back at Kevin, who was still eating his snack. I lowered my voice. "Um, she's... she's missing."

"What?"

I walked out of the garage and began telling him everything. When I was finished, he was stunned.

"Was she microchipped?" he asked.

"No. I'm kicking myself now for not having it done."

"Don't beat yourself up. You didn't know something like this was going to happen. Do you have any idea of who it could be?"

"No," I replied, leaving out the part about Brad's family. Until there was actual proof, I wasn't going to drag their names into it.

"This just blows my mind. I can't even begin to imagine what you're going through. I'll keep an eye out, and if I see anyone snooping around the area, I'll call the police and let you know. Hopefully the sheriff will locate this asshole soon."

"I hope so, too."

We talked a little more about the stalker and then reconfirmed dinner plans before hanging up.

"Did you tell him what's going on?" Mom asked, as I walked back into the garage.

"Yeah. He was pretty shocked, too."

"I'm glad you filled him in. Like I said before, he should know what's going on, especially since he's going to be around us. Who knows? Maybe he's even seen something that can help."

"It didn't sound like it, but I suppose something might come to him," I replied.

Rocky, who was off of his phone now, mentioned that Sheriff Baldwin hadn't been able to locate either of Brad's brothers, but had learned that both of his parents had passed away a few years ago.

"Great," I said dryly. "The brothers are both unreachable. If that doesn't sound fishy, I don't know what does."

"I tell you what I know… I *know* that one of them might be in Summit Lake," said Rocky dryly. "Looking to get shot."

"Now, we don't know for sure if either are involved," Mom scolded. "You shouldn't jump to conclusions."

"We don't know they aren't," Rocky answered. "Anyway, I don't care who this guy is. If I get my hands on the bozo doing this, he's a dead man."

"Rocky," Mom warned, nodding toward Kevin, who was quietly listening in.

"Rocky nothing. This guy has gone too far and needs to be stopped. If the police aren't going to put an end to this madness, I sure as hell am."

"This is 'hangry' talk. You need to eat," she said. "I'll get you something from the cooler."

"This is 'frustrated' talk. But, I'll still take you up on the offer of food," he replied, winking at Kevin.

"Grandpa, did the sheriff find Lacey yet?" Kevin asked.

Rocky's eyes softened. "No, bud. We can't give up hope though, right?"

He nodded and then asked if he could go back down to the lake.

"You just got out of the water," I said, staring at him in surprise.

"I know, but I want to show Grandma my new dive," he said, smiling proudly.

My mother smiled back. "Did Rocky teach you?"

He nodded.

"I gave him pointers, but Kevin learned all by himself," Rocky said. "He's a good swimmer. You should consider joining a swim team someday."

Kevin's eyes lit up. "Yeah!"

"Sure. If that's what he wants to do," I said.

Mom looked at her watch. "What time is Parker and his son coming over for dinner?"

"They should be here around five," I replied.

"I suppose you can go back into the water for a little while," Mom told Kevin. "If you're okay with that, Amanda?"

"Of course," I replied.

"Let's go, kiddo," she said to Kevin. "Show me these new dives of yours. Meanwhile, go and grab something to munch on, Rocky."

"Will do," he replied.

The two left the garage and Rocky looked at his watch. "Is there anything we need to pick up from the grocery store?"

"Maybe something to drink?" I replied.

He nodded. "Good idea."

"I can drive into town and pick up some things."

"I'll go with you," Rocky said.

"You should stay here with Mom and Kevin."

"After everything that's happened, you know very well that I'm not letting you go anywhere alone," he argued.

"He's not going to come after me in broad daylight, especially in the middle of town. If anything, he'd show up here. And those two are more vulnerable than I am."

He sighed.

"Seriously, Rocky. I'll be fine. Besides, you need to eat. Remember? Hangry-man?"

He grunted and rolled his eyes.

"I'll see you later."

"Wait, maybe we should all drive into town together?" he suggested.

"Kevin wants to swim. I'll be fine," I repeated.

He rubbed his forehead. "Why do I feel like this is a bad idea? Promise that if you see anything out of the ordinary, you call me or the sheriff," Rocky said sternly.

"Of course."

Chapter 20

Amanda

WE LOADED A cooler into Rocky's pickup and then I drove into town, constantly glancing into the rearview mirror. As I pulled into the parking lot of Becker's, the local grocery store, I noticed a woman walking her dog and a lump formed in my throat. Blinking back tears, I got out of the truck and went into the store to purchase what I needed. As I was grabbing two large bags of ice from the freezer, someone said my name. I turned around and noticed a woman standing behind me. She was my height, slightly older, with blonde hair and glasses. At first I didn't recognize her, but then remembered she and her husband, Michael Jergan, owned Aunty K's diner, just down the street.

"Karen," I said, smiling. "It's been a long time."

Brad and I used to eat at the diner frequently. I hadn't returned, mostly because my mother was always serving such great meals when we visited Summit Lake.

"It sure has. Wow, I didn't know you were back in town," she replied, looking me up and down. "You look great."

Surprised that the town gossip hadn't been aware of it, I wondered if she'd lost her touch. The woman usually knew everything about everyone, and wasn't afraid to ask questions. "Thank you. I just got in a couple days ago."

Her eyes searched mine. "I heard about Brad. We didn't go to the funeral, of course. But, it was such a shock to hear what happened."

"I was shocked as well."

She nodded slowly. "So, did you two keep in touch before he died?"

I shook my head. "No. To tell you the truth, I hadn't seen him in years."

She glanced up and down the aisle, and then moved closer. "Michael thought maybe he killed himself," she murmured.

My eyes widened. "Why would he think that?"

"The guilt, maybe? I don't know. Of course, who knows what went on in his head? I'd like to think there'd be some remorse, but one never knows with those kind of people."

Remorse?

Those kind of people?

Confused, I asked what she meant.

Her eyebrow arched. "You didn't know?"

"Honestly, I have no idea what you're talking about."

"Well," she lowered her voice again, "Brad left his laptop in our diner several weeks ago. We didn't know whose it was at first, so Michael opened it up, to see if he could identify the owner. Apparently, Brad hadn't logged out of a website he'd visited." She waited for someone to pass us by and then continued. "It was filled with filthy pictures of children."

Had I heard her right?

"Wait, *what?*"

Her lips pursed together. "A website for pedophilia," she said and then made the sign of the cross over her chest.

Speechless, all I could do was stare at her in horror.

She sighed. "We were just as stunned. We had no idea that Brad was into sick things like that."

"Are you sure it was *his* laptop?" I asked, still in disbelief. The man I'd known hadn't been interested in children. Not sexually. At least… not when I'd known him. The idea made my skin crawl.

She grunted. "Oh, it was. He came by fifteen minutes after, asking if we'd seen it. You should have seen how worried he looked, for obvious reasons. We gave it back and pretended we hadn't seen anything, but it was very upsetting. Michael and I just couldn't believe it. We thought you knew and it was why you'd left him."

"I really had no idea. This sounds so unlike Brad," I replied and then remembered the random photos of children we'd found in his phone They'd all been wearing clothes, but it certainly had been odd. Now, hearing this, the photos made sense.

"I wanted to contact the police, but Michael talked me out of it. He promised to confront Brad himself, eventually, but then we learned about the crash." She clucked her tongue three times. "If it wasn't suicide that killed him, it was karma, huh?"

"Yeah," I replied, still trying to collect myself.

"So, you really didn't know about him being a pedo?" she asked, wrinkling her nose. "This must be such a shock. I'm sorry to be the one to break it to you."

"Uh, it's okay. I have to go," I said, unable to talk about it anymore. The idea that someone I'd been madly in love with at one time could be into something so horrible, made me sick to my stomach.

Is that why he'd wanted children?

Bile rose to the back of my throat.

Kristen Middleton

"Well, it was nice seeing you," she called out as I hurried away with my cart. "Stop by at the diner so we can catch up some more!"

Chapter 21

Amanda

ON THE WAY back to the cabin, I couldn't stop thinking about Brad. I tried coming up with a rational explanation as to why he'd been browsing child pornography on the Internet, but couldn't think of anything good.

"That was fast," Rocky said, when I pulled up.

"Not much to get," I replied, turning off the engine. I rolled up the window and got out.

"Any problems?" he asked as we walked around the truck together to the tailgate.

"No."

He opened up the back and smiled when he saw the case of beer.

"I figured Parker might want something other than water and soda," I said. I sure in the hell did at that moment.

"No complaints here," he said, opening up the cooler.

We loaded it with ice and then began filling it with beverages, leaving room for food if needed.

"You doing okay?" he asked, noticing how quiet I was.

I took a deep breath and told him about my conversation with Karen.

He frowned. "You believe her?"

"Why shouldn't I?" I replied, surprised at the question.

He twirled his finger next to his ear. "She's a strange bird. Both her and her husband."

I had to admit, I'd only met Karen a couple of times. As far as Michael, I never talked to him, but had heard he was a hothead. Still, why would anyone make that up?

"You think she might have lied to me?"

He shrugged. "Honestly? I don't know. She was spreading some rumors about Parker last year. Said he was trying to charge her for an operation her dog didn't need."

"Really?"

He nodded. "I don't know much about it other than the animal died a couple weeks later. I assume she didn't bring him in for surgery, like what was recommended. As far as Brad goes, did you ever suspect that he was into pedophilia?"

"No. Which is why it threw me off. But there were those photos in his phone. We all thought that was strange."

He nodded. "Yeah. It certainly was."

"She said they actually 'saw' the website he'd been looking at. I just don't know why anyone would make that up. Even her."

"I hope it's not true." He looked toward the cabin with distaste. "The idea of a pedo actually having lived in our community makes me sick."

"What about me? We…" I shuddered, "were intimate."

"No problems for him there?" he asked, looking uncomfortable.

I shook my head. "No. Like I said, I would have never guessed him to be into… that."

He sighed. "Maybe we should do some investigating of our own. You didn't see a laptop anywhere in the cabin, did you?"

"No. But, I didn't look very hard for one either."

He looked toward the house. "We should go inside and search for it."

"Wouldn't he have taken it with him to the North Shore?" I replied, almost afraid to find it.

"It's always possible," he replied. "But then again, if he committed suicide, he might not have been in his right mind. He may have left it behind."

At that moment, I was beginning to suspect that Brad had *never* been in his right mind.

I followed Rocky to the cabin and we began searching for the laptop. Almost everything in the place had been cleared out, so there wasn't much to go through.

"Have you checked the attic?" he asked me, when we came up with nothing.

I stared at him in surprise. "I didn't even consider that. Did you see the entrance to it anywhere?"

"Actually, I did, and was going to remind you to check it out, but forgot all about it myself. You can access it from the laundry room." He began walking toward the door. "I'm going back outside to get a ladder. We'll take a look and see what's up there."

Hopefully, nothing.

In fact, I didn't know how I'd handle actually finding evidence of Karen's claims. The photos in his phone were one thing, but if Brad had hid something up there, then it wasn't going to be good.

Fifteen minutes later, Rocky had the attic door open and was poking his head inside.

"See anything?" I asked from below, my stomach in knots.

"Yeah, actually. Here, take the flashlight," he said, handing it down to me.

I grabbed it from him.

He began climbing back down the ladder with a large, metal box. He set it down on the linoleum and we looked at each other.

"This can't be good," he said, looking pale.

"Nope."

"I suppose one of us should open it up."

I nodded.

Sighing, He knelt down next to it.

"Wait," I said, my heart thumping wildly. It wasn't big enough to hold a laptop, but there had to be something important enough to keep hidden. Something that had been valuable to Brad.

He looked up at me. "You don't have to look… If we're lucky, it's just some old coin collection or baseball cards. If not, well… I've seen some pretty gruesome stuff in my time, having been a paramedic."

"No. It's okay. I just needed a second to collect myself." I let out a breath and nodded. "Okay. Go ahead. Open it."

He undid the latch and opened up the lid.

"Uh oh," Rocky said, pulling out a stack of photographs. My heart sank as I caught a glimpse of the first one. The model in the photo was naked and young. Too young.

I gasped in horror and looked away.

"Brad, you sick son-of-a-bitch," Rocky muttered angrily.

188

Realizing what Karen had said about Brad was true, I turned and ran out of the laundry room to the bathroom and barely made it to the toilet before vomiting.

Chapter 22

Amanda

AFTERWARD, WE TOLD Mom about the discoveries and she was just as shocked and repulsed as we were.

"Did he ever do anything that would have suggested he was into…" she curled her lips in disgust and shook her head. "You know, I can't even say it."

"No, Mom," I replied, again thinking back to when we'd been together. There'd been nothing to suggest Brad had been into something so vile. Sure, he owned a video arcade, so he'd been around kids quite a bit. But I would have never guessed it might have been because of anything immoral.

"I wonder if he ever abused anyone?" she said, staring off into space.

"Let's hope to hell not," I replied.

"He obviously liked women, too," she said, looking at me again. "There was you and I know he'd dated others in the community."

I shrugged. I didn't know and didn't care. The only thing *obvious* now was that we were uncovering secrets about Brad that would have been buried with him, had he not slipped up that day at the diner.

We called the sheriff and he raced right on over.

"You're keeping me busy," he said, as I handed him the metal box.

I snorted. "Believe me, I wish I wasn't."

"Was there anything else?" he asked grimly.

I shook my head. "Not that we've seen."

There didn't need to be. There were dozens of pictures, all of children, and not the kind that should ever be taken. As far as a laptop, we searched everywhere but never found one.

"I would have never guessed this about Brad," he said, shaking his head in disgust.

I told him about my conversation with Karen earlier.

His face turned red. "And she never reported this?"

"She mentioned that her husband was going to confront Brad, but then he died shortly after, so they let it go," I replied.

Sheriff Baldwin growled in the back of his throat. "I wish people wouldn't try taking things into their own hands. If we'd have known, maybe we could have arrested him and learned where and how he was getting the pictures."

Rocky, who'd been listening quietly, cleared his throat. "Yeah. Too bad indeed. You know, they seemed rather old. Most taken by a Polaroid camera."

"Okay. I'll bring this down to the station and look through them after I eat, so I don't ruin my appetite." He looked at me. "I'm sorry this is happening to you, on top of your stalker. I'm sure it came as quite a surprise. I know I was shocked to get your call."

I nodded. "It's been crazy."

He sighed. "Yep. That it has. Well, thanks for the evidence. If either of you find anything else, let me know."

"Will do," Rocky answered.

"Have you learned anything new about Barry's or Ben's whereabouts?" I asked.

"Not really. We finally have an address for Ben. I called the phone number listed and talked to his roommate, a guy named Terry. He mentioned that Ben is out of the country on a photo shoot. Apparently, he's some kind of fashion photographer. As far as Barry goes, his last known address was in Florida, but he's not there anymore, apparently. Don't worry, if we find out anything more, I'll call you," he replied.

"Thanks," I said, feeling deflated.

"We should both be hearing back soon about your blood test, too," he added, heading toward his car.

"Yeah," I replied. Not that it was going to help any, but I was interested in finding out what the wacko had injected me with.

As the sheriff was getting into his car, we saw Parker's black Hummer heading down the dirt road toward us. The two men waved to each other in passing.

"What did the sheriff say?" Mom asked, walking toward us from the house.

"Not much. He's going to take a look at the photos to see if he can find out who may have taken them," Rocky replied.

"Did he mention whether or not he'd found Lacey?" she asked.

"Nothing yet on her, either," Rocky said.

"What a nightmare," she mumbled, staring away pensively. "Kevin keeps asking about his dog. It breaks my heart that we don't have an answer for him. The poor kid."

"I know what you mean. Where is he?" I asked, looking around the yard.

"Inside the house," she replied. "Playing on the iPad. I think all of the sun and swimming tired him out."

"That, and worrying about Lacey," I said.

She nodded.

"We'd better see if they need help," Rocky said as Parker and Austin got out of the Hummer.

The three of us walked over to them.

"Hey, everyone. I hope you're all hungry," Parker said, opening up the back of his SUV. There was a large Yeti cooler and a couple of grocery bags from the deli. "Just so you know, I brought enough food to feed an army."

"Perfect," Rocky said, grinning. "Jan's been starving me, so I'm hungry enough to *eat* an entire army."

"Oh, you," she scolded, swatting him playfully on the back.

Rocky chuckled.

"Thanks for doing this," I said to Parker, curling my thumbs through the loops of my jean shorts. "This is very sweet of you."

"You're welcome." He smiled. "Thanks for letting me take the dinner party to you."

"Any time." I had to admit, seeing Parker's handsome, smiling face was bringing a little light into the dark day I'd had.

Rocky reached for one of the paper bags. "Here, let me help you grab some of this stuff."

"Thanks," he replied, moving out of the way.

"Hi, Austin," I said, looking over at him. "How are you?"

He gave a nervous smile. "Okay."

"Good. What did you do today? Anything fun?"

"Not really. Just hung out. Um, did you find Lacey yet?" he asked.

"Austin," Parker scolded. "Really?"

"What?" he replied with a frown. "I'm just asking. What's the big deal?"

"It's okay," I said quickly. "No, unfortunately we haven't located her yet."

Parker sighed and rubbed the back of his neck. "I'm so sorry. That's gotta be especially hard on Kevin. Where is he?"

"Inside," I replied, nodding toward the cabin. "Which is where we should probably bring everything right now."

"I agree. With the kind of luck we've been having, a hungry bear is going to show up here and take off with our food," Mom said dryly.

Austin's face lit up. "Have you seen any bears?"

"Fortunately, no. But, I'm sure they're out there somewhere," Mom replied. She looked at Parker. "Can I help with anything?"

"Sure. Here," Parker said, offering her a plastic bag. "I brought along some paper plates, forks, and knives. I wasn't sure what you had here."

"We've already packed away the dishes for the garage sale, so I'm glad you were thinking ahead," she replied, taking the bag from him. "Thank you."

"Oh, of course," he said.

After bringing the food into the cabin, Rocky and Mom went outside to get the grill started while Austin went in search of Kevin, who was in the guestroom.

"So, did the sheriff have any news for you?" Parker asked quietly as we unloaded the items from the bags onto the counter.

"No. Unfortunately," I replied, not telling him about the photos. I was still too ashamed to share that kind of information about a man I'd been married to. Not to mention I felt naïve and stupid, too.

"That's too bad. What are you going to do now?"

"I don't know. When I first saw the cabin, I seriously wanted to move in. It seemed so magical," I sighed. "With everything that's been going on, however, I feel like there's a dark cloud hanging over everything. Even this place. I don't think I want it."

"I'm sorry you feel that way. It would have been nice having you live so close," he replied, looking disappointed. "Hopefully, the sheriff will come through and find this asshole. Maybe you'll change your mind?"

After what I'd learned about Brad, I didn't know if I'd have the stomach to live there. Even if they caught the stalker. "I guess anything is possible," I replied.

"The idea that this lunatic is harassing you pisses the hell out of me. This is supposed to be a quiet, safe town. That's why I moved back here. Well, one of the reasons."

I nodded. "I always thought the same thing, although, the person doing this might not even be from around this area."

"You know, I was thinking, could this nonsense somehow be related to Brad?"

Sighing, I decided to tell him about Brad's brothers. "We don't really know if either are involved, but the sheriff is looking into it."

He asked me if I'd ever met either of them.

"No. And Brad refused to talk about them either. The funny thing is that he and Barry were actually twins, too," I replied. "I imagine that whatever had come between them had to have been pretty significant, considering twins are supposed to be close."

He agreed.

We talked more about what had happened as I helped Parker prepare the food. Eventually, the subject changed and soon we were laughing about some of the memories from high school.

"Are you still friends with Tara?" he asked.

"Yes. We're actually supposed to get together next week."

"I ran into her a few months ago at Merv's," he said, talking about one of the local dive bars. "She was playing in a dart tournament."

"She always did love playing darts. And pool," I said, thinking back to the times we used to sneak into the bars in Stover, which was the next town over. We'd been underage, but had gotten our hands on some fake I.D.s. Fortunately, we'd never gotten caught.

"She tell you about her divorce?"

I nodded.

"It's too bad, although, I'm surprised they stayed together as long as they did. Back in high school, Josh used to brag about all of the 'chicks' he was getting lucky with. The guy was out of control, even back then."

"Sounds like him. I tried telling Tara, but she didn't want to listen," I said. "I guess that it wasn't all bad, though. She has her sons and wouldn't trade them for the world."

He lowered his voice. "That's how I feel about Austin. My marriage was a disaster, but at least I ended up with a terrific kid. I wouldn't change that either."

I wanted to ask him about Austin's mother, but Rocky walked into the kitchen with a beer in his hand.

"The grill is ready whenever you are," Rocky said, looking more relaxed than earlier.

"Great, I think we're all set," Parker replied.

Rocky looked at the plateful of ribeye and chicken breasts and pretended to wipe saliva from the corner of his lips. "Wowza, look at this spread. You weren't kidding. That's enough meat to bring tears to man's eyes. Especially one who's been forced into eating kale and tofu for the last several weeks."

"She's making you eat tofu, too?" I said, wrinkling my nose.

He nodded. "You ever try tofu, Parker?"

"No," he admitted.

"Let me tell you… it tastes just as bad as it sounds. I like to call it 'toe fool'. Cause it looks like toe-jam and I'm a fool for eating it," he joked.

I grimaced. "Oh, yuck."

Parker laughed.

Kevin and Austin appeared in the kitchen.

"What's so funny?" Kevin asked.

"Don't ask. It might ruin your dinner," I said.

Kevin looked around the kitchen. "We're both hungry. Is the food ready yet?"

"Nope. We're just getting ready to put the meat on the grill, though," Rocky said. "Shouldn't be too much longer."

"Can Austin and I go into the woods? He said there's a treehouse not far from here and he wants to show it to me," Kevin said.

"A treehouse?" repeated Rocky. "Really?"

"Yeah," Parker said. "We noticed it last year when we went hiking. It's actually on this property."

I smirked. "If it's anything like the treehouse Tara and I tried building, it's not going to be worth the trip."

"It's pretty rundown," Parker admitted. "But not too shabby, considering that it's probably the work of some kids or teenagers."

"Can we go and see it?" Kevin begged. "Please?"

"It's almost dinnertime," I said. "Besides, I don't want you wandering around the woods. Not after everything that's been happening."

"Tell you what, if your mother is okay with it, I'll take you both there after dinner." Parker looked at me. "It's really not far from here."

"That's fine. I'll even go with you," I replied. "I'm curious to see this treehouse myself."

"So, when did you say we were eating again?" Kevin asked.

"Unless you like your meat raw, in about twenty minutes I'd say, right, Parker?" Rocky asked.

"Yep," he replied.

"Why don't you boys see if Jan needs any help getting the picnic table ready?" Rocky said.

"Okay," Kevin replied.

The boys left the kitchen.

"Those two seem to be getting along nicely," I said, pleased.

"Austin's been bored, so I figured they would," Parker replied.

"You want a beer?" Rocky asked Parker. "Or a soda?"

"I'm good. I brought along some bottled water," he replied. "Thank you, though."

"No problem. You need any help?" Rocky asked, looking down at the counter.

"I think we're good for now," Parker said. "When the picnic table is ready, you can help us bring everything out."

"Sounds good. Let me see what's happening out there." Rocky opened up the sliding door.

"We'll follow you out," Parker said, picking up the heavy plate of meat.

"I've got this," I said, grabbing the foiled package of potatoes and onions, which also needed to be grilled.

"I should probably tell you," Parker murmured as we headed toward the patio. "I quit drinking cold-turkey when I moved out here."

"Oh? Well, honestly, I really don't drink much myself. Maybe a glass of wine now and again," I replied.

"Nothing wrong with that. I, on the other hand, can't stop with one, which is why I just avoid it altogether now."

"I respect that," I replied, remembering he'd mentioned visiting Merv's bar. I knew that didn't mean he'd been drinking alcohol, but I was a little curious as to why he'd been there.

As if reading my mind, he brought up the bar again, explaining that he'd been at a bachelor party and had been one of the designated drivers.

"And the group wanted to go to *Merv's*?" I asked, amused.

He shrugged. "Not much else to go to in this town, besides Shoop's. We stopped there as well."

"What's that place like?"

"Typical meat-market, filled with music and bad decisions."

I chuckled. "In other words, Josh's kind of place?"

He grinned. "Exactly."

"What about you?"

He gave me a surprised look. "What do you mean?"

"You're single and attractive. Where do you hang out to meet 'chicks'?" I teased.

"At work. Not to mention that I get to see my share of dogs, cats, and gerbils there, too," he joked back.

I laughed.

We stepped out onto the deck together.

"The truth is, I've been too busy to date. And… there hasn't been anyone in town who I've wanted to ask out." He smiled. "Until now."

"Oh, yeah?" I replied, smiling back.

"Now, I just have to get the nerve to ask her."

I hadn't flirted for many years, and this was actually giving me butterflies. "I think you have a pretty good shot. You should just take the leap of faith and do it."

"You know what? I'll call her when I get home. Thanks for the advice."

My jaw dropped.

Parker threw his head back and laughed.

Chapter 23

Amanda

AFTER EATING PARKER'S mouthwatering meal, we cleaned up and then took the boys into the woods to see the treehouse. Just like he'd said, it wasn't far from Brad's cabin.

"Whoa, cool!" Kevin shouted, running toward the treehouse, which almost looked like a floating shack from where we were standing. It was built into an enormous oak tree, and a pretty good size at that.

"Wait!" I hollered, staring at the tree-fort. "It could be dangerous!"

As we drew closer, I was a little impressed with ingenuity of the builders. It looked like they'd used whatever they could get their hands on to make the thing, including pieces of siding and vinyl skirting from a mobile home.

Kevin stopped and turned to look at me, a frustrated look on his face.

"I'll go and check it out," Parker said, walking ahead.

After testing out the wood pieces used for the ladder, he climbed up and looked inside. After a few minutes of inspection, he gave a thumbs-up and climbed back down.

"They'll be fine. The flooring is pretty stable," Parker told me, as the boys disappeared into the treehouse. "Everything else is questionable."

"Don't lean against the walls! You could fall!" I hollered and then looked at him. "Great, I'm starting to sound like my mother, now. A perpetual worry-wart."

"Nothing wrong with being careful," he said with an amused look on his face.

I looked back at the tree. "Does it look like anyone has been using the thing?"

"It's hard to say," he replied, swatting at a mosquito. "It's completely empty, not even any candy wrappers or other things you'd imagine a kid would forget inside. It's probably been abandoned for quite some time. I'm surprised it's been holding up with the kind of winters we get."

"Me, too. You mentioned there weren't a lot of kids around this area."

"No. there's not."

"It's kind of strange that it was built on Brad's property. I wonder if he knew anything about it?" I said, my mind returning to the pictures we'd found. It creeped me out to think that he may have known about the treehouse and if *he'd* actually used it for anything.

"It's hard to say. Was he a hiker?"

"He used to be really into fitness, so I would think that he might have walked out here. But, who knows…"

"Brad seemed like a nice enough guy. He probably didn't care," Parker said.

If he only knew.

The door of the treehouse opened and Kevin stuck his head out. "Mom, can we sleep in here tonight?"

"Absolutely not," I replied.

He began to protest.

"Kevin, enough," I replied. "It's too dangerous. Not to mention, you'd get eaten alive by mosquitos," I said, slapping one on my arm. "In fact, we should get back to the cabin. It's going to be getting dark soon, and the bugs are getting worse."

"She's right," Parker said. "It definitely wouldn't be a good idea to sleep in that thing."

Looking frustrated, Kevin closed the treehouse door.

206

"You know, if he really wants to 'camp', we have a large tent back at my place. We could set it up outside and the boys could sleep in that."

"It sounds like fun, but I'm too nervous about him being outside at night while *you-know-who* is running around."

He nodded. "Good point."

Although Parker was with us, now that darkness was starting to set in, I couldn't help but begin to feel a little anxious.

"We should really get moving," I said, looking through the trees.

"Yeah."

He called the boys and they both climbed out of the treehouse.

"Can we come back tomorrow?" Kevin asked, swatting at mosquitos.

"We'll see," I replied.

"Speaking of tomorrow, is Kevin still able to join us?" Parker asked.

I stared at him blankly.

"Fishing?" he reminded me with a smile.

"Oh, yeah. I'd forgotten all about it. Of course. What time?"

"I wanted to leave around seven a.m., but Austin isn't a morning person," Parker mused, putting his hand on his son's shoulder. "So, probably around nine?"

"Nine o'clock is perfect," I said. "I'll drop him off at your place on the way to the cabin."

"Perfect. Are you all set for the garage sale?" Parker asked as the boys took off ahead of us, back toward the cabin.

"I think so. By the way, thanks for inviting Kevin. I doubt tomorrow would have been much fun for him," I said.

"I'm glad he's able to come. It will make it more enjoyable for Austin, too."

We caught up to the boys and I could hear them chatting about the treehouse and what they wanted to do with it. There was the age-gap between them, but at the moment, both boys were excited about the same thing and it was nice seeing the smiles and excitement on their faces.

When we arrived back at the cabin, I could tell Mom and Rocky were tired and ready to head back to their place.

"We were getting worried that you'd be out there in the dark," Mom said with a strained smile.

"Don't worry. I'm a second-degree black belt. I had her back the entire time," Parker said.

"Really?" I replied. "I had no idea. Taekwondo?" Parker nodded.

"I'm impressed. Maybe you could teach me a few defense moves," I said, smiling.

"It would be my pleasure," he replied.

"Dad, can we go?" Austin said, swatting at mosquitos.

"Yeah," he said.

"Parker, thank you so much for the wonderful meal," Rocky said, putting his arm around Mom's shoulders. "I haven't had anything that tasty for a long time. Like I said before, Jan's put me on a diet. Hell, I'm surprised she let me eat as much as she did."

"It was a special occasion. Don't think you're going to be eating like that every day, now," Jan replied.

"Oh, I know. Believe me," he said dryly.

"I'm going fishing with them tomorrow," Kevin announced happily.

"Cool," Rocky said. "You can use one of my poles, Kevin."

"Otherwise, we have plenty of them as well. I also have a life-jacket he can use," Parker said.

Rocky smiled. "Man, you guys are going to have fun."

"You're welcome to join us," Parker said.

"I'd love to, but I promised the ladies I'd help with the garage sale. Next time you go out though, count *both* of us in," Rocky replied.

"Definitely," he said.

"I'm getting eaten up alive. I knew we should have brought along some bug spray," Mom said, scratching her ankle. "We should go before I don't have any skin left to scratch."

We agreed.

"Thanks again, Parker," I said, walking him and Austin to their SUV. "It was a nice evening."

"It was," he replied. "We'll have to do it again, soon. I'm getting a new grill in the next couple of days. I'll have you all over."

"*We're* bringing the food, though."

He smiled and shrugged. "Either way."

I watched as Austin opened up the passenger door. "Goodnight, Austin," I said.

"Goodnight," he replied before getting into the SUV.

"So, I'll drop Kevin off right at nine," I said as Parker and I stared at each other in the darkness.

"Sounds good."

There was suddenly an awkwardness between us. Not sure what to do, I told him "goodbye" and then stepped in to give him a hug. He hugged me back and I was suddenly reminded of how long it had been since I'd been embraced by another man, besides Rocky. It didn't hurt that he smelled good, too.

We pulled apart and I smiled up at him. "Drive safely."

He opened up the door. "Thanks. See you tomorrow."

I nodded.

He got into the Hummer and I watched as he backed out and they went on their way.

Chapter 24

Amanda

WE LEFT SOON after and settled in for the night at Mom and Rocky's. As I was tucking Kevin into bed, he asked again about Lacey. I knew it was looking as if we might never see her again, but I didn't have the heart to tell him. I knew it would crush Kevin.

"The sheriff is still doing his best to try and find her," I said softly as I brushed the hair out of his eyes.

"Maybe we should make some flyers?"

"Now, that's a great idea," I replied. "We'll work on that tomorrow morning. We'll see if Rocky can go into town and make some copies for us, too."

He grinned and then looked troubled again.

"What is it, sweetie?" I asked.

He ran his thumb back and forth over his favorite blanket, like he used to do when he was very young. "What if that man hurt her?"

"Let's not think about that," I replied, not knowing what else to say, especially considering the same thought had crossed my mind many times. "We have to try and stay hopeful. For Lacey."

His eyes filled with tears. "I know. I just miss her so much."

"Me, too." I leaned down and kissed him on the forehead, cursing the devil who was breaking my son's heart.

Kevin used the back of his hand to wipe the tears from under his eyes. "Maybe they'll find her tomorrow?"

"I hope so."

He was silent for several seconds and then his eyes widened. "They should send out a search party for Lacey. Like they do in the movies."

"Unfortunately, they usually don't do that for pets."

He frowned. "Maybe we should make our own then."

"Let's talk about it tomorrow. After you get back from fishing. We'll start with the flyers and go from there, okay?"

He nodded.

I stood up. "Goodnight, Kev. I love you."

"I love you, too," he replied.

I headed toward the doorway and he asked if I was coming to bed soon.

"Yeah. I'm going to take a shower and then I'll turn in."

"Okay."

I could tell from the look in his eyes that he was anxious about being alone.

"You're safe in here. You know that, don't you?"

He nodded.

"Good. I'll be back soon."

"Okay."

I left the bedroom, more determined than ever to keep him safe and by whatever means I had to.

I headed downstairs, where Rocky was watching the news and eating almonds. Next to him, on the ground, was his rifle.

"We should go target shooting again," I said. "Maybe early tomorrow evening? After we get back from the garage sale?"

"Sure," he replied, reaching into the almond bag.

"Okay. Thanks."

"You bet."

I told him about the flyers.

"Great idea. I'll stop at the library and make some copies, once you guys make the flyer."

"Thank you. Where's Mom?" I asked.

"Kitchen."

213

I found her standing by the sink, in the dark. She was staring out the window with a pensive look on her face.

"Everything okay?" I asked, walking over to her.

She looked at me. "I was just thinking again about what happened last night."

"Oh."

Mom looked out the window again. "What if he's out there right now, watching us?"

The hair stood up on the back of my neck. "Chances are he very well might be," I mumbled, moving next to her.

We stood there silently, this time both of us looking out the window.

"Did you get a call from the hospital yet?" she whispered after a short time.

"Actually, I forgot to check my phone. I'll be right back." I left the kitchen and grabbed it from my purse. When I checked my calls, I noticed one from Sheriff Baldwin that I'd missed. He left a message.

"Hi, Amanda. I called the hospital and talked to Dr. Fisher, the physician you saw yesterday. It looks like the drug used to knock you out was flunitrazepam, otherwise known as Rohypnol—A.K.A. a Roofie. You were very, very lucky that he didn't attack you while you were unconscious."

Or murder me.

214

"Also, I went through the pictures and didn't recognize any of the victims. I sent the photos to our Sex Crimes division and hopefully, they'll be able to come up with some more information. They definitely look like they were taken quite a while ago. By the way, if you find a Polaroid camera in Brad's place, make sure you turn it in to us. Anyway, that's all I have for you right now. I wish I had more for you, especially about Lacey. If you have any questions for me, give me a call. Talk to you soon."

I put my phone away and then told Mom, who'd followed me into the living room, and Rocky, about the call.

"I thought it might be something like that," Rocky said, getting up out of his chair. He walked over to the window and pulled the curtain aside. "You were very lucky, Amanda. I know he took Lacey, but things could have been a lot worse."

I agreed.

He let go of the curtain and walked back to the recliner. "You should get some sleep. Both of you," he said to us, sitting back down.

"You're the one who needs some sleep," Mom said. "Why don't you let me keep watch?"

They began to argue about who would stay up.

"This is ridiculous. Neither of you should be having to keep watch," I said, frustrated about the situation. "This is my fault. Both of you go to bed and I'll keep an eye out."

"This definitely is not your fault," Rocky replied.

"He's right," said Mom. "You get yourself to bed and let us worry about this."

"But—" I replied.

"No arguing," she said tersely. "Get some sleep. Rocky and I will handle this. Tomorrow is going to be a busy day for you, with the garage sale and everything."

"Exactly. Besides, I can take a nap during the day," Rocky added.

"Fine," I replied, remembering I'd promised Kevin I'd be up shortly anyway. I walked over and gave them each a kiss goodnight. "Tomorrow night, I'm keeping watch, though."

"Hopefully, the sheriff will have caught this asshole by tomorrow," Rocky muttered.

The way things were going, I wasn't going to hold my breath.

I headed upstairs, took a shower, and then snuck back into the bedroom. I slid into bed and was fluffing up my pillow, when I noticed something underneath it. When I saw what it was, my heart stopped.

Lacey's collar.

Chapter 25

Amanda

"THE BASTARD," ROCKY growled when I brought it downstairs and showed him and Mom. Looking furious, he picked up the gun and stood up.

Mom's face went white. "He's been in our house?"

"Looks that way," Rocky said. "This guy is playing a game he isn't going to win, I tell you that."

"What if he's still inside?" she whispered.

I walked over and grabbed her hand. She looked like she was on the verge of hysteria. "He's probably gone by now," I said, although it was obvious this guy enjoyed scaring me and was probably watching from somewhere outside. "He's not upstairs. I looked before coming down here."

"I'm going to check all the doors and windows to see how in the hell he got in," Rocky said.

"Should I wake up Kevin?" I asked.

He was silent for a few seconds and then sighed. "No. Why don't you go upstairs and stay with him, though?"

"Should we call the police?" Mom asked.

He nodded. "Definitely. Call Sheriff Baldwin and let him know the bastard is still taunting us," he replied.

I hurried back upstairs and snuck quietly into the bedroom. Fortunately, Kevin was still fast asleep. I crept over to the window and peered outside. Although I couldn't see anyone, I had a feeling he was out there, watching and waiting.

"Mom?" Kevin murmured.

I turned around and saw that he was sitting up.

I walked over to the bed. "I'm sorry. Did I wake you?"

He nodded and yawned. "What are you doing?"

"Just looking outside."

Kevin's eyes widened. "Why? Is there someone out there?"

I forced a smile to my face. "No, honey. I was just looking at the moonlight."

He relaxed.

I sat down on the bed next to him. "Try and go back to sleep. You have a big day ahead of you tomorrow."

"I can't sleep. I'm too itchy," he said, scratching at the mosquito bites on his leg. I'd tried rubbing some ointment on them earlier, but it didn't seem to be helping.

"Let me get you some Benadryl," I replied, standing back up. "That sometimes helps."

"Okay."

Luckily, I'd thought ahead and had brought some with us. I opened up the suitcase and pulled out the medication. After giving him the recommended dose, I tucked him back into bed and then waited until he fell back asleep, which didn't take long. Afterward, I slipped out of the bedroom again to see if Rocky had found anything.

"It looks like he got in through the basement window," Mom said, when I went back downstairs. "It's broken."

"Great," I said dryly.

"I talked to Sheriff Baldwin and he's sending over a couple of deputies to check things out," she added. "He has the night off."

"I'm so sorry this is happening," I said. "Maybe Kevin and I should move to a hotel?"

She frowned. "Absolutely not."

"I don't want this nutcase hurting either of you."

"And we don't want you getting hurt either. Separating everyone isn't going to help," she said firmly. "We've already discussed this. Not to mention that you leaving is only going to make you more vulnerable."

She was right, but it seemed like the longer I stayed, the more dangerous the situation was becoming for all of us.

"Where's Rocky?" I asked.

"Outside. Taking a look around."

"I wish he'd just wait until the police came," I said, worried.

I walked over to the window and looked outside. I could see the glow from Rocky's flashlight as he searched the property.

"The man is so stubborn. I tried telling him the same thing, but you can imagine how that went." She sighed. "I still can't believe that horrible man broke into our house. I feel so... violated. Hopefully he left some fingerprints somewhere."

"I have a feeling he's too smart for that," I muttered, still watching Rocky roam around the yard. "He wore gloves last night. I'm sure he wore them today, too."

She sighed again.

Noticing Rocky was heading toward the back, I released the curtain. "I'm going to make some tea. Would you like a cup?"

"No. I'm fine. Thank you," she replied.

"Okay."

When I stepped into the kitchen, I froze.

The sliding glass door was wide open.

Knowing that neither Rocky, nor Mom, would have left it like that, I almost peed my pants. Heart pounding, I grabbed a knife from the butcher block, and raced over to the door. Not seeing anyone on the patio, I slid it shut and was locking it when something small and round hit the glass on the other side of the door, startling me. It landed a couple of feet away and began to smoke, a deep red color.

"What's going on?" Mom asked, coming up behind me.

Before I could say anything, we saw the silhouette of a man stepping through the smoky haze and both of us gasped in horror.

It was guy from the woods and he was whistling the same creepy song, *Pop Goes The Weasel.*

"It's him," I said in a strangled voice.

He was dressed once more in the menacing hunting outfit. This time, however, instead of a gun, he held something even more terrifying—a machete.

"Oh, my God, where's Rocky?" Mom cried.

"I… I don't know." I backed away as the man approached the glass door slowly. Although his face was covered, I imagined that he was probably smiling at our terror.

"The police are on the way!" Mom screamed. "You leave us alone!"

He remained where he was.

"I'm calling them again. They need to know he's back." Mom grabbed the kitchen phone and gasped. "Amanda, the line is dead. He must have cut the line!"

"It's okay. You already talked to the sheriff. The deputies should be on their way," I replied, not knowing what to do. I wanted to run, but suspected that he'd just break down the glass door and do something terrifying, like cut off our heads. It seemed like standing our ground might slow him down until the cops showed up. As for Rocky, I had no idea what had happened to him and was too afraid to think about it.

The man touched the end of the machete to the slider and slowly slid the tip down the glass, taunting us with it.

"Mom, why don't you go upstairs and keep Kevin safe," I whispered, gripping the butcher knife firmly in my hand.

She hesitated.

"Mom, go. Protect Kevin. Please."

She turned and raced out of the kitchen.

The man on the patio began tapping the end of the machete against the slider.

"Why are you doing this?" I called out.

He ignored me.

Tap. Tap. Tap.

Shaking, I tried again. "What in the hell do you want from me, asshole?!"

This time, he lowered the machete. "Resolution."

Yep, the man was a total whack-job.

"Please, go away. I've never done *anything* to you! This is ridiculous!"

He took a step back and adjusted his grip on the machete. Paralyzed, I watched in horror as he viciously swung the handle into the door once and then twice, shattering the glass.

Screw standing my ground.

I turned around and ran like hell into the living room and toward the front door, but realized I had to protect my mom and son. They were still inside.

Shit.

I turned around and looked at the staircase. If I went to them, he'd probably follow and kill all three of us.

Think, Amanda!

Think!

There was nothing to think. I needed to do everything in power to make sure he didn't go up the stairs and hurt the people I loved.

Swallowing, I raised the knife in front of me and waited for him to walk into the living room, shaking from head to toe. As the seconds ticked by, I wondered what the hell he was doing.

Maybe he'd come to his senses and left?

I certainly wasn't about to go back into the kitchen and find out.

Noticing that my cell phone was sitting on the end table, I picked it up and dialed 9-1-1. An operator answered and I quickly whispered what was happening.

"Is the assailant still in the house?" she asked.

"I really don't know."

"Where are you?"

"In the living room," I whispered, my hand shaking so badly I could barely hold the phone.

"The police should be there any moment," she replied. "Can you get out of there or are you trapped?"

"I can't leave. He might get to my son or my mother."

"Where are they?"

"Somewhere upstairs," I whispered.

"Amanda? Jan?" hollered Rocky from the kitchen.

Relieved, I ran back there and found him alone.

"What happened to you?" I cried, as he stepped over the broken glass.

"The son-of-a-bitch hit me in the head with something and knocked me out," he said angrily. "Where's your mother?"

I glanced at Rocky's forehead and noticed blood around his right temple. "Upstairs with Kevin. You're bleeding. Are you okay?"

Scowling, he touched the blood with his fingertips and then wiped it off on his jeans. "I'm fine. Is the asshole in the house?"

"No. He broke the patio door and must have run off."

He looked outside, toward the woods. "Unbelievable."

Realizing the 9-1-1 operator was still on the phone, I thanked the woman and told her we could hear the sirens approaching.

"What happened to the assailant?" she asked.

"Good question," I replied.

WHEN THE DEPUTIES arrived, they searched the property but, of course, couldn't locate the madman anywhere. After taking our statements, they called in a crime-scene analyst, who took pictures and then attempted to gather prints for testing. Unfortunately, there didn't appear to be any decent ones. Like that was a surprise.

"I told you. He knows what he's doing," I said, while one of the medical examiners checked the wound on Rocky's head. "It doesn't seem like I'm his first target, either. He's too good at this. Not to mention he knows something about sleeping drugs. Are you sure there haven't been any similar cases?"

"No," said Deputy Rogers, who we'd met the night before. He was a muscular young man, in his late twenties. "We haven't come across anything like this before in Summit Lake. Let me tell you, this one sure takes the cake."

"It takes the whole damn bakery," I said bitterly.

The deputy's lip twitched. "Besides the machete and the smoke bomb, is there anything else that stood out to you? Or did he make any other new threats?"

"Yeah, he mentioned that he wanted 'resolution'. Considering he brought along a machete tonight, I think he's getting closer to getting it," I replied.

Mom gasped and began wringing her hands. "Why is he doing this?"

"I wish I knew." I looked back at Deputy Rogers. "This guy is getting more dangerous by the minute. Isn't there anything more you can do to help us? Like station one of your men here?"

"Yes. I'm sure we can get that authorized," he replied.

I relaxed. "Okay. Good."

Rocky walked over to us from the paramedic van.

"How's your head?" Mom asked.

"The bleeding stopped, but they think I may have a concussion," he replied, looking more annoyed than anything. "And they feel I should go to the hospital for a CT scan. Just to be on the safe side."

"Then you should," she replied.

226

"Screw that. I'm fine," he said firmly. "I just have a small headache."

She pursed her lips. "Rocky, I think—"

"I'm fine," he repeated sternly. "I had a concussion back in high school. When I was on the football team. This is nothing like that. Plus, I was a paramedic, remember? If I thought I needed to go in, I would."

Mom sighed. "Okay, but for the record, if it were up to me, I'd send you in for the CT scan. It's better to be safe than sorry."

"I'd be sorrier to see the bill come for a scan I didn't need," he replied flippantly. "Anyway, enough about me. Has anyone checked on Kevin lately?"

Shockingly, he'd slept through the entire commotion. I attributed it to the Benadryl, although Kevin was a deep sleeper normally.

"He was fine the last time I checked," Mom said. "Sleeping like a rock."

"I'm surprised he didn't hear anything," Rocky said, in disbelief.

I explained about the Benadryl.

"I didn't try to wake him," Mom said. "I was too busy barricading the door. He didn't even wake up for that."

"I'll go and check on him," I said, concerned. "Do you have any more questions for me?"

"I don't think so," said Deputy Rogers, clicking his pen shut.

I left them and walked back into the house. When I reached the bedroom, I saw Kevin was still sound asleep. He seemed to be breathing fine, and in fact, was snoring a little.

Grateful that he was safe, I climbed into bed and closed my eyes, emotionally and physically exhausted. I wasn't sure just how much more I could take and was thankful that the police were getting more deeply involved. Obviously, the freak-show wasn't finished terrorizing us and I prayed that he was caught before he found his "resolution."

Chapter 26

Amanda

THE NEXT MORNING, it took us longer to get moving, but I was able to drop Kevin off at Parker's on time so he could go fishing. After everything that had happened, I almost had second thoughts, but then realized that he was probably safer being with him than me.

As we were getting out of my SUV, Kevin groaned. "We forgot to make the flyers."

I sighed. "Darn it. I'm sorry."

"What are we going to do? We need to put those up."

I leaned down. "Listen, I'll make one and have Rocky run to the library, like he mentioned. He can put some of them up around town, too."

"But, I wanted to help," he pouted.

I gave him a sympathetic smile. "I know. We can wait until tonight if you want."

I sighed. "No. We need to hurry and get them up. Just let Rocky do it."

I nodded. Kevin was growing up and this was obviously speeding along the process.

We walked up to Parker's front door and knocked. A few seconds later, he opened it.

"Hi," I said, putting my hand on Kevin's back and rubbing it. "We're here and he's excited about spending the day on your pontoon."

"Good. The weather is supposed to be on our side today, too. At least until tonight. You look tired," Parker said, studying my face. I knew there were shadows under my eyes and there hadn't been any time for makeup. Telling me I looked tired was probably the nicest thing anyone could have said to me.

I smiled grimly. "When you have the kind of night I did, you'd be tired, too."

Of course, I'd gotten more sleep than Rocky and Mom. Rocky had spent a good hour boarding up the patio door and basement window. As for the telephone line, it had definitely been tampered with and the phone company was supposed to be out on Monday to fix the problem.

He frowned. "What happened?"

"I'll explain it later," I replied. Kevin still didn't know what had happened, although he'd seen the boarded-up patio door. When he'd asked, we'd told him that an animal had crashed into it. The lies were growing, but I didn't want his day ruined.

"Okay." Parker turned to Kevin and smiled. "So, you're looking forward to fishing?"

"Yes," he replied enthusiastically.

"So is Austin. He's already down by the pontoon. By the way, love the cap. Did Rocky give it to you?" Parker asked, touching the oversized white fishing hat on Kevin's head. There were several lures attached to it, which he and Rocky had hand-selected, in case Kevin wanted to try one of them out.

Kevin smiled proudly. "Yep. He said it was a lucky hat," he exclaimed.

"I bet," Parker said, grinning again.

"And, I already know how to cast," Kevin added.

"Excellent. Maybe you'll be teaching me a few things about fishing, huh?"

"Probably not," he replied, looking serious. "I've only gone a couple of times. That's why Mom signed me up for the fishing camp."

"Really? Well, don't sell yourself short. You might be better than you think," he said.

He shrugged. "Rocky says that it's not always about how you fish, but where you fish. That most of it is luck," Kevin said, looking up at him.

Parker nodded. "He's right. Although, even if you catch a fish, it doesn't always mean you're going to reel him in successfully. Especially the big ones. The monsters. That's where things usually get tricky. In fact, they can get away easily if you don't know what you're doing."

"Are we going to try and catch some monsters?" Kevin asked, his eyes wide.

"You'd better believe it," he replied with a smile. "This lake is supposed to have some giant Northerns and Bass."

Their conversation reminded me of the monster from last night. I began to wonder if that's what we needed to do—reel him in and catch the jerk.

"I saw a Northern at the fair last year. I hope I catch one of those," Kevin said.

"Me, too," Parker replied. "They're pretty tasty. So are Sunnies, although they're much smaller. If we catch enough fish, maybe we can talk your mother into having dinner here this evening. After I teach you boys how to filet them first, of course."

"Cool! Mom, can we?" Kevin asked, turning to me.

"Sounds like a plan," I replied and then gave him a hug. "You have fun, okay?"

"Okay," he said and then gave me a serious look. "If you hear anything about Lacey, could you call and let us know?"

"Of course I will," I replied, staring at him tenderly.

"They haven't found her yet, huh?" Parker asked.

"No," we replied in unison.

"That's a shame," he said. "Hopefully you'll hear something today."

"Mom is going to make some flyers to put up in town," Kevin said.

"Good idea. I was going to suggest it myself," Parker replied.

"By the way, thanks again for taking him out with you, Parker," I said.

He grinned. "No problem. It's our pleasure. Good luck with the garage sale."

"Thanks. And… good luck with the fish," I answered.

"They're the ones who need the luck," Parker answered with a sly grin. "'Cause their hours are numbered. Right, Kevin?"

"Right," he answered.

"You two have fun. Say hello to Austin for me," I said, getting ready to leave.

"Will do," Parker replied.

WHEN I ARRIVED at Brad's cabin, Mom and Rocky had the garage open and there were already customers, picking through things. I noticed, in dismay, that one of them was Karen, from the diner. She was talking to Mom when I approached, and from the gleam in her eyes, I had to wonder if the woman was gossiping again.

"Hi, Amanda," she said, spotting me. "Boy, you guys put this garage sale together quickly."

I smiled. "Yes. It kept us busy, let me tell you."

"I'm sure it did," she replied.

"Where's Rocky?" I asked.

Not only did I want to tell him about the flyers, I knew he'd need help carrying the sofa and some of the heavier furniture outside with him.

"Taking a nap," Mom replied.

"Oh. Okay." Lord knew he needed it.

"By the way, I have some people interested in the dining set and possibly the living room furniture," she said. "They're stopping by later this afternoon, so I figured there was no rush with bringing anything out here."

"That's great," I replied, relieved. The sooner we sold everything, the better.

"Excuse me, do you have the other shoe to this?" an older gentleman asked, holding up a brown loafer.

"It should be over there," Mom said, walking over to him and leaving me alone with Karen.

"You know, I talked to the sheriff yesterday," Karen said. "He asked me about Brad."

I looked around nervously. Fortunately, nobody was in earshot. "Oh, really?"

"Yes. He asked me about the, um, the incident I told you about the other day," she said.

"Let's talk where there's more privacy," I said, nodding toward the driveway.

"Okay."

She followed me out of the garage.

"So, what happened?" I asked, folding my arms under my chest.

"I just told him what I told you. Of course, he wasn't happy that we'd never reported it," she said, looking uncomfortable. "I mean, *I'd* wanted to. It was Michael who stopped me. Then, of course, Brad died and it didn't seem to matter anymore. Anyway, I was a little surprised that the sheriff questioned us about it. Especially now that he's gone." Her eyes bored into mind. "Did something happen?"

"Why would you ask that?" I replied, not wanting to tell her about the photos. Everyone in town would find out about it before lunchtime.

She shrugged and brushed a piece of lint off her black shorts. "I don't know. I just thought it was odd that he was asking about Brad's online activities and the man is dead and buried now. Sorry," she said, smiling sympathetically. "I keep bringing that fact up."

"Brad and I separated many years ago. We hadn't been close in a very long time."

Karen studied my face. "So, you must have been very surprised to learn that he'd left you the cabin?"

I frowned. "How did you know about that?"

Her face flushed. "Honestly, I just figured he never remarried and never mentioned anything about family. Also," she waved her hand toward the items we were selling, "you *are* having a garage sale."

I shrugged. "Yeah, well…"

"Anyway, I imagine you're planning on selling the place?"

Before I could answer, we noticed Sheriff Baldwin's car pulling up.

"Well, speaking of the sheriff," Karen said, raising an eyebrow. "I wonder why he's here?"

"Maybe he wants to buy something," I said, walking away from her and toward his car. The woman was so nosy. It was starting to bug the hell out of me.

Sheriff Baldwin got out and smiled at me grimly. "Do you have a few minutes?"

"Yeah," I said, feeling suddenly anxious. I'd just left Parker's place. *Had something happened?* "What's going on?"

"Nothing," he said, staring past me. "Hello, Karen. Enjoying the garage sale?"

Karen walked over. "Yes. Unfortunately, I have to get going. Michael just sent me a message." She held up her phone. "One of the waitresses called in sick."

"That's too bad," he replied. "Hopefully it didn't ruin your day too much."

"It is what it is." She smiled. "By the way, you should stop in at the diner, Sheriff. We have peach cobbler this week. If I recall, that's one of your favorites."

He grinned. "It certainly is. I just might have to do that."

"I'll make sure to save you a piece or two." Karen looked at me. "Good luck with your sale, Amanda. It was nice talking with you."

"Thank you," I replied, relieved that she was leaving.

Karen waved to one of the other shoppers and then headed toward her vehicle.

"Thank God," I mumbled under my breath.

The sheriff chuckled. "Let me guess, she was grilling you about Brad?"

Grunting, I turned to him. "Yes. She brought up the fact that you questioned her and Michael about the incident at the diner."

He sighed. "Yeah, well… they should have reported it."

"I agree. So, any news?"

"No, sorry. I just wanted to talk to you about last night. I read the report, but wanted to hear what happened in your own words."

I told him the story.

He sighed. "Well, we're stationing someone at your mom's place this evening. If anything, it should at least deter the creep from antagonizing you again."

"I hope so. You know, I was wondering if maybe we should try and set a trap for this guy?" I replied.

"That might be easier said than done. Not to mention, dangerous."

"At this point, I don't care. I want him caught and I'm willing to be the bait, if that's what it takes."

He frowned. "I doubt your mother, or Rocky, will agree to that," he said, glancing toward the garage.

"Maybe not, but I'm a grown woman. One with a son I need to protect. Until he's caught, we're in constant danger."

"I guess it's something to definitely consider. Let me think about it and get back to you this afternoon."

"Sounds good."

"Phew. It's a hot one today. Where's Rocky and Kevin?" he asked, wiping the sweat from his brow. "Down by the dock?"

"Rocky is in the cabin, taking a nap. Kevin is with Parker Daniels. They're fishing."

He nodded. "Good. Hopefully it will take his mind off of things for a while."

"Yeah, I hope so, too."

He looked down at his watch. "I'd better take off. Like I said, I'll call you later."

238

"Sounds good."

He waved at my mother and then got back into his squad car.

"What did he have to say?" Mom asked, coming up behind me as the sheriff left.

"He wanted to know about last night."

"Oh. So, no new news?"

"Not yet," I replied, not wanting to tell her about my idea of setting up a trap. Not yet, anyway.

She sighed. "Well, at least Karen left. She kept asking me about Brad. Talk about a busybody."

"Yeah, she's something else," I replied as a dark blue Audi headed down the gravel road toward us.

"Oh, I think that's Marcus and Julie Gibbons," Mom said. "They're the ones who are running the fishing camp you signed Kevin up for. They own the restaurant on the lake. Very nice couple."

"Oh, cool."

We watched as they parked and got out of the vehicle. Marcus was very handsome, with dark hair and dimples. Julie had long blonde hair that swung behind her as she moved, and bright blue eyes. They were a very striking couple.

"I forgot that she was expecting," Mom said as Marcus took his very pregnant wife's hand and they headed toward us. "The poor girl. She must be miserable with this heat."

I nodded. I'd been pregnant in the summer as well and knew firsthand how uncomfortable it could be.

"Welcome," Mom said as they approached.

"Thank you," Marcus said, grinning warmly at us.

"We heard you were having a garage sale," Julie said, "and had to check it out. We're looking for a couple more items for our nursery."

"Unfortunately, most of what's here belonged to a bachelor," I said, holding out my hand. "By the way, I'm Amanda. We spoke on the phone. I signed my son up for fishing camp."

She beamed a smile at me and shook it. "That's right. Thanks for enrolling him. He's going to have a blast and Marcus is such a great teacher."

"Flattery will get you everywhere, my dear," he said with a twinkle in his eyes. "And I'm thinking you're still craving that ice cream cone you mentioned on the ride over, thus the buttering up?"

"He's also a great husband," she said, winking at us. "Who doesn't miss a beat."

We laughed.

Marcus offered me his hand. "Nice to meet you, Amanda. Julie and I are very sorry about your loss. We heard you and Brad were married once?"

I shook it. "Yes. It was a long time ago. Did you know him?"

"I never met him, personally," Marcus said and looked at his wife. "You did, though, didn't you?"

"I just spoke to him on the phone. He called to volunteer with the fishing program one summer," Julie said.

Oh, God. Of course he did.

"Did he?" I asked, in a hoarse voice. "Help, that is?"

"No. I had to turn him down, unfortunately. We had two other volunteers," she replied. "Along with a waiting list."

I breathed a sigh of relief.

She continued. "Marcus and I have actually considered expanding the program, since we've had to turn kids away because the camp fills up so quickly."

"You should," Mom replied. "It gives children something fun to do in the summer besides playing on their phones."

"Exactly." Marcus patted Julie's belly gently. "Things are hectic right now, as you can probably imagine. If we do expand, it won't be until next year."

"I'm sure you have enough on your plate right now. So, is this your first?" Mom asked.

"Yes," Julie replied, her eyes sparkling. "Of many."

Marcus made a gulping noise and pretended to loosen up his collar. "Many? I think we're definitely going to need to expand fishing camp."

We laughed.

"Congratulations," Mom said. "I'm sure you two are going to make wonderful parents."

"Thank you," Marcus said.

"Yes, thank you. We're so excited. Me, especially. I'm counting down the minutes for our little one's arrival." She rubbed her belly. "Speaking of which, we've been looking for a rocking chair to put on our three-season porch. Preferably a wooden one. You wouldn't happen to have anything like that?"

"Unfortunately, no," I replied. "I wish we did."

She looked around the garage. "They're so hard to find. I'm afraid we might have to find someone to make us one, and that could get expensive."

"You know… the Johnsons are having a garage sale next weekend," Mom said. "Blair and Sam? They have four young kids, and from what I've heard, are planning on selling a bunch of baby items. You should check that out," Mom said.

"The Johnsons…" Marcus repeated. "Doesn't ring a bell."

"They're up the road from us," she said. "We live over on Wayfair Street."

He nodded. "Ah. Good to know. We'll have to check that out next weekend." He looked at Julie. "Who knows? We might even gain some future campers."

"Exactly," his wife replied.

"I see there's a lot of cool stuff here. I'm going to look around," Marcus said. "See if I can use anything."

"If you have any questions, let us know," Mom replied.

Julie began fanning herself. "I can't believe how much there is to do when you're expecting."

"It's just the beginning, too," I said.

"I know. That's what everyone keeps telling me," she replied, wiping some beads of sweat from her brow.

"Would you like any water?" I asked, concerned that she might become overheated. "We have some in the cooler."

"No. I have a bottle in the car. Thank you, though," she replied.

"No problem. Let me know if you change your mind," I replied.

"Okay." She smiled and then joined her husband. The couple looked around and then eventually left without buying anything, which we'd expected.

"I'm glad I was able to meet them," I said to my mother. "With everything going on, the thought of leaving Kevin with strangers, even if it is to fish, is nerve-wracking."

"Yeah. Tell me about it," she said.

The rest of the morning went by quickly and we had a lot of visitors. Apparently, we'd priced the items smartly, because things seemed to be selling quickly.

It was a relief, considering that I wanted to be done with it already.

Around noon, Mom left me in the garage to go and check on Rocky, who was still napping.

"Would you like a sandwich? There are some in the cooler," she said before walking away.

"Yeah. That sounds good. Thank you."

"You're welcome."

She headed into the cabin just as a red Volvo pulled up. A man with blond hair got out, and right away, I felt as if there was something familiar about him. He stepped into the garage and we greeted each other.

"Nice day for a sale," he said, looking around.

"Yes."

The man didn't seem like a typical 'garage sale' customer, so I had to wonder if he was looking for something in particular.

"Can I help you find anything?" I asked.

He smiled at me. "Actually, yes. You can. I'm looking for a woman named Amanda Schultz. Are you her?"

I nodded.

He held out his hand. "My name is Ben Shaw. I believe you were married to my brother a few years ago."

Chapter 27

Amanda

MY LEGS ALMOST gave out from under me. "Uh, yeah," I answered, almost afraid to shake his hand.

Is he the stalker?

It seemed like too much of a coincidence that he was here, in Summit Lake.

And yet, I didn't know for sure.

"It's nice to meet you. I'm… sorry for your loss," he said quietly.

I forced my hand to shake his. Now that I knew who he was, the resemblance to Brad was very noticeable. Even though he wasn't his *twin*, they looked a lot alike. He was slim, handsome, and from the Rolex on his wrist, had expensive tastes.

"Thank you. I… we'd been estranged for many years," I replied uneasily.

He smiled grimly. "I can certainly relate."

"So, what brings you to Summit Lake?" I asked, moving toward the open toolbox, where I knew there was a hammer. I was unnerved by his presence and didn't know what to expect.

"I just recently found out about his death," he answered, walking over to a stack of old records. He began looking through them. "I guess I just needed some kind of closure."

"Oh?"

He pulled out a record and smirked. "Ozzy. Brad sure loved his heavy metal."

"Feel free to take it. No charge. In fact, you can have anything you want of his," I said. As far as I was concerned, he deserved Brad's things much more than I did.

Ben put the record back. "Thank you, but I'm going to pass. I'm more interested in classical music myself these days."

And maybe children's nursery rhymes?

I watched him move around the garage, picking things up and studying them. Remembering that he was a photographer, I almost asked him about his work, but then changed my mind. I didn't want Ben to think I'd been checking up on him. Instead, I decided to ask about Barry.

"We haven't spoken in years," he replied, looking at me as if surprised I'd brought him up. "I couldn't tell you where he is."

"You weren't close?"

"None of us were," he said, looking outside, toward the cabin. "Do you know if this place is going to be on the market soon?"

"I'm not sure. Why, are you interested?"

"No. I was just curious."

I nodded.

"Did you and Brad ever have children?" he asked suddenly.

"No."

"Did he ever have children by anyone else?"

"Not that I'm aware of."

A look of relief crossed his face and I had to wonder if he'd known about Brad's secrets.

"What happened between him and your family?" I blurted out. "I mean, if you don't mind answering. Brad would never tell me why you all were estranged."

It took him awhile to answer. "He never told you?"

"No. I'm sorry. That's rude of me to even ask, I suppose."

He looked away. "It's okay. I didn't think he would tell anyone, although… I had to wonder if you may have figured it out and that's why you divorced."

"Brad refused to talk about any of you," I said.

247

He smirked. "That doesn't surprise me."

"Did it… did it have anything to do with Brad's obsession with…" I stopped, unable to get the words out.

"With what?" he asked, locking eyes with me.

Just say it. "Children?"

"It had everything to do with that," he replied with a stormy look coloring his face.

It suddenly occurred to me that Ben may have been a victim himself. I imagined him to be eight to ten years younger than Brad. Something like that would have definitely torn the family apart.

"Did he ever molest anyone?" I asked, afraid of the answer.

He picked up a marble cigar ashtray and examined it. "You were married to him. What do you think?"

"Honestly, I didn't know he was capable of anything like that," I confessed. "Not until recently."

Ben's cell phone began to ring. He put down the ashtray and checked it. "Sorry, I need to take this," he said, looking up from the screen.

"No problem."

Ben stepped out of the garage and I realized I'd been tense the entire time he'd been in the garage. In fact, my hands were shaking. Wondering if I should call the sheriff and let him know that Ben Shaw was at the cabin, I pulled out my phone.

"Can you believe it, Rocky was *still* sleeping," Mom said, startling me as she entered the garage. Noticing me jump, she smiled. "Sorry. I didn't mean to scare you."

"It's okay," I replied as she stepped closer carrying a wrapped sandwich.

"Here," she said handing me the food. "It's ham and cheese with mustard and pickles."

"Thanks," I said, glancing over at Ben again, who was pacing out by his car and looking a little agitated.

"Who's that out there on the phone? He doesn't look like anyone I've seen in town before," Mom said, looking at him.

"That's Ben. Brad's younger brother," I whispered.

Her face turned white. "What? Is he the guy who's been harassing us?"

I watched him as he moved around the driveway. He didn't seem threatening or as big as the man from last night. "I don't think so. I really don't think it's him."

"But you don't know for sure. What did he say to you?"

I went over our conversation quickly.

"You should call Sheriff Baldwin and let him know he's here," she said, looking uneasy. "He at least needs to be questioned."

"I was about to do that when you walked in."

We watched as Ben hung up and then walked back over to us, a frustrated look on his face.

"Everything okay?" I asked, moving closer to the hammer again. In case I was wrong about Ben and he really was HIM.

"I don't know. I just got off the phone with my roommate. He received a call from your town's sheriff the day before, and forgot to tell me about it. Apparently, the man has some questions for me. Talk about a coincidence," Ben replied.

"Yeah, that's odd," I said, feigning surprise.

Ben looked at my mother and smiled. "Hi, I'm Ben Shaw. Brad's younger brother."

"Nice to meet you. I'm Jan. Amanda's mother."

"You as well." He looked back at me. "Do you have any idea as to why the sheriff would want to talk to me?"

I shrugged. "I don't know. Maybe it's about what we discussed earlier."

He sighed and ran a hand through his blond hair. "I don't know why. I haven't talked to Brad in years. I don't have any information about him."

"Speaking of brothers, have you talked to Barry lately?" Mom asked.

"I already asked him," I said to her. "He hasn't."

"Oh." She looked back at him. "Do you think he even knows that Brad is deceased?"

"I have no idea," Ben said. "We lost contact a long time ago. I don't even know if *he's* alive, to be honest."

From the pained expression on his face, he was saddened by that fact.

"Did Barry ever… was he into the same things as Brad?" I asked.

"You mean did he like children?" Ben sighed. "I don't think so. When he found out about Brad, he was pretty upset about it."

"Is that why Brad moved here?" Mom asked. "Because everyone found out about him?"

"Something like that." He sighed. "Anyway, I'd rather not talk about it anymore. Brad was a sick man. He was still my brother, though. Which is why I came out here. To visit his grave and let him know that… I've forgiven him."

Mom and I both nodded.

"Do you know where he was buried?" he asked. Mom told him.

"Thank you," he said. "I'm going to head out there and call the sheriff on the way. See what he wants."

"Okay," she replied.

"It was nice meeting the both of you," Ben said, smiling grimly. "Too bad it was because of such unfortunate circumstances."

"Yes. It was nice meeting you as well," I replied.

"Yes. It was," Mom said.

He turned and walked back to his car. Once inside, Mom commented that she didn't think he was the man terrorizing us either.

"He seems too nice," she said. "And… normal."

I thought about Brad. He'd once seemed "nice and normal" too.

"Maybe Brad's family isn't even involved, and the person threatening me has nothing to do with him," I said as Ben began driving away. "Maybe it's just some sicko who thinks I've done him wrong somehow."

"Maybe." She shuddered. "Funny, that almost scares me more."

Me, too.

Chapter 28

Amanda

ROCKY WAS UPSET when he found out that Ben had been there and we hadn't informed him of it.

"He wasn't here for very long at all. Just a couple of minutes," I said, after going over our conversation. "Besides, he seemed harmless enough."

Mom agreed with me.

He ran a hand over his face and I could tell he was trying to keep his cool. "Don't you think it's a coincidence that this guy is in town and you're being terrorized?"

"I thought so, too. But he was here because of Brad's death. He wanted to visit the gravesite and find some kind of closure," I replied.

"Or 'resolution'?" he asked dryly.

I laughed nervously. "Maybe, but I just don't think it's him."

"Look, just because Ben seems like a nice guy doesn't make it so," Rocky replied angrily.

"There wasn't anything threatening about the guy," Mom said. "I can vouch for that, and you know how paranoid I am."

He was silent for several seconds and then sighed in exasperation. "Well, did you have a chance to ask him about the twin? What's his name, Barry?"

"Yeah. He hasn't heard from him in years," I said.

"I don't suppose he knew about Brad's darker side?" Rocky asked dryly.

"We talked about it, actually," I replied.

Rocky looked surprised.

"I'm sure that's why Brad moved here. Because the family found out about it. In fact," I sighed, "I think Ben may have been victimized by him."

"That's a shame," Rocky said, looking down and shaking his head.

"Yeah," I replied, wondering if Brad had also been abused. Of course, we'd probably never know.

A couple of cars pulled up to the cabin, so we dropped the subject, although I couldn't stop thinking about Ben meeting up with the sheriff. I still didn't feel as if he was a threat to me, but I couldn't shake the feeling that he still might somehow be linked to what was happening.

"HAVE YOU HEARD from Parker at all?" Mom asked me, around four p.m.

"No, I haven't. I'm sure they're having a blast, though."

"I'm sure. He was pretty excited this morning."

Thinking I should check in, I sent Parker a text asking how things were going. He replied that they were just getting ready to head back to the cabin and had caught quite a few fish.

"It sounds like they're having a lot of fun and are now returning to Parker's to clean fish," I told her. "By the way, we're all invited over to his cabin for a fish fry."

"That sounds lovely," she said, grinning. "I was going to say we should pick up something on the way home, but now we don't have to. What time?"

"He said to just head on over when we're finished for the day," I said, reading his text.

We'd decided to shut down the sale around six at the latest. Fortunately, we'd sold more than half of Brad's things and I was going back-and-forth about what to do with the remaining items. Mom had suggested continuing the garage sale the following weekend. But, with everything that was happening, I wanted to clean out the house and talk to a realtor. Living in Brad's cabin was no longer *anything* I wanted to pursue.

"Sounds good. Did you hear that, Rocky?" Mom said loudly. "Parker is having a fish fry and we're invited."

Rocky, who was watching a baseball game on a small tablet, gave us a thumbs-up.

"Should we bring something?" Mom asked, tapping a finger to her chin. "One of us could run into town and pick up a dessert. Maybe a pie or something?"

"I will," I said, putting my phone away.

"No, let Rocky go," she said.

"He's watching the game. I'll be fine," I said, pulling out my key. "Besides, I need to pick up some things at the drugstore anyway."

Mom looked worried.

"I'll be fine," I repeated.

"What's going on?" Rocky asked, looking at us over his shoulder.

I told him.

"Why do you insist on going it alone all the time?" he said, looking exasperated.

"Someone needs to stay here with Mom. Look, I was fine yesterday. I'll be fine today.

He let out a weary sigh. "You're too stubborn for your own good. Just like your mother. Only, she's cautious and you're… not."

"I'm cautious enough. Anyway, I doubt he's going to risk coming after me on the road or in the middle of the day."

"You don't know that," Mom said.

"I'll be fine," I repeated once again.

THE TRIP INTO town went smoothly, just like the day before. Unfortunately, I'd forgotten all about making a flyer for Lacey, which I knew would disappoint Kevin. Knowing he'd never forgive me if I didn't do something about it, I went into the drugstore first and purchased what I needed. I also included a ream of paper, a box of markers, and tacks and tape. I then quickly wrote up a "LOST DOG" flyer and raced over to the library, only to find that it had closed for the day. Fortunately, there was a photo shop nearby and they were nice enough to help me out when they heard what it was for. Not only did they assist me with the copies, they were able to add a picture of Lacey I'd taken from my phone.

After thanking them profusely, I sent my mother a message to let her know what was taking me so long, and then put some of the flyers up in a few of the shops. Realizing it was getting late, I found a couple of teenagers and paid them to help with the rest.

"Good luck finding your dog, Mrs. Schultz," said one of the teens, a sweet girl name Emily. When she'd learned our dog was missing, and saw a picture of Lacey, she almost cried.

"Thank you. And thanks for helping with the flyers."

"You're welcome," she replied.

Fortunately, the bakery was still open, so I purchased a blueberry pie and it was then that I ran into Tara's ex-husband.

"I heard you were back in town," Josh said, after giving me a hug. "How long are you going to be here?"

"I don't know," I replied, noticing that he seemed to be thriving as a single guy. Not only had he lost weight, his hair looked thicker and his teeth, whiter. He nauseated me, though, and I was happy Tara had dumped him for good.

He gave me his condolences and then asked about Kevin.

"He's doing great," I replied. "In fact, he's fishing with Parker Daniels and his son right now."

"Really?" he said, arching his eyebrow. "So, are you two dating?"

"No. We're just friends."

He smiled in amusement.

"What?"

"You might want to tell *him* that. I ran into Parker yesterday and he made it sound like you two were a thing."

"Oh, really?"

"A word of advice—keep your distance from the guy. He was cool in high school, but I'm telling you… Parker has changed," he said, looking serious.

"What do you mean?"

"When Tara and I broke up, he came sniffing around like a dog in heat. He wouldn't leave her alone."

"Is that so? She never mentioned anything about it to me," I replied, surprised. And Parker had made it sound like he hadn't spoken to Tara much either.

"She probably just wanted to forget about it. Anyway, he was relentless. He kept stopping by unexpectedly and sending her text messages. Honestly, I think they might have hooked up in the beginning, but she never admitted it. Either case, he became a little too aggressive, *if* you know what I mean."

His story didn't jive with the guy I knew. Parker seemed sweet and had been so helpful with Kevin. Of course, it was always possible that he'd changed.

"Anyway, I'm not trying to tell you what to do. Just… be careful," he said.

"Sure. Thanks," I replied.

We talked for a couple more seconds and then went our separate ways. As I got into my car, I made a mental note to call Tara and ask her about Parker. I wasn't sure what to believe, but if Josh was right, it would be nice to know.

Chapter 29

Amanda

I ARRIVED BACK at the cabin and found a rental truck parked outside and Rocky helping someone load the leather sofa into the vehicle.

"We sold most of the furniture to a half-way house over in the next town," she explained, smiling.

"Great," I replied, relieved.

"How did the trip go? Did you put up a lot of flyers?"

"Yes." I showed her what they looked like and gave a rundown of what I'd had to do to get them printed.

"It looks good," she said, smiling sadly at the picture of Lacey. "That was nice of the photo store to do that and not charge you anything."

"I know. The people there are really nice."

After the furniture was loaded, it was close to six, so we shut down the garage sale. I also sent Tara a text message to call me. I was curious as to what she had to say about Parker and if it was even true.

"I can't wait to find out about Kevin's day," Mom said, as Rocky locked the garage door. "I bet they had a lot of fun."

"I'm sure," I replied. "He was pretty excited when I dropped him off."

"Hey, have you heard from Sheriff Baldwin at all?" Rocky asked.

"Nope," I replied.

He grunted. "I wonder if Ben even went in to talk to him."

"I'll call and ask," I replied, pulling my phone out of my purse again.

"Find out if they've sent someone to watch the house, too. I know we're not there, but someone should be keeping an eye on the place in case that bastard tries breaking in again," Rocky said gruffly.

"Okay," I replied.

Since Mom and Rocky drove separately, I got into my vehicle and called Sheriff Baldwin on my way to Parker's. He didn't answer, so I left him a message.

When we arrived, the boys were tossing a football back and forth in the yard. As soon as Kevin noticed us he raced over and started talking about the fish they'd caught.

"I got one this big," he said, holding up his hands.

"You did?" Mom said, ruffling his hair. "That must have been exciting."

"I thought I was going to lose him, but Parker told me what to do and I reeled him in all by myself. He was a strong fish, so it wasn't easy," he said.

"What kind of a fish was it?" Rocky asked.

"A Northern," he said proudly.

Rocky gave him a high-five. "Great job, kiddo. Told you that fishing hat was lucky. Speaking of which, where'd it go?"

Kevin looked toward the lake. "Oh, I forgot it on the boat. Don't worry, I'll go and get it."

"I'll come with you," said Austin.

"Where's your dad?" Rocky asked him.

"I think he's in the house, or on the patio, setting up the new grill," he replied, noticing I was carrying a paper bag. "What's in there?"

"A pie," I replied. "Blueberry."

"Sweet," he said, breaking into a smile.

Kevin, who I'd forgotten wasn't much of a blueberry fan, looked disappointed.

"Sorry, Kev," I said. "There wasn't much to choose from at the bakery. They also had cherry, but I know you're not a fan of that either."

He shrugged. "It's okay."

"You don't like blueberry pie?" Austin asked. "You're crazy."

"I like it," Kevin said, looking embarrassed. "Sometimes."

"I'll have your piece if you don't want it," Austin said.

"Sure." Kevin looked at me again and asked about the flyers.

"I took care of it," I said, relieved I'd remembered.

"Oh, good. Can I see what they look like?" he replied.

I told him I had extras in the SUV. "You can see them when we leave."

"Okay," he replied.

"Let's go back to the pontoon and look for your hat," Austin said. "We can skip some more rocks, too."

Kevin nodded and the two boys took off.

"Austin and Kevin are getting along very well, aren't they?" Mom asked as we headed toward the front of the cabin. "Austin is so much older. I wasn't sure if they would."

"They're both bored. That helps," Rocky said.

"I'm sure," she replied.

As we were about to knock on the door, Parker stuck his head around the side of the house. "Hey, guys! I'm on the patio. Come on back!"

"Okay!" I replied.

"What a nice place," Mom said as we headed toward the backyard.

I couldn't agree more.

The cabin was about the same size as Brad's, but newer. The landscaping was also very nice, especially the garden, which ran alongside the house. It was surrounded by bricks and featured colorful flowers and shrubs.

When we met Parker on the patio, I handed him the pie.

"You look refreshed," Mom said.

His hair was damp, he smelled good, and wore a blue Hawaiian shirt and khaki shorts. He was a sight for sore eyes.

"I feel better now that I've had a shower. How did you know that blueberry pie was my favorite?" he said, looking pleased.

"I wasn't sure, but I figured that if you liked it back when we were teenagers, you probably still did," I answered, remembering eating a piece of blueberry pie his mother had made years ago. She'd commented on how quickly her pies disappeared because Parker loved them so much.

"There are a lot of things I find I'm enjoying from those days. Now, I just appreciate them that much more," he said with a twinkle in his eyes.

I blushed.

"I do, too," Rocky said, not picking up on the flirting. "Especially pie, considering Fran has stopped baking."

"If I make pie, it's gone in a day. Now, you know that's not good for you," she chastised.

He rolled his eyes. "Don't exaggerate, woman. I can make it last for two."

She snorted and then turned to Parker. "My goodness, you certainly have made this nice and inviting," Mom said, admiring the potted plants and bamboo torches surrounding the patio. "I didn't realize you had such a green thumb."

Parker opened up a large cooler and began digging inside of it. "I'd love to take credit for it, but I can't. I had someone do the landscaping. I'm pretty happy with it. By the way, I have soda, water, and beer. Rocky, can I get you a cold one?" he asked, holding up a bottle of beer.

"You read my mind. A cold brewskie sounds great right now," Rocky replied, grinning. He stepped over and grabbed the beer. "Thank you."

"No problem. Ladies?" Parker asked. "I picked up some wine coolers, if you're interested in something sweeter."

"You didn't have to go through all of that trouble for us," I said, knowing he wasn't a drinker.

"No trouble at all," he replied and held one up. "Want one?"

I took it. "Thank you. Mom, would you like one?"

"Yes, actually. It sounds wonderful after the long day we've had," she replied, walking over to him.

He opened up a bottle and handed it to her. "I bet."

"Thank you, Parker," she replied.

"You're welcome. Make yourself at home," he said, nodding toward the patio furniture.

The three of us sat down.

Rocky took a drink of his beer and wiped his mouth. "Looks like you found time to pick up a grill."

He glanced over at the new Weber charcoal grill in the corner. "Yeah. After we went fishing, we ran into town and picked that up. I thought it would be healthier to grill the fish than to fry it."

"Oh, hell. See, now everyone is going out of their way for me because you put me on this diet," Rocky said to Mom. "Look what you've started."

"It was actually Kevin who reminded me," Parker said with a grin. "But, don't worry. I didn't go out of my way. I'm not getting any younger myself and usually try to stay away from a lot of fried foods. Anyway, we needed a new grill, so I figured, why not grab one today?"

Rocky sighed. "I guess I should be happy that Kevin is trying to watch out for my health."

"Exactly," Mom said. "He's a good kid and loves his grandpa."

"He's a *great* kid and very well behaved. He and Austin had a great time fishing, too," Parker said, looking down toward the dock, where Austin and Kevin were now skipping rocks across the lake.

"Yeah, Kevin was grinning from ear-to-ear when we arrived," Mom said. "He couldn't stop talking about all of the fish you caught."

"It was incredible. They were practically jumping onto the pontoon," Parker replied, smiling. "Every time we dropped a line, we'd catch something."

"I wish I could have joined you guys," Rocky said, staring toward the lake. "Next time, huh?"

"Definitely. By the way, how did the garage sale go?" he asked.

Mom started giving him the details and that's when my phone buzzed. I pulled it out of my purse and noticed it was Tara replying to my text. Instead of answering me about Parker, she asked if I could meet her someplace.

Me: *I thought you were out of town?*

Tara: *Change of plans. We need to meet. You free?*

Me: *Is this about Parker?*

Tara: *Yes, among other things.*

Me: *Can't I just call you?*

It took her a while to reply.

Tara: *No. We have to meet. I have something to show you. Where are you now?*

Me: *At Parker's.*

Tara: *Don't tell him that you're meeting me.*

I looked over at Parker and our eyes met. He gave me a questioning look. It made me ill to think that he might not be the guy I thought he was.

Me: *Okay. Where?*

Tara: *I'm actually near your Mom's place. Would that work?*

Me: *Sure. I'll be there in fifteen minutes.*

Tara: *Great. See you soon.*

I put my phone away.

269

"Is something wrong?" Parker asked, his blue eyes searching mine.

I forced a smile to my face. "I'm okay. It's just that… I have to run into town for a few minutes. Brad's lawyer forgot to have me sign a few things."

Mom's eyebrows shot up. "*Now?* Can't it wait until tomorrow?"

"Apparently, it can't. It shouldn't take long," I said. "I'm sorry, Parker. I'll be back as soon as I can."

"No worries," he replied. "We'll just start the grill when you return."

"Nonsense. You guys eat. Just in case it takes me longer than planned," I replied. "I'm sure Rocky is starving."

"Hey, I can always eat some of that pie while we wait for you," Rocky said with a smirk. "You know, if my blood sugar starts to run too low."

Mom rolled her eyes.

"I'll let you know if I'm going to be later than planned." I stood up and pulled my key fob out of my purse just as Kevin and Austin jogged over to us.

"Hey, you found the lucky fishing hat," Rocky said to Kevin.

"Yeah." Kevin noticed I had my key out. "Are we leaving already?"

"Just me. I have to run into town," I replied.

"Why? Did someone find Lacey?" he asked, his eyes full of hope.

"Not yet," I replied softly. "I'm going there to take care of some business."

His face fell. "Oh. When are you coming back?"

"Soon." I gave him a hug and noticed he looked embarrassed afterward. Knowing it was because Austin was watching, and he probably didn't want to look like a baby, tugged at my heart. He was growing up too quickly. "I'll be back."

He nodded.

"Call us if you run into any trouble," Rocky said.

"I will," I promised.

Chapter 30

Amanda

WHEN I ARRIVED at my Mom and Rocky's place, Tara wasn't anywhere to be found. I did notice a squad car parked on the property, however, which was a relief.

I pulled up next to it and rolled down my window. Recognizing one of the other deputies from the night before, a guy named Adam, I smiled and thanked him for being there.

"No problem. Have you had any problems today?" Adam asked.

"No. We haven't been home, though." I looked toward the dirt road that led to the house, wondering what was taking her so long. "A friend of mine was supposed to meet me here. Did you see anyone pull up?"

"No. Sorry."

"Huh. Well, I guess I'll just send her a message and see where she is."

He nodded and took a sip of his coffee.

I pulled out my phone and sent Tara a text. She replied that she'd been scared off by the cop sitting outside of the house and decided to park near a neighbor's dirt road instead.

Me: *Why were you scared off?*

Tara: *Some old habits never die… lol*

Me: *You goof.*

Tara: *Guess where I am?*

Me: *Where?*

Tara: *The treehouse.*

Me: *You mean our lame ATTEMPT at a treehouse?*

Tara sent a smiley face.

Me: *I'll be there in a minute.*

Tara: *I'll be waiting.*

I turned off the ignition and got out of my car.

"I'll be back," I told the deputy, as I began to walk toward the woods.

"Where are you going?" he called out.

I turned around. "To meet my friend."

"Hold up." Adam got out of the car. "Are you sure you want to go wandering out there by yourself considering everything that's happened?"

He had a point. The creep could be hiding in the woods, which meant that Tara was also in danger. I pulled out my phone and sent her another message, telling her to come to the house instead.

Tara: *Do you know how long it took me to get my fat ass up this tree?*

I had to chuckle. She was anything but fat.

Me: *Sorry. It's too dangerous being out in the woods. Some guy has been stalking me and he could be out there. Please, just come to the house.*

Tara: *What?!!! Stalker? Why didn't you tell me?*

Me: *I thought you were out of town and didn't want to bother you.*

Tara: *You are never a bother. I'll be right there, unless I fall and break my neck trying to get down.*

I cringed.

Me: *You want some help?*

Tara: *Maybe. Is the cop still there?*

Me: *Yeah.*

Tara: *Is he cute?*

Me: *Yeah, but I think he's married.*

Tara: *Figures. I'll get down on my own. Be right there.*

I put my phone away and looked at the deputy. "She's on her way. I'm going inside. Would you like anything?"

He held up his Styrofoam cup, which I saw was empty. "Maybe some more coffee?" he asked with a sheepish smile. "If it's not too much of a bother?"

"Not at all. We have a Keurig, so it won't take long to brew," I replied.

"Thanks. I appreciate it."

"No problem. How do you like your coffee?"

"Black."

"Okay." I turned and headed to the house. As I unlocked the door, and stepped inside, I froze.

What if the wacko was hiding inside?

I knew that the deputy hadn't been at the house all day, so anything was possible. Just to be on the safe-side, I grabbed the rifle out of the closet, walked to the kitchen, and put one of the K-cups into the Keurig. As the coffee began percolating, I decided to search the rest of the house. Fortunately, nobody else was inside.

I headed back downstairs just as the doorbell sounded. Thinking it was Tara, I opened up the front door with a smile on my face. Instead of my friend, however, I found a large white box, with a brightly colored red ribbon, sitting on the WELCOME mat.

"Tara?" I called out, stepping outside, the alarm bells going off in my head.

No answer.

I picked up the box, which wasn't very heavy, and glanced over toward the squad car. Deputy Adams appeared to be inside but not paying any attention.

I shook the box gently.

"Tara? Where are you? This isn't funny!" I called out.

No answer.

I looked over at the squad car again and then at the package.

Sighing, I opened up the box and when I saw the contents, was completely baffled. Stuffed inside of it was a light brown teddy bear. One of the button eyes were missing and it looked fairly old. I pulled it out and noticed a slip of paper on the bottom of the box. I pulled it out and read the message.

You'll pay for what you've done.

The hair stood up on the back of my neck. Terrified, I dropped everything and ran to squad car.

"Adam!" I hollered, pounding on the window.

He didn't move.

I took a closer look and it almost look like he'd fallen asleep.

Confused, I opened up the door and shook his shoulder. "Hey, wake—" The words died on my lips as he slumped forward and I realized why he really wasn't answering me; the man was dead.

Gasping at the bloody wound on his back, I lurched backward and that's when strong arms grabbed me from behind. I tried to scream, but it became muffled by the strong-smelling rag shoved over my mouth.

Chapter 31

Amanda

I CAME-TO SOMETIME later with a headache and throbbing pain in my back and limbs. I opened my eyes and found that not only was I inside of someone's trunk, I was hog-tied. To make matters worse, the vehicle I was in seemed to be moving and I had no idea how long I'd been trapped inside.

Terrified, I struggled with the restraints, but it was useless. My captor had used zip ties and they weren't budging.

"Help!" I screamed. "Please, someone help me!"

The car suddenly came to a halt. Seconds later, the trunk was thrown open and a broad-shouldered man stood there in the darkness, wearing a ski-mask and black clothing.

"Shut the fuck up," he snarled, grabbing me by the throat. "Or, I'll cut your tongue out."

"Please," I begged through my tears. "Let me go. I don't understand why you hate me so much. Why are you doing this?"

Growling, he released my neck and reached behind me for a roll of duct tape.

"Is it money you want? I'll give you anything. Just let me go!"

"This isn't about money," he whispered harshly.

"I have a child who needs me. Please, don't do this."

"You don't even deserve kids," he snapped before slapping the tape over my mouth. "Hell, I'm doing him a favor."

Crying, all I could do was watch helplessly as he slammed the trunk closed and got back into the vehicle. He turned on some loud rock music and we began to move again.

IT SEEMED LIKE we'd been driving for hours. At least long enough that I knew people would know that I was missing. Of course, Mom and Rocky would be looking for me in town and may not even know about Adam yet.

As for Tara, I had no idea what had happened to her and hoped that my captor had missed seeing her. And if, miraculously, she did happen to have seen my abduction, I prayed that she had caught his license plate number.

All of this ran through my head as we continued on the road. Although things weren't looking good, I refused to give up. I couldn't let him kill me. One thing I did know for certain was that he could have murdered me back at the house. Instead, he'd kept me alive.

More games?

I had a feeling he was taking me someplace to torture the hell out of me before finally finishing me off. From the hatred in his eyes, he truly believed I'd done him wrong and I was going to pay… unless I did something about it. As terrified as I was, I need to stay strong for Kevin and not lose hope. I was determined to get myself out of the situation and would do whatever it took to get out of it.

***

HIM

THINGS WEREN'T GOING as planned and I was boiling with rage. I hadn't meant to take Amanda. Not yet, anyway. But, I'd been forced into killing the deputy, which had been unplanned, stupid, and reckless. Hell, I'd wanted to play with her some more, even use her son to cause some hysteria. But, our little game was being cut short. Now, she would have to die sooner than expected. I just needed to find a secluded place to finish her off.

As I drove, I thought about the night I'd killed the bitch's ex-husband. After butchering him at the truck stop, I'd shoved him into the trunk of his car and drove away. In fact, I drove *all* the way from Summit Lake to the North Shore, where I recalled him telling "Terence" about how much he loved the area. It had taken over three hours, but I didn't want the town knowing that Brad had been murdered. I'd even rigged his car to drive off of the cliff, making it look like suicide or a tragic accident. Afterward, I caught a ride, from a semi driver to Two Harbors, where I stayed at a motel. The next morning, I took a bus down to Minneapolis and then called an Uber to drive me back to Summit Lake. It was a lot of bullshit, but worth the trouble.

Thinking back to the pleasure I'd felt watching Brad's car go over the cliff, I considered driving Amanda to the same place and dropping her into Lake Superior. The thought of keeping her alive and watching the terror in her eyes before pushing her over would almost be worth the drive. But, I knew it would be too risky and I wanted to prolong her death as long as I could.

My cell phone went off, and when I saw who it was, answered immediately. After speaking to the person on the other end, I realized that *all* of my plans were now botched and I had no choice but to get rid of her now.

Shit.

After driving around a few more minutes, I found a quiet, residential area advertising one-level retirement homes, starting at $499,000.

"What a steal," I muttered dryly as entered the dark construction site at the end of the block.

I turned off my headlights and drove to the framed home on the end. After shutting down the engine, I grabbed my knife and got out of the car.

Chapter 32

Amanda

THE CAR SLOWED and then stopped. The music turned off and then I heard him get out of the car. Holding my breath, I listened as his footsteps approached the trunk and it opened.

We stared silently at each other and it was terrifying.

"Waste of time," he grumbled, raising his knife.

Panicking, I tried rolling away, but my restraints made it impossible.

"Knock it off!" he growled, grabbing ahold of my arm.

Crying, I struggled and thrashed around as much as I could, terrified that I was never going to see Kevin again.

"Stop fighting me! I'm letting you go."

I froze.

Was it a trick?

He cut the zip ties from my wrists and then my ankles. I stretched my legs and arms, my skin raw from being in such a position for so long.

He leaned over, ripped the duct tape from my lips, and smiled when I gasped from the pain.

"Tell me my name," he ordered as I rubbed the tender area around my lips.

"I… I don't know," I whispered hoarsely.

He stared at me hard for a few seconds and then pulled a rag out of his jacket.

"What are you doing?" I asked as he reached behind me and pulled out a brown bottle.

"Giving you a raincheck," he muttered, unscrewing the cap.

I still didn't trust that he was letting me go. It didn't make any sense.

Why go through all of this trouble?

He poured the liquid onto the rag. Realizing I would be knocked out again, I tried getting out of the trunk, but he shoved me back down. I screamed and thrashed my head from side to side, but he managed to force the rag over my face. Gasping, my eyes teared up as he held the fabric over my nose and mouth. I clawed at his hands, but he was too strong. Seconds later, everything went black.

Chapter 33

Amanda

SOMETIME LATER, I woke up to the smell of new lumber and someone's hand on my arm, shaking me. Startled, I opened my eyes and found a man wearing an orange hardhat kneeling down next to me. I blinked again, confused as to who he was and what was happening.

"Are you okay?" the man asked, giving me a strange look.

And then it all came back to me.

He'd actually let me go...

Dazed, I sat up and brushed the sawdust from my shorts. "I... I don't know.."

In the distance, I could hear hammers banging and the whine of an air compressor. From what I gathered, he'd dropped me off in some kind of construction site.

"Can we call someone for you?"

I nodded, looking down at the bruises on my wrists. My eyes welled with tears. "Yes, the police."

IT TURNED OUT that I'd been left in the next town over, so I was only forty-five miles away from Summit Lake.

After being questioned by the police, I was taken to the hospital and examined. They kept my clothing, to try and collect hair or fibers from the kidnapper's trunk, and took more blood. A short time later, Sheriff Baldwin showed up at the hospital with Mom and Rocky. The relief of seeing them, brought tears to my eyes.

"We were so worried about you," Mom sobbed, rushing to my bed. She pulled me into her arms. "We didn't know what to think. Especially after finding that poor deputy murdered."

Memories came rushing back from the day before. I couldn't believe the stalker had killed Adam. "I'm okay."

"I hate to start badgering you with questions already, but… did you witness the kidnapper murder my deputy?" Sheriff Baldwin asked with a troubled look.

"No. He did it when I was in the house. I went inside to make Adam a cup of coffee," I said with a lump in my throat. "That's when I heard someone knocking on the door. When I went to go answer it, I found another package from the kidnapper."

"Was that the teddy bear?" Rocky asked.

I nodded. "You found it?"

"Yeah. Along with the note, 'You'll pay for what you've done'." He scratched his whiskers. "I wonder what in the hell he thinks you did?"

"I have no clue," I replied. "It's obviously something he's created in his demented mind."

"Apparently," he said. "So, what happened after you discovered the bear and the note?"

I told them how I'd raced over to Adam's car and found he'd been murdered. "That's when the kidnapper came up behind me and put a rag over my face. I blacked out again and woke up in his trunk."

Mom gasped. "Oh, my God, you poor thing!"

I told them the rest of the story.

"You are *so* lucky to be alive," my mother said, hugging me again. "I don't know what I'd have done if he'd killed you. Or Kevin. He would have been devastated."

I closed my eyes and hugged her back. "How is he doing?"

"He's with Parker right now," Rocky replied. "He wanted to come, but we weren't sure if it was a good idea."

"It's okay. I'll see him soon," I replied.

Mom reached into her purse and pulled out a tissue. "You should have told us where you were going," she scolded, wiping the tears from under her lashes. "And… *why*. We were so confused when you didn't return and then Rocky called the lawyer. Of course, when he mentioned that there was no meeting set up between the two of you, we had no idea what was going on."

I apologized. "I was supposed to meet Tara and didn't think that I was in any danger," I replied. "She didn't want Parker to know, for some reason. It's why I couldn't say anything."

"We figured that out when we found your phone at the house and read the text messages," Rocky said.

I swallowed. "Has anyone found her?" I asked, afraid of the answer.

Sheriff Baldwin nodded. "She's fine. Apparently, she's out of town and thought she'd left her cell phone at home. From the looks of things, it was stolen."

"How did you get ahold of her?" I asked, relieved that she was okay.

"Through Facebook. Which reminds me." He handed me a slip of paper. "That's her business cell number. She wants you to call her as soon as you can."

"So, the person texting me was my kidnapper… pretending to be her?" I replied, surprised.

He nodded. "Apparently."

Mom's eyes widened. "How did he know about the tree?"

"I have no idea," I answered, thinking back to our messages. It was hard to believe they hadn't been from Tara. The lunatic had impersonated her to a "T."

"My guess is that this guy is closer to you than you realize," the sheriff said. "Especially if he knew about you and Tara's old meeting place."

It wasn't exactly a secret that we used to hang out there years ago. Even our boyfriends had known about it.

My heart skipped a beat. "Could it be Josh?"

Sheriff Baldwin's eyebrows shot up. "Josh?"

"Yes. Tara's ex," I replied, trying to remember the color of the kidnapper's eyes.

Brown?

"Wait a second, you think that he might be the one terrorizing you?" Mom asked, looking startled.

"I don't know. I never did anything to the man, and the guy who's doing this clearly hates me. But, Josh could have somehow gotten to Tara's phone, if he still has a key to their house, and he definitely knew about our old hangouts. Not to mention that he bad-mouthed Parker."

"What do you mean?" the sheriff asked.

I told them what Josh had said about Parker aggressively trying to date Tara.

"The guy texting you also made it look as if Parker wasn't to be trusted," the sheriff said with a smirk.

I nodded.

"Well, what more do you need?" Rocky said. "It's just too much of a coincidence that both the kidnapper and Josh brought Parker into this mess."

"It's definitely fishy, but not enough to arrest anyone. So, why did Tara and Josh divorce? Did she confide in you?" Sheriff Baldwin asked, taking out a pen and a small notepad.

"He cheated on her," I said. "Quite a few times, I'm guessing."

Mom grunted. "He always was a flirt. I saw him hitting on one of the waitresses at the diner long before they were divorced. She brushed him off, but I was appalled by his behavior. Of course, I never said anything, since it wasn't my business."

"Tara knew about his behavior for many years and chose to ignore it. She didn't actually leave until catching him red-handed, and that was after giving him a second chance. I'm just glad that they finally divorced," I replied.

"Did *you* help persuade Tara into leaving him?" the sheriff asked.

I shrugged. "I mean, I always told her that she was too good for Josh. But, they split up *after* Kevin and I went back to Chicago, last summer. I didn't break them up. He did that all on his own with his actions."

"Well… it could be that he partly blames you. I just never thought he was a violent man," Rocky said, crossing his arms over his chest. He looked over at the sheriff. "Maybe we should go over and pay him a little visit."

"You are doing no such thing," Mom said, looking cross. "This is a matter for the police. If Josh is involved, he's also a murderer and too dangerous for you to be confronting, Rocky. Let them take care of it."

"She's absolutely right," the sheriff said. "Don't you worry, Rock. We'll definitely going to be questioning him, though." He looked at me again. "By the way, did the perp speak to you?"

"A little," I answered.

"What do you think? Did he *sound* anything like Tara's ex?" the sheriff asked.

"Honestly, he didn't say much and when he did, it was more of a growl," I admitted.

"Do you think it could really be Josh?" Mom asked.

"I suppose it's possible," I said. It could have also been Ben. Both men were of similar stature, from what I could tell. I pointed that out to the sheriff and asked if he'd spoken to him.

"Yes. I interviewed Ben yesterday afternoon. He claimed that he'd just arrived in Summit Lake," he replied.

"And you believed him?" Mom asked, not looking so convinced.

"Honestly, I don't know what to believe. But, there wasn't much I could do," he replied. "There isn't any evidence against him, so I had to let him go."

"Did you happen to notice what color eyes Ben has?" I asked.

His eyebrow arched. "No. Why?"

"I'm pretty sure that my kidnapper had brown eyes," I said, recalling his cold stare.

The sheriff's face lit up. "Good. Was there anything else that you remember about him?"

"Not really. I was in shock and terrified. I'm just surprised he let me go," I said.

"You were very lucky, indeed."

"He said he was giving me a raincheck," I said, the words making the hair stand up on the back of my neck. "He's not finished with me."

A vein began to throb in Rocky's temple. "Raincheck, my ass. He's not getting his hands on you again."

"He'd better not," Mom said. "But, you can't go off on your own anymore, Amanda. Not until he's caught. I don't know how many times we have to drill that into your head…"

"I know," I replied.

"Are Josh's eyes brown?" the sheriff asked, scribbling in his notepad again.

"I don't remember," I said, trying to picture his face.

"Looks like I have some things to check out," Sheriff Baldwin said, putting his notepad away. "Including foot size."

We all looked at him in surprise.

"I spoke to one of the officers. He said they found a footprint impression in the dirt," he explained. "One that doesn't match the construction worker who found you. Apparently, the perp has long, wide feet."

"A real Sasquatch, huh?" Rocky said dryly.

"Yeah. He's been eluding us like Bigfoot, too. But not for long." The sheriff looked at me. "We're going to get this guy, Amanda. I swear to you; I'm not resting until we nab him."

I wasn't either.

Chapter 34

Amanda

AFTER BORROWING SOME scrubs from the hospital to wear home, Sheriff Baldwin took us back to Summit Lake. He dropped us off at Mom and Rocky's and once again, promised to work vigilantly on finding the kidnapper.

"I'm heading on over to Josh's right now," he said.

"You need backup?" Rocky asked.

Mom glared at him.

The sheriff chuckled and shook his head. "Rocky, you just stay here and keep an eye on your family. Let me deal with the rest."

He nodded.

I TOOK A shower and put on a pair of jean shorts and a thin, peach hoodie. After wrapping my hair into a loose bun, I went downstairs to the kitchen, where mom was. Seeing me, she announced that Parker was bringing Kevin home to us.

"Good," I replied, noticing that my hair was still damp and leaking water down my neck. I dried it with my fingertips. "Does Parker know why I really left last night?"

"Yeah. We told him."

I swallowed. "Was he angry?"

Her eyes widened. "At you? No. He's mad at Josh, though. He was very adamant about the fact that nothing had happened between him and Tara. He said that Josh made it up."

"Oh, good."

"Have you spoken to Tara yet?"

"No. But, I did leave her message, telling her that I was okay and to call me when she had some free time." I noticed a couple of kettles on the stove. The kitchen smelled wonderful and my empty stomach growled. "What are you making?"

She smiled at me. "One of your favorites— chicken and dumplings. I figured you could use some comfort food."

I thanked her and sat down at the table.

"You want some coffee or iced tea?" she asked. "I'll get you whatever you want."

"Thank you. Tea would be nice. Where's Rocky?"

"Sitting on the porch with this shotgun. I think he believes he's Clint Eastwood now or something," she mused.

I sighed. "Well, we could use *Dirty Harry* right about now," I said. I closed eyes and rubbed my forehead. "I hope to God they find this guy."

She went into the refrigerator and took out the pitcher of tea. "Me, too. I don't want to believe that it's anyone we know, but I just want this over with. I want my family safe."

My cell phone began to ring. I took it out of my pocket and saw that it was the sheriff.

"I just wanted you to know, that we've arrested Josh on suspicion of kidnapping," he said when I answered.

Stunned, I turned to face my mom. "You did? I thought you needed evidence?"

"Yeah, well… we have it. In fact, I'm bringing it by as we speak."

I didn't understand. "You're bringing it *here*? What is it?"

He was quiet for a few seconds. "I'll call you right back."

"Okay."

We hung up and a few seconds later, he sent me a message with a photo attached. When I saw the image on it, my eyes filled with tears.

"What's going on?" Mom asked, walking over to me. She looked at my phone and gasped. "That's—"

"Lacey," I finished, smiling so wide, my cheeks hurt. "He found her."

NOT LONG AFTER Parker and Austin brought Kevin home, the sheriff arrived with Lacey. I hadn't told them about the surprise, so when she leaped out of the squad car, and charged Kevin's way, he gasped in shock.

"I can't believe it," Rocky said, squeezing my shoulder as we watched the heart-wrenching reunion. "She's alive."

Too emotional to answer, all I could do was nod and smile as Kevin hugged his dog and cried tears of joy.

When she was finished with Kevin, Lacey headed my way. Teary-eyed, I kneeled down, still unable to believe that she was with us.

"I missed you," I murmured, pulling her into my arms. She let me pet her for a brief minute and then went down the line, greeting everyone with excitement.

"She's limping a little," Mom said, watching her move.

"That's from the trap, I'm sure," I replied.

Parker smiled. "She seems to be getting along pretty well, though. I'll check her out and see how she's doing after she's calmed down."

"And fed. I bet you're hungry, huh, girl?" Kevin said. "You want some food?"

Lacey barked and then followed him toward the house.

"I'll go with them," Austin said.

"Can you tell us what happened?" Rocky asked the sheriff when the boys disappeared into the house with the dog.

"Besides finding Lacey, it doesn't appear that he has an alibi for yesterday, and when I brought your name up," he looked at me, "Josh became quite agitated."

I rolled my eyes. "So, he actually blames me for their divorce?"

"Let's just say that he's decided to put the blame on everyone else for the problems in his life." He looked at Parker. "He tried bad-mouthing you as well. He claims you and Tara had something going when he was trying to get back with her."

Parker looked stunned. "That's B.S. Tara and I never dated. We exchanged phone numbers once, but that was as friends and nothing more. He's obviously paranoid and delusional."

"It certainly looks that way from where I'm standing," the sheriff replied. "Now, I know you mentioned to the cops that you didn't know what kind of a car the kidnapper had, but did you at least see the color of it?"

"I was in the trunk the entire time and it was dark," I replied. "I'm sorry. I couldn't tell you."

"Maybe if she saw the trunk again, she'd recognize it?" Rocky said. "What kind of a vehicle does Josh have?"

"All that is registered is a Jeep Wrangler, which was in his garage," the sheriff said. "But, that doesn't mean he didn't rent or borrow a car from someone else."

"Of course he did," Rocky said. "Hell, he may have even stolen one. Nobody in their right mind would use their own vehicle to kidnap someone."

"Probably not," Sheriff Baldwin replied. "Of course, you'd have to be completely out of your *right mind* to kidnap someone."

"Touché," Rocky said.

I crossed my arms under my chest. "And… what did he have to say about Lacey?"

"Josh claimed that he found her limping down the road the other day and picked her up. Since she didn't have any I.D., he decided to keep her."

Rocky rolled his eyes.

"He said that he figured his sons would love her," the sheriff added. "And Tara. He made it sound like he was going to win Tara back with the dog."

"Considering that he's more of a dog than Lacey, it would have never happened," I said dryly.

The sheriff smiled.

"Did Josh admit to *anything*?" Rocky asked.

"Nope. But, he's going to be calling his lawyer," he replied. "I'm sure they'll deny everything. My guys are doing a search of the property right now, to see if there's any other evidence, and I'm headed back there myself. I just wanted to bring Lacey back so I could personally see the look on Kevin's face."

I smiled. "You made his day. You also made mine. Thank you."

He grinned back. "You're welcome. Now, I don't want to get your hopes up or anything, but from where I'm standing… I think this case is solved."

"I hope so," Mom replied, looking relieved. "We couldn't take much more of this."

"Especially Amanda," Parker said, putting an arm around my shoulder. He squeezed it gently. "She's lucky to be alive."

He nodded. "I agree. Anyway, I've got to get back to Josh's. If we find any more evidence, I'll let you know. He's our number-one suspect right now, though."

"He's guilty as hell, as far as I'm concerned," Rocky said. "Amanda doesn't have any other enemies."

"None that we know of at least," I replied.

"You're too nice of a person to have enemies," Parker said, looking down into my eyes. "Although, Josh always was an egotistical, arrogant hot-head who always had to get his way. I just can't believe that he pulled something like this, though."

"Me neither," Mom said. "I guess you just never know about people."

"No, you don't," he replied.

My cell phone suddenly began to ring. I pulled it out and saw that it was Tara calling me back.

"I have to take this," I said. "It's Tara."

"If you wouldn't mind, I'd like to speak to her when you're finished," the sheriff said.

I nodded and answered the phone.

"How are you?" she asked, sounding concerned.

"Much better now," I replied.

"That's a relief. What in the hell has been happening out there?"

I went over all of the events, leaving Josh's name out until she asked if there were any suspects. When I told her, she gasped in shock.

"My Josh? No way," she said firmly. "I know he's a womanizer and a real jerk, but Josh isn't violent and would never kill anyone."

"He had Lacey," I told her.

She sighed. "There has to be some logical explanation. I've known Josh for half of my life and he would never kidnap anyone. As far as blaming you for the divorce, he knows why I left him. It had nothing to do with you."

"Apparently, he had a lot of bad things to say about me when they arrested him," I muttered.

Tara gasped again. "He's been arrested?"

"Yes. They're also searching his house."

She sighed. "This is crazy. Look, I'm sorry about everything that's happened to you. I love you, you know that."

"I know. I love you, too."

"I just... there is no way that anyone could convince me that Josh was the one responsible for killing the deputy or that he terrorized you like that. That's not the man I know."

I sighed. Just like she'd been in denial about him cheating on her long before she caught him red-handed. Of course, I didn't want to argue with her about it. Finding out that the father of your children might be a cold-blooded murderer would shock anyone. Plus, I was sure she still had feelings for him.

"I know. Hopefully they'll figure out what's going on, and if he is innocent, they'll catch who really did it," I said.

"I hope so. I know one thing; I need to get my ass back to Summit Lake. It looks like both of you need me right now."

"Sounds good. Oh, Sheriff Baldwin wants to talk to you."

"Good, I have a few things to say to him, too," she replied dryly.

I walked over to the sheriff and handed him the phone. He greeted her and then I watched his face as Tara spoke to him. From the look on it, he was getting an earful.

"I understand your concern," he said. "And we'll take all of that into consideration."

They spoke for a few more minutes and then the two hung up and handed the phone back to me.

"So I take it she didn't take the news very well?" Rocky asked.

"No. She's convinced that he's innocent. And," he shrugged, "technically… he is, right now. Until he confesses or is found guilty in a court of law. I still think we have our guy, though."

I did, too. At least, I hoped he was. I knew that if, by chance, Josh was innocent however, I'd be the first one to find out. By raincheck.

Chapter 35

Amanda

JOSH WAS ONLY detained for twenty-four hours, because of lack of evidence. Apparently, having my dog wasn't enough to press charges and they had to let him go.

The next couple of days seemed like a whirlwind. Not only did we have the media showing up at our doorstep, I couldn't go into town without being bombarded with questions from friends and neighbors. Although they were horrified by what had happened to me, nobody wanted to believe that Josh was the guilty party.

"He might be a fool," Karen said, when Tara and I grabbed a bite to eat at Aunt's K's on Wednesday. She'd gotten back the night before and was still trying to process everything that had happened herself. "But, he's no cop killer. Hell, he and Adam used to talk to each other all the time. They were practically friends."

"I agree," Tara said, twirling the straw in her raspberry lemonade. "Josh has made a lot of mistakes, but he's not a murderer." She looked at me. "Or a kidnapper. The sicko behind all of this is not him. I'd stake my life on it."

After a while, even I began to question Josh's innocence. That was... until more evidence was found—the camouflage suit the stalker had worn. It was actually Tara herself who stumbled upon the outfit hidden in Josh's garage. She called me up after finding it and then sent me a photo.

"Yeah. That looks like it," I said, calling her back. I was relieved and yet sad for my friend. As much as I wanted him convicted, I knew what it was like to find out your ex was psychotic. It was even worse knowing that you'd lived with the guy and never knew. "Did you ask Josh about it yet?"

"No. I stopped by to see if he could fix the chain on my bike. Actually, I just wanted to see what he had to say about this thing with you. Anyway, when he went into the house to get us something to drink, I noticed a covered barrel tucked back in the corner of the garage. I'd never seen it before, so I looked inside and that's when I found the suit." She lowered her voice to a whisper. "Uh oh. I have to go. I think he's coming back. You'd better call the sheriff."

"Okay."

She hung up and I dialed Sheriff Baldwin. When he heard the news, he promised to check it out.

"What's going on?" asked Rocky, who'd walked into the kitchen while I'd been on the phone with her.

I told him.

"I'm surprised the investigators didn't find it already," he replied.

"Maybe he hid it there afterward?"

From what I'd learned, they'd searched his place a couple of times, but hadn't found any other evidence.

"Probably. Oh, hell. I knew it was him all along. Ever since he was arrested, things have been quiet around here. He knows people are watching him."

"True."

"I'm glad it was Tara who found the suit. Hopefully she'll come to her senses and quit falling for his bullshit."

"After today, I don't think that will be a problem," I replied, thinking about how angry Josh was going to be when the police showed up.

An hour later, Sheriff Baldwin called and asked if I could take a drive over to Josh's place to identify the suit, so Rocky took me. When we arrived at the house, there were three squad cars parked in front of his garage.

"Is he here?" Rocky asked the sheriff, after we got out of the truck.

"Yes. Josh is being detained in the house," Sheriff Baldwin replied and then introduced us to Detective Davis, a nice-looking man in his thirties.

"I was going to head out your way to ask you some questions when I received the call from the sheriff," Detective Davis said as we headed to the garage.

"I guess now you can kill two birds with one stone," I replied.

"Looks that way," he replied.

"Hopefully we'll wrap this thing up and you boys will get what you need to put him behind bars once and for all," Rocky said.

"Let's hope," Sheriff Baldwin said.

When we reached the garage, Tara was inside, talking with another officer. Seeing me, she got up and we hugged each other.

"Are you okay?" I murmured, noticing her makeup was ruined from crying.

"I just can't believe this is happening," she said softly as we pulled away. "I was so sure he was innocent."

Rocky gave her a sympathetic look. "It's hard believing that someone you love could do hurtful things like this. Nobody blames you for wanting to defend the man. At least now you know the truth."

She nodded and then started crying again. "I just don't know how I'm going to tell our boys. This will wreck them."

Thinking about it made my heart heavy. "Tara, it'll be okay," I said, hugging her again. "They have you and you'll work through this."

"I'm sorry. I should be the one comforting you," she said.

"I'm fine," I replied. "Don't worry about me."

"Just be thankful you two also have each other," Rocky said. "You'll get through this. You and Amanda have more balls than most of the men in Summit Lake."

Tara laughed sadly.

"Here it is," said Detective Davis, who was now wearing plastic gloves. He raised the camouflage outfit up for my inspection and there was no doubt in my mind that I'd seen it on the person terrorizing me. It even had the fake leaves and twigs. "This wasn't in the barrel when we did the initial search. I know that for a fact."

"Do you recognize it?" Sheriff Baldwin asked as I stepped closer.

"Oh, yeah. It's the same one my guy wore," I replied.

"You're certain?" Detective Davis asked.

"Unless this is Summit Lake's new fashion trend, I'm pretty sure it's a one-of-a-kind suit," I replied.

"What did Josh have to say about it?" Rocky asked.

"He claimed he'd never seen the suit in his life," said the detective.

"That's odd," Rocky replied dryly.

"He also says that someone is trying to frame him," said Detective Davis.

"Of course he is," Rocky said with a scornful look. "The man is a liar. A cheat. A stalker *and* a cop killer. The evidence keeps piling up and he's scared shitless now. What else *would* he say?"

"Not the truth, that's for sure. He'll never admit to this," Tara said in a hollow voice. "He would never admitted anything to me either. Why should he start now?"

I grabbed her hand and squeezed it.

"Let's bring him down to the station," Sheriff Baldwin said.

Chapter 36

Amanda

THREE WEEKS LATER

CHARGES WERE FILED against Josh and he was denied bail. The court date was set for the following month, which meant that Kevin and I wouldn't be leaving Summit Lake anytime soon. After everything that had happened, however, I couldn't wait to return to Chicago. The town had lost its charm and even though Josh was behind bars, I felt uneasy and out of place there.

As we waited, I put Brad's cabin up for sale and it sold within twenty-four hours. During this time, I also received the funds from the inheritance, so Kevin and I finally had some money in the bank—and a substantial amount at that. To celebrate this, along with the fact that my birthday was the following day, I decided to take my friends and family out to dinner.

"So, what are your plans when this thing is over?" Tara asked, while we were gathered at Antonio's Italian Restaurant. There were seven of us, including Kevin, Mom, Rocky, Parker, and Austin.

"We're returning to Chicago," I replied. "I'm renting a house there but we're going to purchase one in the same school district. That way, Kevin can still see his friends."

Kevin grinned. "Yaay!"

"So, you're not staying here?" Parker said, pretending to pout.

"No. Although we love you all, I feel that Kevin and I need to put some distance between us and the memories of the last few weeks," I replied softly.

They all nodded.

"I understand. I was hoping you'd stick around, but after what you've been through, I'd probably do the same thing," Parker said, reaching over and squeezing my hand.

"We'll come back next summer," I promised. "Especially now that Kevin is a 'master fisherman'."

Although Kevin had missed the first couple of days of fishing camp, he'd been going for the last two weeks and loving every minute of it. He'd made a bunch of new friends, learned when and how to use different lures, and had even gotten a taste of fly-fishing and trolling.

"Don't forget, *Parent Night* is Friday," Kevin reminded me.

"Don't worry. I could never forget, considering it's all you talk about," I replied with a grin.

"Oh, that sounds like fun. What happens on *Parent Night?*" Mom asked.

"There's going to be a fish fry and Marcus is going to be giving away awards," Kevin replied.

"What kind of awards?" Rocky asked, looking intrigued.

"Like… who caught the biggest fish," he replied.

"Or the most," Austin added.

"*You* caught the most," Kevin said to him. "You're bound to win."

Smiling, Austin shrugged. "Yeah. Maybe."

Parker ruffled his son's hair. "Don't be modest. You learned from your old man, so I know you could teach Marcus a thing or two."

"He was hinting at that when I picked the boys up yesterday," I said, grateful to Marcus and his wife for everything they'd done.

After learning about what had happened with Josh, the couple had refused to cash the check I'd written for the camp, claiming that it would be an honor to help take Kevin's mind off things.

"Marcus said that I was a natural-born fly-fisherman," Kevin said, looking pretty proud himself.

"We have to come back here next year so that I can go to their camp again."

"Of course we will," I replied, happy to see such enthusiasm on my son's face.

"Or you could just buy a house in Summit Lake and try your hand at ice-fishing," Parker said with a wink. "It's beautiful here in the winter."

"Good try," I said, smirking.

"Hey, I have to keep trying," Parker said with a twinkle in his eyes. "Otherwise I'm giving up too easily and that's unattractive in a man. At least that's what Tara told me the other day."

"Oh, really?" Rocky asked, looking amused. "Was she trying to give you some pointers?"

"Apparently, I need them," Parker replied. "Because my charms don't seem to be working very well these days."

"Right," I said dryly.

Parker and I had actually been spending a lot of time together. Although we hadn't "slept" together, we'd made out like horny teenagers more than once. I hadn't wanted to take it any further, especially knowing that I'd be leaving town soon. Although I did have some feelings for him, they weren't compelling enough for me to stay. Not when my sanity needed a vacation from Summit Lake.

Tara, who'd been quiet, chuckled. "I was talking about the butcher, Steve Jacobs. I know he wants to ask me out, but something tells me he's too afraid of rejection. If he waits to long, I'm going to have to say 'no', though. I like my men assertive."

"And loyal," I added.

"And sane," she said. "Let's hope that when Butcher Steve finally gets the nerve to ask me out, he leaves his cleaver at home."

We all laughed.

Tara raised her wine glass in the air. "I feel like making a toast. May we *all* walk out of here tonight and live normal, happy lives. No stress. No craziness. Nothing but love and peace."

We clinked our glasses together.

The waiter returned to the table and brought our appetizers.

"Mom, I need to use the bathroom," Kevin whispered.

"Okay. I'll go with you," I replied.

"Do you have to go, too?" he asked, frowning.

"No."

"I can go myself," he whispered, giving Austin a sideways glance.

"Alright. Go ahead," I replied, realizing that he didn't want to look like a baby around the older boy. "Do you know where it is?"

Kevin stood up. "Yeah, by the entrance."

"Okay. Hurry back," I said.

He walked away from the table.

"I thought he just went to the bathroom before we left?" Mom asked.

"Well, he has to go again," I replied.

She gave me a look of disapproval. "It's all that orange soda he had today."

"It's a special occasion," I said. "He'll be fine. Could you pass me the artichoke dip and some of those chips, please?"

"Sure," she replied, reaching for the plate.

"So, Austin, when are you going back home?" I asked, directing my attention to him.

"The end of this month," he replied.

"You miss your mom?" I asked.

He nodded.

We began talking about his school and he mentioned joining the football team in the fall.

"Your father was on the football team," I said, smiling at Parker. "That's how we met. I was a cheerleader."

"The prettiest one in Summit Lake," he replied, touching my hand.

"Hey, I was a cheerleader, too," Tara said, pretending to pout. "But, I have to admit… Amanda *was* the prettiest."

"I think you're both crazy," I replied.

"I wonder what's taking Kevin so long?" Mom said, when the waiter returned with our salads. "There won't be any wings left." She slapped Rocky's hand away from the Buffalo wings. "Leave those. You've already had two of them. Remember your blood pressure."

"Woman, *you're* the only thing raising my blood pressure," he grumbled.

I looked toward the entrance again.

Still no sign of Kevin.

"I should probably go and check on him," I said, standing up.

"Would you like me to go?" Parker asked. "I doubt they'll let you into the men's room."

"Don't worry about it. I'll wait for him outside. I need to stretch my legs anyway. I'll be back."

"Okay," he replied.

I left the table and headed to the front of the restaurant. It was busy and there were a lot of people waiting to be seated. After finding the restrooms, I stood by the men's and waited for Kevin to walk out. After a couple of minutes, I began to wonder if he wasn't feeling well.

"Excuse me," I said, as an older gentleman walked out. "Did you see a boy in there? He's eight, with curly brown hair?"

"As far as I could see, there wasn't anyone in there but me," he said before walking away.

Alarmed, I walked into the restroom. "Kevin?" I called out, checking under the stalls for his shoes. "Are you in here?"

Nobody answered.

Even worse, I found that the bathroom was, indeed, empty.

Trying not to panic, I walked out of the restroom and straight over to the hostess, who looked like she wasn't much older than sixteen. I asked her if she'd seen Kevin and described what he'd been wearing.

"I'm sorry, ma'am. We've been so busy, trying to seat guests. I didn't notice him," she replied.

"Your child is missing?" an older woman with a cane asked, looking concerned.

"I… I don't know," I replied, my heart racing now. "He needed to go the bathroom and he's not there."

"Check the women's restroom," someone else suggested.

I raced inside, and when I didn't find him there either, I left and headed outside. My eyes scanned the parking lot, which was busy with cars coming and going.

"Kevin!" I hollered.

No answer.

I raced over to Rocky's truck and searched the area, but there was no sign of him there either.

Maybe he went back to the table?

I began to relax, thinking that I was probably panicking over nothing. The restaurant was huge and it was likely that Kevin could have found a different route back to our table.

I went back inside.

"Did you find your son?" the older woman asked as I stepped past her.

"No, but I'm hoping he might have taken a wrong turn somewhere in the restaurant," I replied, turning back to look at her. "I went into panic mode and didn't think to check back there."

She gave me a sympathetic smile. "I know how that goes."

"Have a good night."

"You, as well. Thank you."

When I stepped back into the dining room and saw that Kevin's chair was empty, my legs felt like they were going to buckle underneath me.

"Where's Kevin?" Mom asked, looking past me.

My eyes filled with tears. "He's missing," I said, turning back around to talk to the maître-d. "Call the police!"

Chapter 37

Amanda

KEVIN WAS NOWHERE to be found. By the time law enforcement showed up, almost everyone from the restaurant was out searching the streets for him. Meanwhile, I was on the verge of hysteria. Tara had mentioned something about child trafficking and it was all I could think about. Just imagining what might be happening to him was driving me over the edge.

"You have to find him," I begged, gripping Sheriff Baldwin's forearm.

"Don't worry, Amanda," he said, trying to calm me. "We'll do everything in our power to bring Kevin back to you."

He'd said that about Lacey, but I knew that finding her had been pure luck.

"Now, tell me exactly what happened," he said gently.

I went over everything, watching the front entrance while I spoke. "I shouldn't have left him go alone," I said, sobbing, knowing that I'd failed my son. "This would have never have happened otherwise."

"Now, you can't go blaming yourself," he replied.

"I'm his protector. He's only eight years old and I allowed him to use the restroom by himself," I said bitterly, swiping at the tears under my lashes. "I should have known better."

Sheriff Baldwin sighed and looked around the lobby. There was just us and the hostess at the moment. "Didn't anyone see Kevin leave the restaurant?" he asked.

"Apparently not," I replied. "Nobody was paying attention."

"That's the problem these days," he muttered. "Everyone's too busy staring down at their damn cell phones to see what's happening around them." To prove a point, he nodded toward the young hostess, who was frantically typing on hers.

He was right, although when Kevin had disappeared, the lobby had been packed with people. I was just surprised nobody had seen what happened.

"As much as I appreciate that everyone is searching for him, we need to interview everyone who was here," he said as the restaurant manager approached. "Somebody *had to* have seen something."

While Sheriff Baldwin spoke to the manager, I walked back outside for some fresh air. It was then that I saw Marcus Gibbons and his wife, Julie, walking toward me. They were both dressed up and that's when I remembered that it was their anniversary.

"What's going on? Why are the police here?" Julie asked, a concerned look on her face as she took in the squad cars parked in front of the restaurant.

I broke down. "Kevin is missing," I cried. "Someone took him."

Marcus looked horrified. "Oh, my God. How? *When?*"

Julie put her arm around me as I told them what had happened. When I was finished, she gave me a hug. "Don't worry, they'll find him," she said. "You have to believe that."

I wanted to believe it. "I feel like I've been cursed," I said, wiping my tears with the back of my hand. "I don't understand why all of this is happening to us."

"What can we do to help?" Marcus asked. "I'm assuming they've formed search parties?"

I nodded.

Julie reached into her purse and handed me a tissue. "You poor thing. Marcus, go inside and ask the police if there's anything that we can do."

"Right away," he said and walked into the restaurant.

Both of our phones made a high-pitched sound. I pulled mine out of my pocket and saw that they'd issued the *Code Adam* for Kevin.

"I can't believe this is happening," I said, sobbing again. "And, I don't know what to do. I feel so helpless."

"I know," she said in a soothing voice. "But, you're doing everything you can right now. Just stay strong for him. And don't lose hope."

Marcus walked out of the building with Sheriff Baldwin.

"Julie, look at you. You're about ready to pop any day, aren't you?" Sheriff Baldwin said with smile.

She rubbed her stomach and nodded.

This brought more tears to my eyes as I was flooded with memories of being pregnant with Kevin.

The sheriff's smile crumbled. "Sorry, Amanda. That's rude of me. I didn't mean—"

"It's okay. You didn't do anything wrong. Just… please, find my son," I begged.

He touched my shoulder. "I will."

THE SEARCH CONTINUED, with no luck. Eventually, Mom and Rocky tried talking me into going home with them to get some rest.

"I'm not leaving here," I said firmly.

"I hate to say this, but there's no reason to stay here. Whoever has Kevin wouldn't be sticking around this area," said Tara.

I didn't care. I couldn't bring myself to leave the restaurant. It made me feel like I was abandoning my son. I told them that.

"I understand," Mom said, looking weary. "Believe me, I love Kevin and want him back as much as you do. But, I don't think he's here, either. We should go back to the house, have some coffee, and collect our thoughts."

"Mom, I'm not leaving," I said firmly. "Why don't you two go back home. That way, if we get any phone call leads at the house, someone will be there to answer them. I'm sure the entire town knows Kevin is missing now."

Rocky sighed. "Yeah. That's a good idea."

"If you wouldn't mind, could you bring me home?" Julie asked them. "That way Marcus can stay and help here."

"No," I said. "It's your anniversary. Go and have dinner," I said, feeling guilty.

"Absolutely not. Kevin is a great kid. We want to help, don't we, Marcus?" she said to her husband.

"Yes. Of course," he said. "I wouldn't dream of tapping out now. Kevin means a lot to us."

"Thank you," I said.

"We'll give you a ride home," Rocky said to Julie. "I'm sure Parker and Austin can drop Amanda off at home later."

"I'll take her home. Don't worry," Tara said.

"Thanks," I said, drying my eyes again.

AFTER MOM, ROCKY, and Julie left, the search party broke up an hour later. Parker and Austin returned to the restaurant and asked if I wanted to leave with them. Although I was exhausted, I still couldn't bring myself to go.

"You should really get home and rest," the sheriff said. "There's nothing more that we can do here."

I began to protest when Tara stepped in. "Why don't we go up the street to Aunty K's and have some coffee? Antonio's is going to be closing at eleven anyway."

I reluctantly agreed.

"I'd love to join you, but I need to bring Austin home," Parker said. "He's exhausted."

"I totally understand," I said, glancing over at his son. I smiled. "Thank you for helping out. I appreciate it. Kevin would, too."

He nodded. "I hope they find him," Austin said. I could tell he'd been crying himself. I knew Kevin adored Austin and looked up to him like a big brother. It was obvious that Austin had a soft spot for him as well.

I gave him a hug. "Me, too."

After Parker left, Marcus joined Tara and I at the diner. Fortunately, Karen wasn't working, so we didn't have to deal with the pesky woman.

"I bet you *really* wish you'd never come back here now, don't you?" Tara said, pouring cream into her coffee. "First Josh and now this."

I rubbed my temples. "You have no idea."

"Did Josh actually confess?" Marcus asked.

"No. He's denying everything," I said.

"What a shame. He seemed like a great guy," he replied.

I'd learned that Julie used to babysit Tara and Josh's boys when she was a teenager, which was during the time Julie and Marcus had started dating.

"Well, he could certainly put the charm on when he needed to," Tara said dryly.

"That he could," I said.

"Are you positive that he's guilty?" Marcus asked. "I mean, what if they have the wrong guy? And the person who took Kevin is the same one who killed the cop and went after you?"

Tara and I looked at each other.

"No," I said, the very idea making the hair stand up on the back of my neck. "They have the right person. They found evidence. Not to mention he had my dog."

Marcus shrugged. "I guess there's that. Although," he picked up his coffee. "What if he was framed?"

"Well, that's what Josh keeps telling everyone," Tara said.

Marcus's eyebrow raised. "Really? And you don't believe him?"

"Nope. He wouldn't admit to cheating on me. Why would he admit to murdering a cop? That's a capital crime. The kind that will get you the death penalty," she replied. "Of course he's going to keep denying everything. He wants to live."

"I suppose," Marcus said. He looked at me. "I can't imagine what you're going through. Not knowing if Kevin is dead or alive?"

His words triggered another lump in my throat. "It's… horrible. I'm at the point to where I don't want to think about it too hard or I might just go insane."

"You have to keep hoping for the best, though. Just like my wife always says," Marcus said. "She believes in the Law of Attraction and I guess I do. You think good thoughts, good things come your way. If you live your life badly, you will only attract darkness in the end."

"It doesn't seem like any of that is happening here," Tara said. "Amanda is a good person with a good heart. Kevin is a great kid. If the Law of Attraction really worked, they'd be together right now and sleeping soundly in their beds."

"I've asked my wife why bad things happen to good people and she thinks it's to wake us up. She says that we have the ability to change the world and find happiness. We just have to work and clean up the negative areas in our life. Once you find inner peace, you can project an outer peace."

Obviously, his wife had never been in a situation like mine. I blew out a long breath. "I appreciate your advice, but before all of this... we were happy. And, look where we are now."

He opened his mouth to say more and I held up my hand.

"Marcus, I know you mean well, but do you honestly expect that the evil person who took Kevin is going to suddenly have a change of heart, if we think 'happy thoughts'? That he'd actually return my son to me?"

"I'm just saying, don't lose hope," he said.

"I won't. Hope is all I have left," I said. "And that's one thing I will never give up."

SHERIFF BALDWIN CALLED me about thirty minutes later. He didn't have any news, which broke my heart even further. I knew that every minute was critical in the case of a lost child.

"Go home and get some sleep," he ordered. "You need to be strong for your son and staying up all night isn't going to help anyone."

"I doubt I could sleep if I tried."

"You're still exhausted and need to rest," he said. "Take some melatonin or something."

I promised him I'd try to do what he suggested, but knew that sleep would be impossible until Kevin was back, safe and sound.

After hanging up, the three of us decided to leave the diner.

"I can drop you off," Marcus said. "You're on the way home for me."

"Thank you," I replied.

Tara and I hugged each other and then we went our separate ways.

"Thank you for doing this," I said to Marcus after we got into his Audi. "I feel so horrible that it's your anniversary and you were sucked into this."

He shrugged. "It's okay. I'll make it up to Julie tomorrow. Honestly, she was tired when we left and tried backing out of dinner anyway. She's been trying to get so much done before the baby arrives. I think they call that nesting?"

"Yeah. How far along is she?"

"Her due date is next week."

"Wow. Have you found out what you're having yet?" I asked as we pulled out of the parking lot.

"No. We wanted it to be a surprise. Did you know what you were having with Kevin?"

"It was a surprise for us, too."

"Brad must have been happy to have a son."

I cringed. "Brad? No, he wasn't the father. We divorced many years ago and I remarried."

The idea of him being a father now made me ill. Especially after learning about his pedophilia. Although, the police hadn't been able to come up with much in regards to the photos, it was obvious that he'd been into some illegal stuff. Not to mention what he'd done to his younger brother.

"Oh, I thought maybe you divorced after having Kevin?"

"No. It was long before that."

"So, what was Kevin's father like?"

"Jason?" I sighed. "He was a sweet man."

"What happened?"

"He died of a stroke. When Kevin was a baby."

He looked surprised. "I'm sorry."

"Me, too," I replied, thinking back to how excited Jason had been when he'd learned I was pregnant.

"I guess Kevin really lucked out."

"How so?"

"You remarried. His father wasn't a pedophile."

"How… how did you find out about Brad? Was it Karen?"

He laughed harshly. "No."

"The sheriff?" I asked.

"Nobody told me."

Confused, I stared at him in the darkness. "Then, how did you know?" I asked, terrified of the answer.

"You don't recognize me, do you?"

I studied his face. "I thought we'd just met?"

Looking frustrated, he began tapping on the steering wheel. "My last name used to be Fender. My mother remarried when I was twelve."

The last name rang a bell and then it hit me—I used to babysit an eight-year-old with the last name of Fender. It hadn't been for very long, and we'd called him Marc at the time.

"Ah... I see a lightbulb finally going off," he said.

"I can't believe I didn't recognize you," I said, feeling tense. The atmosphere in the car had turned cold.

"Apparently, you weren't the only one," he replied.

"Are you saying that Brad did something to you?" I asked hoarsely.

"Ding. We have a winner," he said dryly.

"I don't understand? He was never around when I watched you," I said, surprised. "He was always working."

"Apparently, he wasn't," Marcus said.

My thoughts drifted back to those early days. I recalled watching Marc in the summer and sometimes his mother would have to work late. I couldn't recall

Brad interacting with any of the children, but, it wasn't impossible.

"He touched you inappropriately?" I asked, almost unable to get the words out.

"How many times do you need it spelled out for you?" he said coldly. "Yes. He did."

I was horrified. Brad had molested him under my care?

How could I have *not* known?

"I'm so sorry," I said, a lump forming in my throat. I reached over to touch his arm. "I don't know what he did to you, but I am so, so sorry."

"Fuck you," he snarled, shoving my hand away. "Don't pretend you didn't know."

"I didn't, Marcus. I had no idea," My eyes widened as he reached under his seat and pulled out a gun.

"Okay, maybe you're not lying and are just a stupid idiot," he said, pointing it at me. "I mean, if you were smart, you'd have figured everything out by now."

Terrified, I felt like the wind had been knocked out of me. "What do you mean?"

He began to whistle a familiar tune.

Pop Goes The Weasel.

Chapter 38

Amanda

MARCUS DROVE TO a dark alley and forced me into the backseat. He took my purse, and then ordered me to put on a pair of handcuffs. Afterward, he tied up my feet with twine.

"Now lie down and stay down," he ordered. "Misbehave, and your son will suffer."

"You have Kevin?" I gasped, as he produced a roll of duct tape.

"Of course."

I sighed in relief. "Does Julie know what you've been doing?"

I could tell from his expression that she didn't.

"What would she think of all of this if she found out? My God, she's pregnant with your child."

"I'm doing this *for* my child."

I stared at him in disbelief. "What?"

"It all goes back to what we talked about earlier— *The Law of Attraction*," he said, ripping off a piece of duct tape. "Once I get rid of the poison in my life, things can only get better."

"I don't think it works this way, and… why am *I* a poison? I never did anything to you."

"You *allowed* it to happen," he spat. "You should have stopped it."

"I would have if I'd have known," I cried frantically. "I swear to God, I'd have done something."

He hesitated and then put the duct tape over my mouth. "And I swear that people will say anything when they're desperate."

Frustrated, I tried begging him to let me go, but of course, my mouth was taped, so it came out garbled.

"It's better for you if you just stop trying to defend yourself. It's not going to help your situation. It certainly didn't help Brad's."

I stared at him blankly.

"Brad didn't die by driving over a cliff," he explained with a sardonic grin. "He died right here, in Summit Lake. With my help, of course."

It didn't surprise me. Not after everything Marcus had gotten away with so far.

We heard thunder in the distance. Marcus looked outside and his face grew serious. "We should go. It's going to be a long night. Not to mention I need to deal with Tara, too."

My heart slammed against my chest.

He was going to kill her?

Marcus got back into the front seat and started driving.

"This feels good. Getting it off my chest. I've been holding all of this shit in for so long. Especially about Brad," he chuckled. "It was quite hysterical, actually. I'll never forget the look on his face when I pulled the knife on him."

Marcus told me about how he'd set up a meeting with Brad online, and the gruesome details that took place afterward.

"It was risky, but worth it." He grunted. "I'm sure Brad had other victims. I only wish they knew the truth, of how he died, so that they could rejoice in the fact that he got exactly what had been coming to him."

In a way, I couldn't blame him for wanting to strike back at Brad. But Marcus had committed cold-blooded murder. Not to mention, he'd killed the deputy, too. An innocent man who'd risked his life daily to help others.

Marcus began talking about Julie again.

"To answer your question… no. She doesn't know. She'd never understand and I wouldn't expect her to. She's sweet and kind. Hell, she's the best thing that ever happened to me. I… I just want to keep the darkness from her. This is why I have to delete all of it from my past."

The man was using darkness to rid himself of the exact very same thing. It made no sense.

"You know, I'm surprised you didn't figure it out after I gave you that teddy bear. It was from your daycare. You obviously didn't remember it."

I definitely didn't remember the stuffed bear. There'd been so many toys for the kids, though. Plus, it had been almost twenty years ago.

"Anyway, back to Brad," he said, turning the windshield wipers on as it began to rain. "I can still remember that day in the summer, when he took away my innocence. It was the worst day of my life."

My eyes filled with tears as I listened.

"It had been a hot day. Everyone was outside… running through the sprinklers and having water gun fights. After a while, I had to go inside and use the bathroom." He paused and then went on, his voice tight. "Brad was home and invited me into his office, to try out some new dragon pinball machine."

I recalled the one he was talking about. It had been a special collector's edition and he'd decided against keeping it at the arcade. Brad had been very protective of the expensive machine.

He continued. "Of course I went in to play, making the worst mistake of my life."

He was silent for several seconds and then went on, leaving out the exact details of what had happened in the office.

"After he was done molesting me, he threatened to kill my mother if I said anything. He told me that you were cool with it and would immediately tell him if I mentioned it. So, I kept it to myself."

I thought back to when I'd watched Marc and recalled how quiet he'd gotten toward the end of the summer. I'd even mentioned it to his mother, thinking it was something he might have been dealing with at home. She'd brushed it off and, unfortunately, I'd let it go myself. If only I'd approached him all those years ago. Things could have been so different.

"Fortunately, I was able to convince my mother to let me stay home by myself when school started, so I didn't have to go to your place anymore. We were struggling for money, so she agreed."

I could tell we were slowing down and wondered where he was taking me. Meanwhile, Marcus kept talking.

"I never did tell anyone, although when I met Julie, she knew I had something in my past that I refused to talk about. It's killed me that we've been able to share everything, but not what's gutted me the most. But, the hell if I was going to tell her some guy used and abused me. She'd never look at me the same again."

I closed my eyes.

He stopped the car, turned off the engine, and got out. My heart pounded as he opened up the back door and leaned down to cut the twine from my ankles.

When he was finished, Marcus straightened up and ordered me to get out. He then ripped the tape off my mouth and I squealed in pain.

I got out of the car and looked around. "Is Kevin inside?" I asked, noticing that we were parked behind Gibbons' Dockside. Of course, since it was late, the place was closed and there were no other cars around.

"Nope. Don't worry, though. You'll see him soon enough if you do what you're told," he motioned toward the lake with the gun. "Let's go."

It was dark and the mosquitos were biting, which added to the hell I was walking into. But, I managed to get to the dock without tripping. Once there, we boarded an old Sea Ray and he ordered me into the small cuddy cabin down below.

"Don't think about trying anything funny, either," he said icily. "Or, like I said before, Kevin will suffer for your disobedience."

"I won't," I promised.

More than anything, I needed to get to my son and wasn't about to give Marcus any problems. At least not until the time was right.

The cabin was small and musty, but offered a place to sit. There was also a head, and although I was starting to feel like I needed to use it, I decided to wait. I didn't know if it worked and wasn't about to ask Marcus.

I sat down and listened as he started the engine. Soon we were moving and I wondered where he was taking me. I also wondered how he'd gotten Kevin out of the restaurant without anyone noticing.

It took about twenty minutes to reach our destination. I listened as he cut the engine, secured the boat, and then ordered me out of the cabin. As I stepped out and took in our surroundings, I could see that we were in a very remote area.

We got off the boat and then followed a trail that led us to a dimly lit cabin. He unlocked the door and then ushered me inside.

"Where is he?" I asked, my chest tightening. From where I was standing, it looked like we were completely alone and I wondered if he'd lied about Kevin's whereabouts.

"In the cellar," he said with a little smile. "With the rats. Hopefully, he's still in one piece."

I stared at him in horror. "What?"

With an evil glint in his eyes, Marcus nodded toward the hallway. "The door to the cellar is that way," he said, his gun pointed at me again. "Let's go."

Shaking with anger and fear, I headed in that direction, which brought us to the kitchen. As we stepped inside, I noticed a butcher block on the counter.

"This way," he said, leading me to a door on the other side of the room. He pulled out a set of keys, unlocked it, and then stepped back. "Ladies first."

"Can you please remove the handcuffs?" I said, still scrambling for a way to escape. "I don't want my son seeing me wearing them. It will upset him."

He snorted. "I hate to say this, but he's already scared shitless. Seeing you in handcuffs isn't going to make any difference."

"Look," I said in a low voice. "I know why we're here—you're going to kill us. All I'm asking is that you let me hug my son before you do. Please."

He was silent for a few seconds and then pulled out a small key from his front pocket. "Fine. You don't need me to tell you what will happen if you screw with me or try and escape."

"I wouldn't put my son's life in any more danger than it already is," I replied, holding out my hands. Of course, I also knew what our future held if I didn't risk it.

Not replying, he unlocked the cuffs and removed them.

I rubbed my wrists, grateful for the relief. "Thank you."

"Don't make me regret it." He turned the light on for the stairway. "Now, go and see your son."

Chapter 39

Amanda

I HURRIED DOWN the steps and looked around. It was a small, dank cellar, containing nothing but old shelves and empty mason jars. There was no sign of Kevin. Confused, I turned and looked at Marcus, who'd followed me down.

"Where's my son?"

He smirked but said nothing.

Was this another part of his game?

"Marcus, where is he?" I asked angrily, taking a step toward him. "Tell me!"

He raised the gun. "In a quiet place."

My eyes filled with tears.

Had he already killed my little boy?

Trying to remain calm, I released a shaky breath. "I don't understand. What did you do with him?"

"You must be thinking that I am the real monster here, but you are part of the poison that ruined my childhood. You and your sick, twisted ex-husband."

"I told you before, I didn't know what he did to you!" I said, desperate for him to believe me. "If I would have known, I'd have beat the bastard myself. I swear to you!"

A look of doubt flashed through his eyes and then they turned to steel. "Sorry, lady. But you lost my trust a long time ago. Even if it were true, which I'll never know, the hell if I'm going to jail. So, save the begging and pleading for your maker, who you're going to meet very soon."

"Can you at least tell me if he's okay?"

He said nothing.

I tried again. "What are you going to do with him? No matter what you believe about me, you know that Kevin is a sweet, innocent little boy. One whose childhood you're now ruining yourself!"

"Honestly, I haven't figured it out yet."

I had to believe that meant he was alive. I sighed in relief. "So, he's here?"

"Like I said, he's in a quiet place."

"Is he okay?"

"Unless the dosage he received was too strong... he should be."

I didn't know whether to laugh or cry. "How... how did you manage to kidnap him?"

"He met me outside of the restaurant, like we'd planned."

I stared at him in confusion.

He explained. "We talked earlier, about your birthday coming up, so I knew where you were planning on having dinner. I told him that I had a small cake for you and that once you were seated, to meet me in the parking lot. Surprisingly, he kept it a secret, like I asked him to. You're right, he's a good boy. Too good for you. Happy Birthday, by the way."

"Is he here?" I asked angrily.

"He's—"

"In a quiet place," I snapped. "Yes, I get it. I just want to know where you've taken him. Is he here?"

He smirked again. "Maybe," he said, enjoying my frustration. He nodded toward a folded metal chair leaning against the wall. "Sit down and make yourself at home while we wait."

"Wait? For what?"

"Oh, did I forget to mention that we have some other guests arriving?" he said, with a glint in his eyes. He looked down at his watch. "They should be here relatively soon."

"Who?"

"People who are always looking for new product. You're an older model, but you've kept yourself up, so I told them you were in your late twenties. I think you could definitely pass," he said, his eyes roving up and down my body. "I imagine you should turn a little bit of a profit for them."

My heart skipped a beat. "You're *selling* me?"

He smirked. "Yeah. I thought it was only fitting that your husband used my body. Now, I'm selling you to a group so they can return the favor."

I stared at him in horror. "Traffickers?"

Marcus nodded.

"And what will happen to Kevin? Are you selling him, too?"

"No. Now why would I do that? I'm *not* the monster here."

Not the monster? The man was delusional.

He went on. "Although Julie and I could really use the money right now, he won't be sold for anyone's sexual gratification. This thing between you and me," he said, pointing back and forth between us, "is all about revenge. I want you to know what it's like being used and not being able to do anything about it."

Before I could reply, his cell phone went off. He pulled it out of his pocket. "Oh, the wifey is checking up on me. I'm supposed to be fixing some plumbing issues here. It's my uncle's cabin. He's in a retirement home now and can't keep it up anymore."

"Please, don't hurt my son," I replied, not giving two shits about his uncle. "Do what you want with me, but let him go."

"I wish it were that easy. See… I can't let him go. He knows too much," Marcus said. "I can only promise that his death will be quick and painless. You're welcome."

"You *are* a monster!" I cried, rushing toward him with rage. I tried raking my nails across his face, but he shoved me away and then slammed the butt of his gun into the side of my skull. I fell to the ground, my head roaring with pain.

"Knock it off!" he growled. "Or I'll bring Kevin down here and let him watch my guests rape you before killing him. Is that what you want?!"

"No," I replied, sobbing. "Please, just let him go. He's innocent like you were. He doesn't deserve to die."

"I didn't deserve what I got, either, but that didn't stop it from happening," he growled before walking back upstairs and locking the door.

Chapter 40

Marcus

THE WOMAN WAS so irritating, I wanted to just be done with her. But, the bills were piling up, especially with the baby on the way. Then there was the restaurant, which was in desperate need of repairs. The broiler was on its last leg and the cooler was starting to give me trouble as well. It's how I'd come up with a solution—sell the bitch to traffickers. I'd kill two birds with one stone by getting rid of her and making some quick cash. Plus, it would be the ultimate ending to our little game. It had been fun while it lasted.

Finding someone to take her—now that had been the tricky part. I'd spent the last couple of weeks on the Dark Web, which was basically the seedy underworld of the Internet. After much research, and private chats with some sketchy individuals, I was able to set up a meeting with a pimp who had connections with the Russian mafia. Once we got to know each other, and I earned his trust, he put me in contact with the right people. After checking up on me, they'd agreed to meet at the cabin tonight. Even better, for my effort, I would collect five thousand dollars, if they liked what I had to offer. Considering that Amanda was a good-looking woman, and still looked quite young for her age, I knew I'd be leaving the cabin with a fat wallet and the knowledge that I'd gotten my revenge. Sure, the people I was about to do business with were scum, but some things couldn't be helped. Besides, it was only fair that she experienced what it was like to be a victim. As far as her stating that she hadn't known about Brad, I didn't care one way or another. She was supposed to protect the children she'd cared for and had failed. Justice was still due. There was still one problem, however.

Kevin.

I knew I had to kill the kid, but it didn't make me happy. He seemed like a good egg. I couldn't risk going to jail, though, and that was exactly what would happen if I turned soft. I'd never get to raise my own kid and my beautiful wife would never forgive something she couldn't begin to understand. Hell, I was probably doing Kevin a favor. His father was dead and he'd be heartbroken without his mother.

I looked at the clock. It was almost one a.m. and my Russian guests would be arriving any minute. I quickly called Julie back and told her that I was fine and at the cabin.

"I thought you were going there tomorrow?" she replied, surprised.

"Remember? I wanted to get an early start on the repairs I told you about. Besides, the baby could arrive any day. I need to have this done before then."

"You work so hard, Marcus."

"All for you, babe. I take it you can't sleep?"

"No. I can't find a comfortable position. When do you think you'll be finished with the repairs?"

"Hopefully in the early afternoon," I said and yawned. "In fact, I should get going. It's late and you should be sleeping, too."

"I know, but it's impossible. Did they find Kevin?"

"No."

She groaned. "That poor, poor kid. I hope they catch the asshole who took him and castrate the freak. It makes me frightened to think that our baby is going to be born into such a terrifying world."

"We'll protect him," I promised, forgiving her harsh words. She didn't understand what it was really about.

"Or her," she said, a smile in her voice.

I grinned. "Or her."

"I love you, Marcus."

"I love you, too."

She make a kissing sound and I returned it. As we hung up, I felt a twinge of guilt once again for lying to her, but reminded myself that justice sometimes came with a price, as did peace. By ridding myself of the things still haunting me, I knew that I could concentrate on being happy. I could never embrace the *Law of Attraction* otherwise and reap its rewards.

Whistling, I went to the guest bedroom and unlocked the door.

"Kevin?" I said out loud.

The boy didn't answer.

I walked over to the bed and saw that he was still sleeping soundly. Satisfied that he wouldn't wake up, I left the bedroom and was heading back to the basement, when I heard the knock. Relieved the woman would be out of my hair soon, I answered the door and found my Russian contact, a man known only to me as Ivan, standing there alone. Tall, thin, and in his thirties, he wore black chinos and what looked to be a Tommy Bahama shirt. His blond hair was pulled back into a short ponytail, and he had sharp features and thin lips. Not a good-looking man, but a very dangerous one.

"Marcus," he said with a cool smile as he held out his hand. "I was worried we might have the wrong cabin."

Trying not to stare at all of the rings on his fingers, or the long pinky nail, I shook his hand. "Were my directions that bad?"

"No. We're just out in the middle of nowhere. I wasn't expecting that," he said, his accent thick.

It wasn't that bad. We were only a few miles out from my restaurant. "Are you here alone?" I asked, looking past him.

"No. Rigor is tying the boat up. He'll be here in a second. So," he clapped his hands together. "Where is the girl?"

I smiled. "She's in her twenties. Not quite a *girl*. Remember?"

"Really? I must have misunderstood. We pay for young ones," he said, a sparkle in his eyes. "I don't know about a twenty-something woman."

Realizing that he was haggling already, I tried to remain positive. "Let me introduce you to her. She's quite the looker. Nice body and a pretty face. I'm sure you'll find some very interested clients."

"We shall see. How did you acquire her?" he asked as his associate, Rigor, joined us. The man wore all black and made the two of us look like dwarfs. He wasn't just tall, I could tell he was built like a wrestler and one who'd had his nose broken a few times. He was obviously the brawn in their little operation.

"Does it matter?" I asked, my stomach tightening.

"If we are going to invest in her, we should know her background," he said as I stepped back so they could enter the cabin.

"She's from this town. Doesn't have a husband or boyfriend. Healthy and easy on the eyes. Don't worry, she's not a druggie or an alcoholic."

Looking amused, the two men glanced at each other and spoke in Russian.

"I'm sorry, did I miss something?" I asked.

"I just said that if we take her, she will be," Ivan joked, looking back at me. "Drugs keep them calm. And obedient."

"I understand," I said.

"Let's hope that you haven't wasted our time," Rigor said. "Where is the girl?"

"Young woman," corrected Ivan.

Rigor's dark eyebrows shot up. "Oh? I thought she was teenager?"

I didn't think that arguing with them was a good idea and I was very specific in mentioning that Amanda was not a teenager. She'd barely get by as someone in her twenties.

"No. Come on. I'll take you to her," I said.

Chapter 41

Amanda

AFTER MARCUS LEFT, I searched the cellar for something to use as a weapon, but there really was only the mason jars. So, I took a chance and broke one of them. When he didn't respond to the noise, I grabbed a piece of jagged glass, stuck it into my back pocket, and kicked the rest of the pieces under the shelving unit.

Several seconds later, I heard Marcus talking to someone above and then footsteps. When the door opened, and I saw him with two other men, I tried not to panic. Part of me had hoped he'd been lying about the traffickers, to keep terrorizing me. Seeing now that he'd been telling the truth, I was scared to death.

As the two strangers followed Marcus downstairs, they looked at me in a way that made my skin crawl.

Not knowing what else to do, I decided to try and reason with them. If they wanted money, I was willing to pay them anything to help my situation. I cleared my throat. "Please, he's kidnapped me and—"

Before I could finish, the man with the blond ponytail hollered, "Silence!"

Flinching, I stared at him in fright. It was obvious the two men didn't care how I'd gotten there.

"A blonde. She's pretty," the tall, burly-looking one said. He reached forward and touched a strand of my hair. "Does the carpet match the drapes?"

I smacked the thug's hand away, which was a mistake because he backhanded me across the cheek hard. Crying out, I stumbled backward, my entire jaw on fire.

"I don't know," the blond guy said, tapping his chin as he stared at me. "She is attractive, but I can see that she's older than what you stated on the phone."

"Look, Ivan, I don't know *how* old she is but the woman is hot. Any guy would pay money to have her," Marcus said, sounding a little nervous himself.

"What do you think, Rigor?" Ivan said, looking at the bigger guy. "Is she worth our trip out here?"

"I don't know. Maybe we should take her for a spin and see?" he suggested with a smirk.

"Please," I begged. "I'm thirty-eight years old. Your clients are not going to want me."

Ivan's face turned red. "Thirty-eight? That's too old. Not when I can spend the money on fresher meat. You've wasted our time, Marcus. I am very disappointed."

"Hold up," Marcus said, his eyes filling with panic. "Nobody needs to know how old she is. I mean, look at her. She could pass for someone much younger."

"I say we check out what's under the clothes and decide," Rigor said, his eyes raking over me. "At least it won't be a waste of a trip."

Ivan let out an exasperated sigh. "Fine." He pointed toward my clothes. "Remove them."

I stared at him in horror. "No," I said, trembling. "Please, if you want money, I have it. I'll pay you whatever you want."

"She's lying. She doesn't have a pot to piss in," Marcus said, staring at me coldly.

"This isn't television. Even if you had the kind of money you'd need for us to help you, we'd never take that kind of a chance," Ivan said to me, looking amused.

Rigor laughed. "Yeah, we don't take checks and the banks are closed right now."

Marcus looked at his phone. "It's getting late, so if you want to inspect her closer, be my guest. I'll be upstairs."

Ivan frowned. "I have to say, I'm very disappointed in you, Marcus. I think we need to have a discussion on what is expected on your end if we're going to do any business together. You and I will talk. Meanwhile," he looked at Rigor. "You do what you want with her. If you think she's worth it, we'll take her with us."

"Sounds good," he replied.

Marcus and Ivan walked upstairs, leaving me with Rigor, who smiled cruelly. "Don't give me any trouble unless you like it rough." He cracked his knuckles.

Terrified of being raped by the scary-looking buffoon, I thought about the glass shard in my back pocket. Although I couldn't imagine myself killing anyone, I knew Marcus would murder my son, and soon, if I didn't do something quickly.

"Take off your clothes," Rigor ordered again.

"Wait, can we just talk about this?" I said, backing away from him.

His eyes narrowed. "Shut up and do what you're told or I will do it for you."

"But—"

His hand snaked out and he grabbed me around the neck. Gasping, I tried pulling his beefy fingers away from my throat, but they were like steel vices.

Rigor smiled, said something in Russian, and began fondling my chest. Unable to breathe, I reached behind me and pulled the glass out of my pocket. As his fingers moved under my shirt, I reminded myself again that Kevin's life was in danger and found the courage to jam it into the side of his neck. Gasping, Rigor let go of me and tried removing it.

He stared at me in disbelief. "Gah…"

Blood rushed and spurted out of the wound. Backing away, I watched in horror as he began to choking on it.

I'd done that.

He was dying because of *me*.

As much as I despised a man who'd been intent on violating me, I still felt sick to my stomach.

I was now a killer.

"I'm sorry," I whispered.

Rigor stumbled toward me and then dropped to the ground.

Trembling, I waited a few seconds, half expecting him to get up. When he remained motionless, I wiped the blood off my fingers.

God, forgive me.

I leaned down and began searching his jacket for a cell phone and that's when I noticed the gun holstered underneath. I pulled it out. Standing up, I took a deep breath and headed toward the stairs.

Chapter 42

Marcus

I KNEW I was in trouble with Ivan, but wasn't interested in doing any future business with him. Of course, I wasn't about to admit that, either. So, I listened as he rambled on and on about what he was looking for and how he didn't like anyone wasting his time.

"I'm sorry. I didn't realize that age was so important. Especially when they're attractive."

He wagged his finger at me. "Considering it's our first venture together, I will let it slide."

"Thank you."

We were seated in the kitchen and I glanced toward the hallway. I was getting anxious about Kevin waking up and didn't want Ivan seeing him. He'd probably take the kid instead of Amanda.

Ivan pulled out a pack of cigarettes and shook one out. "I guess… she's not completely unusable," he said, lighting the end. "Tell you what—we'll take her for… five hundred. Just to get her off your hands. Obviously, you can't let her go and you don't seem like the killing type."

"Five hundred?" I repeated, not happy. Obviously, he was haggling again. "I can't do that. No offense, but I think I can find someone to pay much more than that for a good-looking woman."

"Fine. One thousand dollars and that's my final offer," he said, leaning back in the chair. "And to answer your question about someone else paying more—we run all the business in this area. So, you see, it's us or nobody."

I was beginning to believe that age had nothing to do with it and that Ivan played this game on all of his investments. Of course, one grand was better than nothing. Plus, there were two of them and one of me. Not to mention that they weren't regular businessmen. Even if I somehow killed the two of them, their mafia friends would come after me and my family.

"Fine. I'll take the thousand. Now, how confident are you that she won't escape? If she does, my ass is grass. She'd go right to the cops and I don't want to do any jail time."

"Oh, they never get away," he said with a confident smile. "We couldn't afford it, either, obviously. Once she's in our care, she'll be employed until we can't use her anymore. Then nobody will ever hear from her again."

I relaxed. "Okay."

Ivan blew out a stream of smoke. "So, we have a deal?"

Before I could answer, the cellar door opened up and we turned to look. Expecting to find Rigor, we were both shocked to find Amanda standing there with a gun aimed at us.

Shit.

"Whoa," I said, raising my hands and standing up. "Amanda, lower the gun before someone gets hurt."

"Where's my son?" she asked in a shaky voice.

"I'll tell you if you give that to me," I replied, trying to remain calm.

"Where's Rigor?" Ivan asked sharply.

"He's dead," she replied. "And you will be, too, if you don't give me my son."

Chapter 43

Amanda

BOTH OF THEM stared at me in shock.

"He's in the guestroom, sleeping," Marcus replied, taking a step toward me.

I slowly began moving around them. "Don't get any closer," I said, swinging the gun back and forth between the two. Marcus had gotten to his feet, but Ivan was still sitting in the chair and I could tell from the look on his face, he wasn't going to remain there long.

"Let me take you to him," Marcus said in a soothing voice.

I wasn't an idiot and knew I was dead if I showed them any weakness. I looked over at the entrance to the cellar. "Get downstairs," I ordered, waving my gun toward the doorway. "Now."

Neither moved.

"Do you think Rigor died on his own?" I snapped, glaring at them. "Now, get your asses down there or you'll be next!"

Ivan stood up slowly. "Relax. We'll go," he said, moving his hand slowly behind him.

"What are you doing?" I said, wondering if he was reaching for a weapon. There was a gun on the counter, which looked like the one Marcus had been using earlier. I just needed to make sure he didn't get his hands on it. "Put your hands behind your head."

Smiling coldly at me, he finally did what I asked.

I glared at Ivan. "Where's your gun?"

"I don't have one on me," he replied.

I didn't believe him. There was a glint in his eyes that told me otherwise. "Turn around."

He scowled at me.

"Turn around," I repeated sharply. "Slowly."

Sighing, he did and that's when I saw a holstered gun sticking out from the waistband of his belt.

Dammit.

Change of plans.

I needed to get Ivan's gun away from him.

I looked over at Marcus. "*You*, get downstairs. Now."

Both Ivan and Marcus headed toward the doorway.

"Not you, Ivan," I said. "Stay where you are with your hands behind your head."

Ivan froze. "You confuse us with all of these orders. First you want me down there. Now you don't."

"Just stay where you are, Ivan. Marcus, keep going."

Marcus went downstairs, thankfully.

I carefully approached Ivan. "Move and I'll blow your head off."

"I wouldn't dream of it."

As I pulled his gun out of the holster, he elbowed me hard in the stomach. So hard that I dropped it onto the linoleum.

Ivan spun around and then scrambled to retrieve his gun from the floor. Before he could grab it, I fired mine, hitting him in the shoulder. He screamed in agony and collapsed. Meanwhile, Marcus was back at the top of the stairs, staring at both of us in shock.

"Get back down there!" I hollered, waving my gun.

He quickly obeyed.

Ivan's shoulder was covered in blood. He was in critical condition, but not dead. I eyed him warily as I grabbed his gun from the ground and locked Marcus downstairs.

"Don't move," I warned him as I backed toward the hallway.

"Does it look like I'm going anywhere?" he groaned, holding his shoulder and panting. "I need a doctor."

Ignoring him, I raced out of the kitchen and began searching the cabin. Fortunately, I found Kevin sleeping in a small bedroom.

"Oh, thank God." I rushed over to him and sat down on the bed. "Baby, wake up. Kevin… come on," I said, shaking him.

"I'm so tired," he mumbled, pushing me away. "Please, let me sleep for just a little longer."

"Kevin. Honey, we've got to get out of here. We've been kidnapped."

His eyes popped opened and he stared at me in confusion. "What?"

Before I could answer, a board creaked behind me. Before I had a chance to react, I was hit in the head with something hard. It knocked me out.

Chapter 44

Marcus

FORTUNATELY, IVAN HAD unlocked the door for me and now I was once again in control. But, everything was now a mess. Not only had Rigor been killed, but Ivan was losing too much blood and I was running out of time. Daylight would be coming soon and I still had to deal with Tara.

After hitting Amanda on the head with a vase, I locked the bedroom door and walked back into the kitchen.

"I need a doctor," Ivan said. He was seated on the floor, with his back to the wall, in shock and ready to pass out.

"Sorry, Ivan," I said, aiming the gun at him. Not having any other choice, I put him out of his misery by shooting him in the chest.

Sighing, I left the cabin and headed to my uncle's shed. I grabbed the shovel and walked into the woods to the shallow grave I'd been working on. Fortunately, the rain had stopped, but there was now a lot of mud.

Swearing to myself, I stepped into the hole and began digging. I now had four bodies to get rid of.

The night had really gone to shit…

AFTER WORKING ON the hole for a while, I realized that there was no way I could make it big enough in the amount of time I had. It would take hours, especially with it being so muddy. So, I decided on a new course of action—I'd only bury Kevin and Amanda and dispose of the other two bodies in the lake. Of course, I'd also need to figure out a way to get rid of the Russians' boat.

I threw down the shovel, went back into the cabin, and poured myself a shot of whiskey to get through what was to follow next. As I was considering a second one, I heard Kevin crying in the next room. Sighing, I put the bottle down, grabbed my gun, and went to check on them.

"My mom isn't waking up," he sobbed after I entered the room. "You need to help her."

"What happened?" I asked, playing dumb. I didn't know if Kevin was aware of what was happening yet. I'd knocked him out, back at the restaurant, when he still thought I had a cake for him.

"I don't know. I was so tired and she was trying to wake me up. I... I can't remember anything," he said, his lip trembling.

I relaxed. "It's okay."

"Is she going to be all right?"

Hopefully, she's already dead, I wanted to say. But, I didn't have the heart to be that much of an asshole to the kid, so I lied. "Don't worry. I'm going to get her some help," I said, approaching them slowly. Amanda's head was bleeding and her face was pale. She definitely wasn't looking good.

Kevin got out of bed. "Okay." He looked around. "Why are we here? I don't remember."

"We're celebrating your mom's birthday. Remember, I made her a cake?" I said.

He rubbed his eye. "I thought we were going to eat it at the restaurant?"

"We came back here to eat it instead." I patted his shoulder. "It's okay. You've had a very busy day."

"I have a headache," Kevin said.

"I'll get you something soon." I didn't want him to see me burying his mother and I was not quite ready to kill him yet. "For now, I need you to get back into bed and stay there while I find her some help. Okay?"

He looked confused. "Why can't I go with you?"

"Because, it's late and my Julie is supposed to be arriving soon," I lied.

"Oh."

"See, that's why you need to wait here and tell her what's happening. Otherwise, she'll get scared."

"Can't you just call her?"

The kid was too smart for his own good.

"Unfortunately, my phone died and I don't have a charger handy."

He looked down at my hand and his eyes grew wide. "You have a gun. Why?"

"For protection. There are a lot of bears in this area."

"Where are we?"

"At my cabin, remember? Geez, you must have forgotten all about the entire night."

He didn't reply, just stared at me in confusion.

Eyeing Amanda, I slid the gun behind my belt and then shook her gently. She groaned but didn't open her eyes.

"Mom, wake up," Kevin said. "Please."

"It's okay. She'll be fine." I took a deep breath, bent down, and picked her up. "Now, you lie down and I'll be right back. Okay?"

Thankfully, he did what I asked without any more questions.

I carried Amanda out of the bedroom, expecting her to wake up and start struggling, but she remained unconscious.

Once I managed to get her out of the house, I carried her toward the hole, grateful she was a petite woman and that I'd been using my gym membership.

I set her down in the mud and stared at her face. For a brief moment, I recalled the very first day we'd met. As a child, I'd thought she'd been the nicest and prettiest daycare lady I'd ever seen. She'd been funny and had kept us entertained with crafty art projects and outdoor activities. Unfortunately, those days had turned into the darkest moments of my life.

Releasing a breath, I rolled her into the hole and she landed with a thud. I stood up, grabbed the shovel, and began filling it with mud. I'd barely covered her when I heard a shrill scream coming from the house.

Kevin.

Chapter 45

Amanda

I WOKE UP to something wet and heavy hitting me in the face. At first, I thought I was dreaming but then heard a scream in the distance and that's when everything came back to me.

I sat up and winced at the horrendous pain in my head. Forcing myself to ignore it, I rose to my feet and when my eyes adjusted to the darkness, I noticed Marcus running toward the cabin. Shaking, I climbed out of the hole and followed him, wondering where my son was.

Marcus went inside.

Quickly. I looked around, trying to find something to use as a weapon. Noticing a stack of firewood, I grabbed a piece of wood, raced to the front door, and quietly snuck inside.

"Who is that?" I heard Kevin crying from the kitchen.

"Don't worry about him. He was a very bad man. He wanted to hurt you and your mom. I had to shoot him," Marcus said. "Now, calm down, okay?"

"I'm scared."

"There's no need. Now, let's get you back to the bedroom," Marcus said in a soothing voice.

"I want to see my mom. Where is she?"

"I told you, I'm going to find her help. I can't do that until you do what you're told," he said sternly.

Help?

Right.

Enough was enough.

I needed to get my son away from the lunatic.

"I want to go with you to get help. I don't want to stay here," Kevin sobbed.

Marcus let out an exasperated sigh. "Fine. You want your mom? I'll bring you her," he muttered angrily.

I quickly hid in the shadows and watched as Marcus snatched Kevin by the arm and led him out of the kitchen and toward the front door. They stepped outside and I hurried after them, clutching the piece of wood tightly, praying that neither of them would turn around and see me. As they approached the hole, Marcus let go of Kevin's hand.

Knowing this might be my only shot, I charged at him with the wood piece and cracked him as hard as I could in the skull with it.

Hollering in pain, Marcus slipped and fell into the hole.

"Mom?" gasped Kevin, staring at me in shock.

"Get behind me," I ordered, my heart racing as I watched Marcus, who was now on his knees and getting back up.

Confused, Kevin obeyed.

Marcus looked up at me. "You… bitch," he growled. "I'm… going… to kill you."

I raised the piece of wood and smashed it into his forehead this time, knocking him back down. He screamed in agony.

"What are you doing?" Kevin screamed, still confused. "You're hurting him!"

I watched as Marcus slowly began to rise again. Before I could take another swing, he pulled out his gun and smiled at me in victory. "Say goodbye, bitch."

"No!" Kevin screamed.

Someone gasped behind us. We turned around to find Julie standing there, holding her belly and looking shocked.

Marcus's smile broke. He lowered the gun. "Baby, what are you doing out here?"

"I've been trying to call you for the last hour-and-a-half," she blurted out quickly. "Amanda's mother called and said she never returned home. I spoke to Tara and she said that you'd driven her. I was worried…" Julie looked at me and then at my son. "I don't understand. What is going on here?"

"Your husband kidnapped him," I said, desperately in need of her help. "Now… he's trying to kill the both of us."

Julie's face turned ashen. "What?" Her eyes filled with tears. "Marcus? Is this true?"

For a second, he looked at a loss for words and I thought he might try to deny it. But, instead, he smiled apologetically. "I have no other choice. I have to do it."

She stared at him in horror. "What do you mean you *have* to?"

"It's for us. I'm confronting my demons so that we can focus on being happy," he said.

"By killing a child and a woman?" she asked, her lips trembling. "Why would you do something like that?"

"I need to find peace," he replied, looking at me for a brief second.

"You're not making any sense." She held out her hand and stepped toward him. "Now, give me the gun before you take this too far."

"If I let them live, I'll go to jail," he said. "For a very long time."

371

Julie froze. She looked at me and then her husband. "I'm sure Amanda understands that you need help."

"It's too late for that," he replied.

"Why do you think it's too late?" Julie asked, looking more confused than ever.

Marcus went silent.

She turned to me. "Is there something *else* I should know about?"

I was going to tell her about him killing the deputy and Brad, but Marcus spoke up again.

"I was abused," he said, sounding broken. "A long time ago."

Julie's face softened. "I'm so sorry, Marcus. Is that what's been bothering you for so long?"

"Yes." He pointed at me. "And it was Amanda's husband who did it. When I was too young to protect myself."

"Oh," Julie replied.

I cleared my throat. "I didn't know about it."

He swept his hand through his hair and laughed shrilly. "Obviously, the shit really messed me up. I don't even know what I'm doing anymore."

"It's okay, baby. We can get you some help," Julie said softly. "We'll get through this."

He shook his head. "No. It's too late."

Julie frowned. "Don't say that, Marcus. It's never too late."

372

"She's right, Marcus," I said, pulling Kevin closer to me. "It's not too late."

He ignored me.

I tried again. "You were right about one thing—I should have known what was happening in my own house. But, I didn't. That was my fault and I'll never forgive myself for what he did to you. I'm so sorry and ashamed for what happened."

Marcus looked at me.

"Please, forgive me," I said.

His eyes filled with tears. He didn't reply but looked at Julie. "I love you, babe. I always will."

She smiled sadly. "I love you, too. Now, come out of that hole and we'll talk some more, okay?"

"I'm either Hell-bound or jail-bound. I won't be there to help raise our child and that's not fair to either of you. I've now realized that what I've done has made me the darkness in your life. Me," he said with a bitter smile. "I don't want that for you or our child." He raised the gun to his head.

"Marcus!" she cried, moving toward him. "Don't! Please! We'll work through this."

"Apology accepted," he said, looking at me before pulling the trigger.

Kevin screamed right before I pulled him into me to try to shield him from yet another horror. I was too late.

Chapter 46

Amanda

TWO WEEKS LATER

"I'M GOING TO miss you so much," Mom said after I loaded the last of our suitcases into my SUV.

Kevin, Lacey, and I were finally returning to Chicago to try and get past the horrors we'd faced in Summit Lake. We'd decided to stay in our rental for now, to put some normality back into our lives. Kevin would have his friends around and I knew it would be the best thing for him, after everything that had happened.

"I'm going to miss you, too," I said, hugging her.

"And to think, we almost had you back," she replied, smiling sadly as we released each other. "Maybe you'll have a change of heart next year and think about coming home for good?"

"We'll see," I said.

"Parker is sure hoping you'll come back," she said with a glint in her eyes.

I smiled. "We talked last night, Mom. We've decided we're just going to stay friends. That way, he can get on with his life and I can get on with mine, without any guilt or expectations."

I'd also talked with Tara, who was planning on visiting us in Chicago in a few weeks. We'd made promises to keep better in touch. As far as she and Josh went, it was over for good. Even though he hadn't been guilty of any crimes against me, the man wasn't trustworthy and she knew it.

"Oh, poo," Mom said, looking disappointed. "I was hoping you two would get together. He's such a nice, young man."

"He is. He's also a great catch, which is why he needs to be available," I replied. "Parker deserves to be happy and someday he'll find someone who can offer him what I can't."

"So, you're serious about never moving back then?" she asked.

"Honestly, I don't know what the future holds. I don't want to make any promises, though. One way or the other."

She nodded.

The truth was, I couldn't wait to get as far away from Summit Lake as possible. Yes, Marcus was gone, but the memories of the last few weeks were still fresh and painful. Not to mention the fact that everyone in town kept asking me about it. More than anything, they wanted to know how Marcus had murdered Brad, which I didn't even know the full details about. Or they wanted to know how he'd managed to frame Josh, who was now out of jail. As for poor Julie, I couldn't imagine what she was going through. She was now a single mother and a widow to a man who'd not only shocked her, but an entire town.

"By the way, did you hear? Julie had a girl," Mom said softly.

"Yeah, I know," I replied, my heart heavy for the young mother. The same night Julie's husband had committed suicide, she'd actually gone into labor from the stress.

"She's leaving town, too," Mom added, with a sad smile. "Going to stay with her sister in Florida."

I sighed. "Hopefully, she'll get through this."

"I hope so. Julie and Marcus had been together since high school. They were childhood sweethearts," she said. "I'm sure she's devastated by everything. Not just what he did to himself, but to everyone else."

"It broke her heart," I replied, thinking back to that night at the cabin. After Marcus killed himself, she became hysterical and started having contractions. I quickly called for emergency services, and not only did the police show up, but they sent a medical helicopter to air-lift Julie, Kevin, and myself to the nearest hospital. From what I'd heard, she spent the next five hours in labor, fortunately having her parents and other family members around. I ended up having a few stitches and a mild concussion from the head injuries I'd sustained, and the bruise on my jaw from where Rigor had hit me was now just a fading yellow. Kevin was given a clean bill-of-health, although after everything he'd witnessed, it was clear that he'd probably need counseling. Truthfully, neither of us would ever be the same and I'd probably need some therapy, too.

"I talked to the sheriff this morning. He said the two men found in the cabin were linked to the Russian traffickers," she said.

"Yeah, I believe it," I replied, grateful they hadn't charged me for Rigor's death. But, it had been clear to him, and Detective Davis, who'd interviewed me at the hospital, that I'd acted in self-defense.

She clucked her tongue. "You both were so lucky."

"So was Tara. She was next on Marcus's hit list."

Mom sighed. "I still can't believe that he was behind it all."

"And I can't believe Brad did what he did to him," I said. "I still feel horrible. I don't even know if he harmed any of the other kids."

"Now that it's been in the media, I'm sure if Brad touched anyone else, you'd have heard about it by now," she replied.

I nodded. The story had been all over television and I'd gotten several calls from journalists, asking for interviews. I'd refused them all, wanting to put the horrible events behind me so we could get on with our lives.

Rocky walked out of the house with Kevin and Lacey.

"You ready to go, kiddo?" I asked as they joined us.

Kevin nodded.

We sadly said our goodbyes and then I loaded Lacey into the back of the SUV. With a final kiss and a hug to both Rocky and Mom, Kevin and I got in and drove away.

"I'm going to miss them so much," Kevin murmured, staring out the passenger window.

"Me, too."

He asked if we'd visit the following summer.

I shrugged. "I don't know. Maybe they can visit us next year instead?"

"But, then we can't go fishing or see Austin," he said with a disappointed look on his face.

"Kevin, I thought you might want some time away from Summit Lake. Because of everything that happened," I said, grabbing his hand and squeezing it.

He gave me a confused look. "But, Marcus is gone, Mom. We're safe now. Right?"

I sure hoped so. "Yeah."

"Then, why can't we go back next year?"

I sighed.

"Rocky said that when bad things happen, it makes us stronger."

"True," I replied, wondering where this was going.

"I know you've been through a lot, Mom," he said, sounding so much older than his eight years. "But, you and I are a team and we can do anything if we set our minds to it."

I laughed. "Did Rocky tell you this?"

"Yeah," he admitted. "But, I believe it. Don't you?"

"I do," I said, proud that my son was intellectually stronger than I'd given him credit for.

"Then we should come back next year. Rocky and Grandma will be sad if we don't. So will Lacey. She loves running around the yard and jumping in the lake."

"She does, doesn't she?" I replied, smiling.

"Yeah."

"We'll talk about it later, okay?"

"Okay."

"Why don't you put on some music?" I said, nodding toward the stereo.

Kevin reached over and turned on the radio.

As we drove past the *'Thank you for Visiting Summit Lake'* sign, and toward Chicago, I knew we'd return the following summer. Kevin was right about bad things making you stronger—and what kind of a mother would I be if I taught him that running from your fears was better than facing them?

"Okay. You win. We'll return next year," I said over the music.

Kevin smiled. "Cool."

"Did Rocky give you any other advice you'd like to share?"

He was silent for a few seconds and then smiled. "I could use a cell phone."

I raised my eyebrow. "He said that?"

He broke into a smile again. "No. But, it would be a good idea, don't you think?"

"And why would it be a good idea for an eight-year-old to have one of those? Convince me and maybe... *maybe*... I'll consider it."

As Kevin gave me his list of silly reasons why, I couldn't help but be thankful for not only having such a witty kid, but a courageous one. I wasn't sure what the future held for us, but he was right—we were a team and anything was possible.

"So, what do you say?" he said, sounding winded.

Considering it was safer for our team to always be able to contact each other, I knew he'd be getting one for Christmas.

"We'll see. Christmas is right around the corner…"

His eyes lit up. "That's it! I'll ask Santa for one."

I cringed inwardly. "That's kind of an expensive request for the jolly-old-elf, don't you think?"

"It's no big deal. Santa's elves can build one for me. They have a shop, remember?"

"I just don't know if they can actually make cell phones," I replied. "I'd stick with asking Santa for Matchbox cars and other toys."

"I can always ask him for one, anyway. I'll just give him a list of a few ideas. Do you have a piece of paper?"

I bit back a smile. "Uh, I think there's a pen and paper in the glovebox."

He reached inside and found what he was looking for. He began writing a lengthy list of items.

"Wow, that's quite the list," I said, glancing down at what he was writing.

"Don't worry. I put something down for you, too."

"Really? What's that?" I asked, amused.

"A swimming pool."

I snorted. "Oh, a swimming pool? That's it?"

"Yeah, I wasn't sure what else you wanted."

"Kevin, I have everything I want," I said softly. "But, I have to admit—a swimming pool would be nice."

He smiled. "I'll circle it so he knows it's important."

I laughed. "You do that."

"Okay."

Honestly, as I glanced at Kevin again, I couldn't think of anything else I wanted or needed. He was my everything. Yes, I knew that someday he would graduate, go off to college, and make a life of his own. Until then, he was mine and nothing would, or could, stop us. Not while I was still standing.

The End